"Her Partner"
Bulbs, Blossoms and Bouquets #3
By Laura Ann

This is a work of fiction. Similarities to real people, places, or events are entirely coincidental.

HER UNEXPECTED PARTNER

First edition. February 3, 2022.

Copyright © 2022 Laura Ann.

Written by Laura Ann.

DEDICATION

To my snake lover.
I love your fascination with all things
creepy and crawly.
Keep being you.

ACKNOWLEDGEMENTS

No author works alone. Thank you, Tami.
You make it Christmas every time
I get a new cover. And thank you to my Beta Team.
Truly, your help with my stories is immeasurable.

NEWSLETTER

You can get a FREE book by joining my Reading Family! Every week we share stories, sales and good old fun. To get in on the action, just visit my website at

lauraannbooks.com

CHAPTER 1

Mr. Snyder whistled low under his breath. "You sure do good work, Charli," he complimented, running a hand over his thinning hair. "Back when I was a young'un, girls spent their time crafting blankets and hosting dinners...not creating workmanship like this." He walked by the fireplace, running his hand over the newly finished mantel.

Charli had to admit that she was pretty proud of the work. She adored fixing up old houses, and in her small coastal town of Seaside Bay, Oregon, old houses were easy to find. More so even than houses, however, Charli loved restoring antiques in general.

She didn't get to do it as often as she wished as most of her income came from doing repairs for the locals in town. That might have been why she worked so hard on projects like this for Mr. Snyder. The mantel over his fireplace had come from an old sea captain's ship and had grown chipped and faded over the years. He'd given Charli free rein to refurbish the slab of wood as she saw fit.

Two weeks later, with a fresh coat of paint and newly carved oceanic designs, the mantel hung in its place of honor, giving a bright new focal point to the sitting room.

"Oh, Charli." Mrs. Snyder came in from the kitchen. "It's just stunning!"

Charli grinned and gave a teasing salute. "Thank you, Mrs. Snyder. I'm so glad you two like it."

Mr. Snyder chuckled. "The grandkids won't be able to keep their hands off it." He frowned and looked to Charli. "Will it become damaged if enough sticky hands run over it?"

She shook her head. "Nope. I used an eggshell finish, which should clean up really easily. Just wipe it with a damp cloth and she should be as good as new."

"What do we owe you?" Mrs. Snyder asked, heading toward where her purse was hanging by the front door.

"Oh, don't worry about it now," Charli said as she gathered her supplies from hanging the piece. "I'll get a bill sent out."

"At least have a piece of pie before you go," the elderly lady said, changing her trajectory back to the kitchen. "Strawberries are in season, you know."

Charli shook her head. "My dad always said that fruit pie is really just a side dish."

Mr. Snyder laughed. "I always enjoyed your dad." He waved for Charli to follow him. "Well then, come have a side dish. If you stick around long enough, we both know Ethyl will give you the rest of the meal."

Charli laughed softly. "As tempting as that would be, I have another job to get to soon."

"They can wait until you eat!" Mrs. Snyder shouted from the other room.

Charli sighed, one of enjoyment and content. Jobs like this were so worth it. Working inside people's homes could go one of two ways. Either the owners hated everything, or they took you into their family. Luckily, the Snyders were family people.

Having spent her entire life in Seaside Bay, Charli knew just about everyone. Though it was hard to tell during the summer when tourists invaded their area for access to Oregon's beautiful coastline and fishing tours.

"Okay, Mrs. Snyder...I've got like..." Charli made a show of checking her cell phone. "Like fifteen minutes."

The grandmotherly woman smiled. "Of course. That's plenty of time to eat."

Charli gave her a skeptical look, then accepted the invitation to sit down.

An hour later, Charli finally managed to slip out the front door. She was absolutely positive she had a food baby at this point and rubbed her stomach with a quiet groan. "Why do old ladies always cook so well?" she whispered. "Looks like it's an extra mile or two on the run tonight."

Just as Charli stepped into her pickup truck, her phone buzzed. She grabbed it from her pocket and looked at the screen. Smiling, she answered the video chat. "Hey, bro. What's up?"

Charli's older brother Felix, who ran a fishing charter off their coast, was grinning widely. "Guess what we're having for dinner tonight?"

Charli groaned and threw her head back. "Felix...we don't need any more fish! Our freezer is so full it's gonna burst!"

He made a disbelieving face. "What are you talking about? I didn't say anything about fish."

Charli narrowed her gaze. "Okay..."

He swung his phone to the side. "Surprise!"

"Felix," she said in a deadpan voice. "That's a fish."

He brought the camera back to his face. "It's not a fish. It's a halibut."

"The fact that you don't think that's a fish is worrisome," Charli said with pursed lips. "You're supposed to be an expert. I mean...people actually pay you for your fishing knowledge, so I would expect you to be a little more...you know...knowledgeable."

Felix sniffed. "Fine. If you don't appreciate my fishing skills, I'll share them with someone else."

"Like who?" Charli did her best to hold back a grin, her lips twitching with the effort. "Your boy toys are so worn out with fish that I think Benny said, and I quote, 'Next time you feed me fish, I'm strangling you with your own fishing line,' unquote."

Felix grumbled under his breath. "None of you appreciate me."

Charli laughed and set her phone in its stand on the dashboard as she cranked her old pickup to life. With the engine chugging along steadily, she pulled out and began to navigate the small town to get to her next appointment. "Sorry," she apologized. "I'm grateful for all you do to put food on the table."

"Darn right," Felix continued to mutter. He sighed. "But you're right. We're about to run out of freezer space. I guess that means we'll just have to eat more fish."

"Or maybe you should just stop bringing it home," Charli said helpfully.

Felix must have decided to ignore her because he kept talking for several minutes about all the ways they could fry, bake, or sautee everything that was in their cold storage.

Ignoring his ramblings, Charli checked the address she had written down and pulled up to the curb near an older-looking cottage. She studied the home from her place in the truck for a moment before getting out. The owners had worked with Charli several times over the years. Slowly but surely, the young couple had been fixing up this home and since they'd booked her for a consultation today, she assumed they were ready to take on another project.

"I'm here, Fe. Gotta run."

"Be safe!" he hollered, his onslaught of useless knowledge stopping immediately.

Charli was close to her brother. He'd become the only family she had left when their parents had been killed in a car accident a few years back. Their relationship growing up had been like most siblings, where they fought and bickered and drove each other crazy. But after they were on their own…it all shifted. Together, they had moved back into their parents' home and ended up growing closer, which had been an unexpected blessing as they mourned for their lost family. "Will do," she answered. "I've got a consult with the Fishers and then I'll be home."

"Fishers? Speaking of fish—"

"BYE!" Charli hollered and closed the call before he could get going again. She blew out a breath. It was amazing her brother was still human since he seemed to eat and live among the sea creatures.

Grabbing her notebook, Charli marched up the front steps feeling quite content with her life. Renovations might not be her absolute dream job, but it was an awfully close second, and she didn't feel like she had anything to complain about.

***

"YOU KNOW I'M HERE FOR you," Canon said with his hands splayed out. "But even I can't change the rules of the will."

Bronson let out a low huff and pushed a hand through his waves. Everything in his life seemed to be falling apart. He'd taken a leap of faith and was currently about to hit the concrete. He turned back to his brother. "There has to be something you can do," he said, leaning on the desk with his palms. "It can't be legal to force someone to jump through these kinds of hoops in order to get an inheritance that's rightfully theirs."

Canon's blue-gray eyes, so similar to Bronson's, looked at him with forced patience. "There's nothing I can do," Canon said firmly. "Dad had it signed and notarized before any of us knew there were changes. If you want your portion of his money, you have to do what he asked."

Bronson shook his head and fell backward into one of the two chairs placed artfully in front of his brother's desk. "Dad and I got along so well," he murmured, more to himself than present company. "I just don't get why he would do this to me. He never once seemed to be upset with my change in careers."

Canon tapped his pen on the wood. "I don't know, Bron. Maybe he just didn't want it to come between you." He smiled tightly. "Dad seemed to grow...soft in his old age. You always did seem to be his favorite."

Bronson rolled his eyes. "Yeah, right. Aria was his favorite. She had the old man wrapped around her little finger."

"Mmm," Canon said, his eyes dropping to the papers in front of him.

Bronson tapped the arm of the chair. "No offense, Canon, but maybe we should let someone else look at the will. We all know you're the best lawyer in L.A., but even the great Canon Ramsay can make mistakes."

Canon's eyes turned more steel than blue and Bronson held back a sigh. He knew it had been a risk to ask about someone else seeing their father's will. After all, Canon specialized in inheritance work and had a reputation for never backing down, but Bronson was beginning to feel desperate.

Bronson put up his hands. "Forget I said anything. I'm just thinking out loud. Sorry." Canon's anger wasn't worth it right now, especially when Bronson was still feeling worn down from the funeral last week.

"I'd worry more about how you're going to fulfill the requirements Dad asked for, rather than testing my competency," Canon snapped.

Bronson nodded, trying not to snap back. He'd worked many years trying to curb the quick temper they'd all inherited from their mother. All three of the Ramsay children were easily provoked, but the older Bronson got, the less he wanted that kind of lifestyle. Janine, his father's old girlfriend, had helped smooth those rough edges and Bronson didn't want them back.

Canon had found a use for his quick mind and tongue, becoming a killer in the courtroom. He had a reputation for shredding people on the witness stand no matter whose witness they were.

Aria, their baby sister, was planning to follow their mother's footsteps and become a model, but was currently getting her undergrad at UCLA. Their father had insisted that she have a back-up plan in case modeling didn't pay the bills, though it wasn't a real concern. Last he heard, the daughter of Evangeline Ramsay had more contract offers than she knew what to do with. Bronson's sister was a stunning beauty, but he secretly hoped that she never made it. The whole family watched how that lifestyle had driven their mother slowly mad. Evangeline had been all the rage in her prime, but the loss of attention and adoring fans as she aged caused her to slip into a shell of the woman she'd once been.

The love of her husband and children hadn't been enough. She'd needed more, and when it had refused to come, Evangeline had grown so depressed that she'd eventually taken her own life, leaving Joshua, her husband, to raise three teenaged children by himself.

Two were succeeding in all the ways the world thought important...but Bronson was different. His mother's death had hit him differently and he'd lost his ambition.

Or maybe I just gained perspective.

He'd gone to college and worked in finance for several years before deciding he wanted a more satisfying lifestyle. The thought of punching somebody else's numbers for the rest of his life had felt like a prison sentence, so he'd gotten out. When his dad's girlfriend, Janine, had suggested he volunteer at a place called Fathers and Sons...

It changed Bronson's life.

He desperately wanted to be able to give back to the organization, but the reading of his father's will had created an obstacle that Bronson wasn't sure he could tacke.

"So what are you going to do?" Canon's question brought Bronson away from his wandering thoughts.

Bronson pinched the bridge of his nose. "Remind me again exactly what the terms of the estate are?"

Canon picked up the top paper on his desk, his eyes flitting around. "Do you want the legal version or layman?'

"Layman."

"Basically it says you have to do a job for a certain amount of time, eight weeks should do it, and do it in such a way that you have something to show by the end."

"What in the world does that really mean?" Bronson asked, leaning forward onto his knees. "Have something to show? Like a certain number in my bank account or a promotion or something?"

Canon shrugged. "I'm not exactly sure what Dad was referring to, but I would think most anything tangible would hold up in a court. The words are quite vague, so it can be interpreted in lots of ways."

Bronson frowned and shook his head. "It's just so out of character for Dad. When I quit my job, he told me that he understood. He never said he was upset with my choices or bothered me about getting back into the regular workforce."

Canon tilted his head to the side to study Bronson, looking very much like their father as he did so. "He might not have said anything, but he obviously thought it."

Bronson nodded and rubbed his hands over his face. He needed to shave and he knew there were dark bags under his eyes. He hadn't slept well since his father's accident, and personal grooming had definitely gone out the window. It was a good thing that he lived in California, because the dark shades he'd worn at the graveside service had looked perfectly normal in the bright sunshine overhead.

"Look, why don't you come over for dinner tonight and we'll brainstorm," Canon said, shuffling the papers in his hands. "I have a client to get to, so I need you to head out."

Bronson stood, not offended by his brother's dismissal. They'd always had a slightly strained relationship, and right now both were under heavy stress. "I'll take you up on that dinner invitation," he said as he slipped through the doorway.

"Seven sharp," were Canon's last words as Bronson closed the door behind him.

His legs felt heavy and his mind overly tired as he walked into the light and down the block to the bus station. He hadn't felt up to dealing with traffic that morning.

What am I going to do? That was the question of the hour. He worked full time for the nonprofit, but apparently that wasn't good enough. Dad wanted him back in the nine-five, rat-race and part of Bronson didn't feel like it was worth it.

If Fathers and Sons wasn't in such terrible financial straits, Bronson knew he probably wouldn't bother fighting for that inheritance. But as it was, the charity was going to go under if someone didn't come up with a way to save their building. Bronson had thought his inheritance would be an answer to their prayers, but now it looked like it might be just another obstacle to keep him from getting what was rightfully his.

CHAPTER 2

"Admit it..." Felix pressed. "Come on, Charli...admit it."

Charli rolled her eyes and shook her head. "Sometimes I wonder why I still live with you."

"Because the rent here is cheap," he shot back. Pressing his hands on the table, he leaned in. "Now admit that my fish is the best in the state."

"I haven't eaten fish throughout the entire state," she said primly, picking another bite of meat off her plate. "So I can't compare."

Felix gave her a look. "You're a brat, you know that?"

Charli gave him her best smile. "Lucky you."

He stabbed at his mashed potatoes. "Lucky whoever your husband is, someday," he grumbled. "I'm totally giving him a rundown of how difficult you are." His grin was purely evil. "Maybe it'll scare him away from the altar altogether."

"Then don't expect me to not pull out the naked baby pictures when you finally bring a woman home," Charli shot back. "She'll be so shocked by your lack of hair until you were five that she'll refuse to marry you in defense of her future children."

"Good thing I don't plan to marry, huh? I've already got two women in my life and that's more than enough."

"Oh, for heaven's sake..." Charli groaned. "Your boat is not a woman!"

Felix made a face. "Don't talk about *Morwenna* that way," he demanded. "She'll hear you!"

"She's down at the dock! That's like five miles down the road!"

"Ahah!" Felix pointed a finger at her. "You call her a *she*. You admit she's a woman."

Charli sighed and laughed. "One of these days we'll find something new to argue about."

Felix chuckled right along with her. "Tired of the same old conversations? You're welcome to come up with a different topic." It was quiet for a moment as they both chewed. "What about your storefront? We could talk about that."

All the humor of their dinner conversation immediately fled. "There is no storefront," Charli said quickly. She kept her eyes down. She hated when her brother pressured her about opening a store. Yes, it was Charli's dream, but she wouldn't do it until she actually had enough money saved to keep them afloat long enough for the business to take off. And she simply wasn't there yet.

"You keep pushing it back and it'll never happen," Felix said, unperturbed by her shutdown.

"Then it'll never happen," she snapped.

"You're too good to not give it a try," Felix said, his voice softer than before. "I can pay the bills until you—"

"No!" Charli shouted, then deflated. "Sorry. But I'm not putting the whole burden on your shoulders, Felix. I want to do this on my own." She gave him a pleading look. "I *need* to. Accepting your money just isn't an option for me. In this, I work solo."

Felix shook his head. "Most people use others' money to start a business, Char. You can always buy me out later when you get going. And we have a decent savings account. We'd be all right."

"I know we can make it for a few months," she agreed. "But I don't want to risk us not being able to pay the mortgage, or property taxes. I want to be in a position where we can afford the hit that'll happen for the first few months."

"I think we can afford it. Which is exactly why you keep using that as an excuse not to take a risk. Are you just frightened? Or...what? I don't get why you don't take a partner and make a go of it. Even if you don't want my money, get a different investor. You're going to wait too long and then your chance will be gone," Felix argued, ending on a quiet tone.

Charli couldn't meet his gaze. He was right. She did use the house and bills as an excuse, but she also just wasn't quite ready, not to mention she had no intention of taking a partner. She wanted to do this on her own. She had saved enough to keep paying her share for about three months and that just wasn't enough. Charli felt positive that she would feel better if she had six months' worth of bills paid, knowing that a new business in a small tourist town would take quite a while to get moving.

Felix sighed. "What about that building you were looking at? What's going on with that?"

"Nothing. It's just sitting there."

"Have you tried talking to the owners?"

Charli shook her head. "If it was for sale, it would have a sign on it." A few months ago, a business had left town, leaving behind a huge warehouse that would be perfect for the antique/restoration shop that Charli wanted to open. The problem was, she didn't know what was going on with the building. No sign for rent or sale had come up since the tenant had left, leaving Charli with more questions than answers. She didn't know who owned it and she didn't know where to begin finding out.

Her frustration mounting, she pushed away from the table. "Got a long run tonight," she said. "Do you mind doing the dishes?"

"Hey! I cooked!"

"No," Charli said firmly. "I cooked, you caught. Not the same."

"It should count," Felix murmured grumpily.

"Not a chance, dear brother," she called over her shoulder. "And hold some ice cream for me!"

"You run, you lose!" he shouted at her.

"That doesn't rhyme!"

"Never said it did!"

Charli laughed, already feeling lighter. She tied her laces and slipped out the back door. She loved her brother, she truly did, but sometimes he was a little too much like a mother, instead of a sibling.

The low sun held little heat as she began to put one foot in front of the other. It took almost no time at all to find her rhythm and Charli allowed herself to take a deep, relaxing breath.

She loved her runs, especially her long ones. It was the best way to clear her head and let go of the struggles in her life. Not that she had a crazy amount of them. Her life, compared to many, was pretty easy.

There was the occasional difficult client, but otherwise, Charli spent her days doing what she enjoyed and helping make the homes in her area not only more beautiful, but more functional as well.

Just because she had a dream that meant stepping out of that comfortable living, didn't mean she had to go after it. Or that she had to risk what she had to accomplish it. She already had enough things to bring her happiness.

Good friends.

Good family.

Good job.

And good exercise.

Her heart was beating strong and steady now that she had completed her first mile.

One down, twelve to go.

She didn't have a race for the next few months, but Charli never let herself get too far from her training. She enjoyed making sure her life was predictable and safe. Any adventure she craved was satisfied with her Ironman competitions, so there really was no reason for her to risk losing all of that just to open a store. It simply didn't make sense.

"HAVE YOU FIGURED OUT what you're going to do?" Elisha asked, folding her arms over the table.

Bronson glanced at his brother's girlfriend. "Not yet."

"No ideas?"

Irritation began to prick at him. He had come to dinner hoping for help, not the Spanish Inquisition. "No."

She tsked her tongue. "You need to take more initiative, Bronson, or you'll never get that money."

"I'm aware, thanks, Elisha." There was a little more bite in Bronson's tone than he wanted, but at the moment it couldn't be helped. He was floundering and everyone seemed to want to point that out, rather than throw him a life raft.

She sniffed and stood. "Well, if you want to continue to fund that carefree lifestyle of yours, then you'd better do something."

Bronson clenched his jaw together. *Why does no one understand that volunteering IS work? I don't go in and loaf all day.*

"Enough," Canon said, his voice cutting through the tension like a hot knife in butter. He wiped his mouth with his cloth napkin. "Sit down, Elisha."

Her nostrils flared, but she did as she was told.

Bronson shook his head. He hoped when he finally found a woman, she wasn't afraid to stand up to him when he got out of hand. It was all too easy to see that Elisha liked Canon's money too much to rock the boat.

"Are you done?" Canon asked, eyeing Bronson's barely touched plate.

Bronson nodded. "Sorry. Not hungry this evening."

Canon nodded and stood. "Come on. We can head to the study and figure things out while the housekeeper cleans up." He frowned at Elisha when she started to rise. "You won't be needed, Elisha. Feel free to go do something else."

Bronson almost felt bad for the shrewish woman when her lips pursed and cheeks turned red. Canon was often just as hard at home as he was in the courtroom. It wasn't a relationship that Bronson envied, that was for sure.

"We'll be back for dessert later," Canon said, his voice a little softer as he spoke to his girlfriend.

Her red lips stretched into a smile. It was moments like this that Bronson could see why Canon was so attracted to her. Elisha was almost six-foot, tan, and high maintenance. She had all the right qualifications to be a gorgeous woman, but her personality was enough to put Bronson off her forever.

"Come on," Canon said, heading out of the room.

Bronson followed like an obedient puppy. The image didn't help his already stressed mentality. He might be struggling to figure out how to work with his dad's will, but that didn't make him someone else's lap dog.

Bronson paused in the doorway and squished his lips to one side. "You know, maybe I should just go home. If I do some research, I'll find something that'll work, at least for the short term."

"Sit down," Canon said, settling himself in a large arm chair.

Bronson balked, then forced himself into submission. His brother was high-handed but was trying to help. Canon was so used to being in charge that he sometimes forgot to step out of the role when he wasn't at work.

"Tell me about your hobbies."

The question seemed to come out of left field and Bronson jerked back a little. "My hobbies?"

"Yeah." Canon waved a hand in the air. "You know, the things you like you to do. You said you quit being an accountant because it wasn't what you really wanted to do. Obviously you work with those...kids, but that's not what we're looking for. So...what have you found that you *do* enjoy?" There was an underlying tone of annoyance in Canon's words, but since he had a good point, Bronson chose to overlook it.

Bronson had to think for a minute. He spent so much time at the safehouse for the kids that he hadn't dabbled in hobbies for a long time.

Canon sighed. "Bron, there has to be something."

Bronson shrugged. "I enjoy fishing, but I don't think that's going to be what we're looking for."

Canon gave him a look. "Probably not," he said flatly.

Bronson picked at his sweater. "I'm good with numbers," he said.

"Which is why you were an accountant."

Bronson nodded. "Yeah, but it could be used in other ways as well. Math is critical to all sorts of careers."

"True." Canon's eyes flitted around the room, obviously bored at their conversation.

"Look, Canon. I appreciate all this, but I think I'm gonna head home. I know I have some stuff to figure out, but I'll probably do that better alone." Bronson stood up. "I'll call you tomorrow."

Canon watched him shrewdly, then nodded. "Okay. If that's what you think is best."

"Yep." Bronson turned and began to walk out. "Tell Elisha goodnight for me and thank you for dinner."

There was no answer as Bronson left, but the deep breath he was able to take when he was out of Canon's stuffy home felt freeing in more ways than one. His brother's disappointment was more than evident, even if he was trying to help.

Bronson rubbed a hand over his face. Unfortunately, this was something he was going to have to figure out himself. If working for a nonprofit wasn't a good enough career...what was?

Once home, Bronson grabbed a soda from the fridge and sat down on his favorite spot on the couch. His apartment was a far cry from Canon's mansion, but it fit Bronson better. Simple, clean and homey. It was exactly the type of place he wanted to come to at the end of the day.

Sighing, Bronson grabbed a computer and let himself flip through social media. Ads for fishing tours, books and even art supplies popped up every so often and Bronson waved them away with a flick of his fingers. Until one in particular caught his eye.

He studied the ad for a homebuilder's competition and found himself growing increasingly intrigued. Opening up a new page, Bronson looked up the group and realized they were based out of Oregon. It seemed a Home Builders Association was holding a parade and awards banquet for newly constructed and renovated homes. The only caveat was that they had to be within certain areas of Oregon and the person entering the competition had to be hands-on with the work.

Bronson tapped his fingers on the side of the laptop, an idea churning in his head. He'd always enjoyed working with his hands. Maybe something like this was just what he needed to get himself off the couch and moving. If he could buy an old house for super cheap and fix it up in time for the deadline, then he'd not only have a monetary gain to show the courts, but winning that competition would be an added bonus the judge wouldn't be able to say no to.

A smile played on his lips for the first time in weeks. Numbers and ideas swam through his head as he figured out a plan to be able to make it work. He'd need help, but that could be found locally. Surely in one of those small towns, there was a handyman of some sort who would be willing to be hired full time in order to help put the house in order.

Bronon grabbed his phone and shot his brother a text.

I think I've got it figured out.

Now all Bronson had to do was find a property and officially enter the contest. Starting tomorrow, he'd take a leave of absence from Fathers and Sons and dive into construction management. *Sort of...*

he corrected himself. He wasn't running a crew, since the fine print had a cap on the amount of hired workers a person could bring on. But he'd still be a boss, and that should definitely count for something.

CHAPTER 3

"Oh my gosh," Charli moaned as she licked her fingers. "You're like a sorceress with chocolate."

Caro, one of Charli's best friends, smirked and buffed her shiny red nails on her shirt. "I know." Her Southern drawl made the quip all the more cute, and the two women broke down in laughter.

"Seriously though," Charli said as they calmed down. "How do you come up with so many new ideas? And all of them good?"

Caro rolled her eyes. "All of them aren't good. I bomb out all the time in the kitchen." She tilted her chin down and gave Charli a look. "But do you really think I would bring the yucky ones out front? Of course, what you're eating is good. I wouldn't dare bring it out otherwise."

Charli made a face and tilted her head from side to side. "True enough." Her eyes went to the glass display case. "I'm trying to decide if I love Felix enough to want to bring something home to him."

"Charli, you mean old thing," Caro scolded. "You take that heavenly hunk of man something good." Still muttering, she grabbed a small, mint green box and began stacking a few truffles inside of it.

"You did not just call my brother good-looking," Charli said with a scowl.

"Of course, he's good-looking," Caro shot back. She pursed her lips at Charli. "Looks obviously run in the family, but still...I'd have to be blind and deaf not to see that."

"Blind and *deaf*? What does being deaf have to do with anything?"

"Hon, have you ever listened to the deep tone of your brother's voice?" Caro shook her head and tsked her tongue.

Charli covered her ears. "No more. I don't want to hear that you've got the hots for Felix. That's just weird." She paused. "Huh. I guess I know how Benny felt when Mel and Jensen got together."

Mel and Jensen were two others within their friend group that had become a couple last year. Now they were engaged, along with Cooper and Genni, and everyone had two huge weddings to look forward to at the end of the summer.

Caro rolled her eyes so hard Charli completely lost track of the bright blue color of them. "Geez, Charli. Don't you know anything? I don't have the hots for your brother. I'm just good at appreciating a fine male specimen when I see one."

Charli pretended to wipe a sweaty brow. "Whew. Dodged a bullet there. I love ya, Caro, but you and Felix just don't work for me."

"Or me," Caro said cheerfully, setting the candy box on the top of the counter. "I need a man who will love me more than his boat."

"Don't we all," Charli mumbled. "What do I owe you?"

Caro's perfectly manicured nails went over her heart. "My dear, dear Charlize. Did I just hear you offer to pay me?"

"Knock it off, Caro," Charli said wryly. "I offer to pay you all the time. You just never take payment."

Caro tapped her plump lips with her finger. "Maybe I should rethink the whole 'friend policy' thing."

"You really should," Charli said, gathering the box. "Come on out for dinner and I'll pay for it out of our freezer."

Caro put a hand to her stomach. "If I eat any more fish, I think I might head into the water and swim away. I know we live on the ocean and all, but still, a body needs something with legs once in a while."

Charli laughed so hard she snorted just as the bell rang over the door. Up until that moment, the two women had been alone in the store, leaving them to talk freely, but now a customer interrupted them.

"See ya later, Caro," Charli said, giving a little wave. She paused when she noticed Caro's expression. Turning to see what the candymaker was looking at, Charli felt her whole body go cold. Then hot. Then cold again.

Standing in the doorway was a Greek god.

Or at least, a man who looked like one. He was tall and thickly built. Big enough that he would give Charli's friend Ken, who was the police captain, a run for his money. His nearly black hair held a blue sheen in the sunlight coming through the glass doors and it almost matched the blue of his eyes. Charli squinted slightly, because his eyes weren't just blue. There was something else there...gray, maybe.

His collared shirt had a button open at the top, just enough to see that his skin was sunkissed everywhere and his worn jeans looked worn and stylish at the same time.

"Hello."

Oh, good heavens. Charli was sure she was going to melt into a puddle. Caro might think Felix had a good voice, but it was nothing on Mr. Handsome standing in the entrance.

"He...llo," Caro purred.

Caro's voice snapped Charli out of her lust-induced staredown. She felt her cheeks flush and she spun toward the counter to give herself something to look at other than the stranger.

"I hate to bother you, but I'm a little lost."

Charli felt her eyes go wide as Caro began to primp and preen herself. It was like a bucket of cold water slapping Charli in the face. With her short, sassy hair and athletic build, Charli knew she was no match for Caro's perfectly curvy frame and Southern hospitality. And she loved her friend too much to even try.

"Tell you what," Caro flirted with a few rapid blinks of her eyelashes. "You buy a four-pack of truffles and I'll tell you what you need to know."

A deep, rich laugh came from behind Charli and she fought the sensation to close her eyes and drown in it. It was so open and carefree, so opposite of how she lived her life. It was glorious.

"I think I can manage that," the man said.

Charli could hear his footsteps coming up behind her. Holding her breath in an attempt to be quiet, Charli began stepping to the side, attempting to sneak out and leave Caro and her well-curated flirting skills with their prey. The thought brought an unexpected rush of jealousy to Charli's stomach.

She gave her friend a discreet wave, which Caro didn't seem to notice, then spun when she thought it was safe to do so and practically lunged for the door. She miscalculated, however, and nearly ran over the tourist.

"Excuse me," he said in that dreamy tone of his.

Charli's mouth flopped and knew she must look like Felix's catch of the day. "Uh...yeah..."

He gave her a funny look, then smiled. The look was just as good as his laugh. *Heaven's above, this is stupid. Since when do I fall for handsome strangers?* The word stranger brought Charli to a halt. Something about the man's handsome face looked familiar, yet she couldn't place him.

His eyes, which she could not tell were indeed gray and blue, meandered down then back up to her face. "On your way out?"

Charli nodded, her words still lost at sea.

He turned toward the door. "Let me get that for you." Taking a few steps away, the man held the door open for her while she walked out, still gaping like a largemouth bass.

"What a gentleman," Caro gushed from behind Charli, helping bring Charli's mind back where it belonged.

"Thanks," Charli squeaked before darting out the rest of the way and rushing down the street. She leapt into her car and dropped the candy on the seat before putting both hands on the steering wheel. "I. Am. An. Idiot."

Leaning forward, she planted her head against the wheel and began to laugh. The whole situation was an absolute disaster, which meant she could either cry or laugh, and there was no way she was going to cry. Charli almost never cried and when she did, it certainly wasn't because of overly pretty strangers with chocolate fondue voices who were soon to be caught in Caro's womanly trap. Absolutely not.

BRONSON COULDN'T HELP but watch the fit, gorgeous woman walk past him and climb into an old beat-up truck. Her dark hair framed her oval face perfectly and added a little edge to her looks. Large, dark eyes and plush pink lips had barely responded to his act of chivalry. If he hadn't seen her laughing and talking with the store clerk before he'd entered, Bronson would have wondered if she actually spoke at all.

"She's something, isn't she?"

His head whipped around. For a moment, he'd actually forgotten his purpose for slipping into the cute candy shop. He gave the clerk a crooked smile and shrugged. "That obvious?"

"Only if the drool dripping from your mouth is considered evidence," the blonde said with a smirk.

Bronson laughed, a little uncomfortable with the woman's forthright way of speaking. "Sorry about that." The woman behind the counter was a very attractive woman herself, but her blonde hair and blue eyes were an everyday occurrence in California, and definitely didn't stand out as much as the woman who'd just left.

She waved him off. "No biggie." She straightened her shoulders but tilted her head to the side expectantly. "So?"

Bronson raised his eyebrows. "So?"

She laughed and pointed her head toward the display case. "I do believe you agreed to a four-pack in exchange for information."

Bronson's smile widened. "So I did. I guess I got sidetracked." He walked up, his hands in his pockets as he studied the goodies. "These look great."

The woman fluffed her hair. "Thanks. I'll tell the baker."

Something about the way she said that made Bronson narrow his gaze. "Are you..." He pointed to the chocolates. "Did *you* make these?"

"Guilty as charged." Her Southern accent was a fun addition to their little conversation. It wasn't something he heard very often back home.

Bronson reached over the counter. "Bronson Ramsay."

She smiled sweetly. "Caroline Douglas. My friends call me Caro."

"Is that a way of giving me permission to do the same?"

"I don't know. I don't usually make friends with tourists." Caro put a hand on her cocked hip.

"It just so happens I'm not a tourist."

"Oh?" Her eyebrows rose high.

"I'm here to renovate a home." He slapped his pockets. "Speaking of which, that's why I need help." He finally found the piece of paper he'd been looking for. "I'm looking for this address." Bronson handed it to Caro.

She eyed it and nodded. "I know that house."

Bronson waited.

She waited.

The silence began to grow awkward until Caro cleared her throat and pointed at the treats again.

A rumble of laughter worked its way up Bronson's chest. This woman wasn't one to give up. "Excuse me, Ms. Douglas. It seems I lost my head today." He looked at the case again. "I'll have a mint, a sea salt caramel, an orange and the vanilla creme."

She boxed it up, tied a pretty white bow on top and rang him up.

Bronson handed over his credit card. "So...am I forgiven? Can I get those directions now?"

She handed the card back and scooted the box across the counter with a grin. "It's always nice to get business out of the way first, isn't it?"

Bronson chuckled and nodded. "It is."

"What you're looking for is the old Miller residence. Go north on Main, turn right on Alder. It's about a half-mile off the main street. It'll be on the left-hand side of the street."

Bronson nodded and took his candies. "I appreciate it. Thank you."

"Good luck," Caro called out. "You're gonna need it."

Bronson frowned. "Why's that?"

Caro smiled, a little bit of the devil in her look. "You'll see."

He shook his head and turned to go.

"And feel free to call me Caro."

Bronson looked back one more time to find her resting her chin in her hands as she leaned over the counter. "Thanks, Caro."

"Can I ask why you're headed out that way?"

Bronson held in a sigh. Obviously he wasn't going to be able to escape as quickly as he'd thought. He turned to give her his full attention. "I said I was here to renovate a home. That's the one I bought."

Her eyes widened. "Wow. You're a construction worker, then?"

Bronson felt heat rush up his neck and was grateful his tan usually kept such reactions hidden. "Uh, not really. I'm planning to hire a local handyman to help me." He gave her an imploring smile. "You wouldn't happen to know who I could call?"

Caro laughed. "That's easy. You'll want Charli."

"Charlie?"

She nodded. "Yep, you know the one...." Caro waved her hand toward the door, then stopped quickly and dropped her head to look under the counter. "Hang on. I've got a card and that'll be easier." After fumbling around under the cash register for a moment, she emerged. "Got it! I knew I had a few left over."

Her smile was extra wide as Bronson retrieved the small piece of paper. "Thanks," he said, reading the name. It was spelled a little funny, lacking the 'e' on the end like normal, but he figured that wouldn't affect whether or not the guy could actually do the work. "I'll be sure to give him a call."

Her laughter followed him all the way out the door. "You do that. We'll see if *he* can speak by then."

Bronson shook his head. He wasn't quite sure what to make of the petite and pretty candy maker. He was, however, grateful for her instructions. Climbing back into his SUV, Bronson backed up and followed everything she'd said. Once in the driveway, he finally understood why she'd wished him luck.

The house looked absolutely nothing like the pictures online. "They must have gotten them from when it was first constructed," he grumbled as he stared up at the dilapidated old thing.

The roof was half-missing, the siding looked like it hadn't been painted in fifteen years and any minute, a leprechaun was going to jump out of the overgrown landscape. "This might have been a mistake."

Slowly, Bronson got out of the vehicle and walked to the front door. He'd thought the low price was because of a motivated buyer, but that was apparently not the case. All his hopes of cashing in on a major real estate deal were looking like they might go up in smoke.

But what will happen to your inheritance if you back out now?

The question was valid, though Bronson wasn't happy about it. Taking a fortifying breath, he unlocked the front door and stepped inside, then promptly came back out. "Cats," he groaned.

The more he studied the inside from his perch on the porch, the more he realized he had bought the home of the town's crazy cat lady. From the smell of the interior, she'd had enough felines to fill an entire animal shelter.

CHAPTER 4

Is this Charli Mendez?

Charli frowned at the text. She didn't usually get messages from unknown numbers. Spam calls came through once in a while, but this person knew her name, which made it unlikely they were spamming her.

Yes.

Great! I'm looking to hire a handyman and was told you're the best.

She relaxed and let out a long breath. Job offers she could work with. "Why don't they just call though?" she muttered as her thumbs moved over the keys.

I know my way around a hammer. What can I do for you?

My name is Bronson Ramsay. Can we meet up for lunch and I can tell you about the job?

Sure. When and where? When the meeting was set up, Charli glanced at her watch. She had a few hours before she needed to get cleaned up. Meeting a potential client was always a lot like a job interview. If she showed up covered in paint and sawdust, most people tended to think it unprofessional. *I mean, it's not like my job involves paint or sawdust,* she thought sarcastically.

Pulling her protective glasses back down onto her nose, she began running the sander again. The beautiful buffet she was working on was exactly the kind of project Charli enjoyed. Old and beat up, with a ton of character just waiting to be exposed.

The piece had come in a few weeks ago, but Charli was just now getting enough time to start stripping it. First, she had worked on fixing hinges and drawer slides, and now she was finally ready for the fun part.

After she got it worked down to the wood underneath the fifteen layers of paint someone had put on it, she would stain the piece, put new hardware on the doors and then put it up for sale in her online store. She didn't always have things for sale, since restoring wasn't her full-time job, but she was blessed enough to have a few followers who always enjoyed seeing the pictures of her projects, and that usually led to someone buying the piece.

Someday I'll do this all day, every day.

She blew out a breath, blowing dust everywhere and making herself choke a little. She turned on her Bluetooth again and let the music begin to play before going back to grinding. The repetitive movements were peaceful and did wonders for the tension in her body. She loved how those slow, easy movements could strip away the bad and bring out the hidden beauty within a piece.

Each time Charli restored something, she felt as if she'd given it a new chance at life, and that feeling was addictive...not to mention slightly dangerous. It made her long for the chance to do that in her own life. To step out of the old and into the new.

Her desire to make it on her own, however, always seemed to overpower the longing. She wanted to start her business, but didn't want to rely on anyone else to make it happen. This was going to be her baby. She would accomplish it alone or not at all. Any failures or triumphs would lie solely on her shoulders. It felt to her, like the only possible way to really prove herself in this profession.

She knew her parents wouldn't begrudge her choice of career, but whenever she introduced herself as a restoration specialist, people's interest always faded. Most didn't care about the history of a piece of furniture or whether or not the gloss was high or matte. They just wanted the pretty finished product. The rest was useless background.

But those parts mattered to Charli and she had this...*need* to prove that what she was doing, the dream she wanted to create, was worthwhile. A storefront filled with pieces of history, most lovingly restored at her hands, would be just the way to do it.

When her music track began to play again from the beginning, she glanced at her cell and jumped when she saw the time. Unplugging her tools, she left them on the counter and ran for the house. If she hurried, she'd have just enough time to clean up before meeting Mr. Ramsay at the cafe.

Thirty minutes later, with the taste of mint still in her freshly brushed mouth, she drove down the road and found a parking spot. It was one o'clock and the lunch crowd was still milling around, letting Charli know it would take a while for them to get a table.

She hopped down from the truck and headed to the front door. The sky was gray today with only intermittent spurts of sunshine, so all in all, a very typical coastal day. Wearing her nicest jeans and a v-neck T-shirt, Charli waited at the door, looking around for her potential client.

"Can't say I expected to run into you again."

Charli spun, nearly falling onto the seat of her pants at the sound of that molten chocolate voice. Even though she'd only heard it once, she'd recognize it anywhere. Mr. Greek God was looking adorably disheveled at the moment and it broke his persona just enough to let him appear approachable. His short-sleeved shirt had dust stains on it and his jeans were frayed on the bottoms, leading to old-looking work boots. His hair looked like the ocean breeze had been playing tag, leaving him with a few pieces sticking up in odd places, which made Charli's fingers twitch with a completely inappropriate desire to smooth them down.

She clenched her fingers into fists, shoving the desire aside. "Hello," she managed to croak, then immediately cleared her throat. *Awesome first impression, Charli. Real winner.*

A knee-melting chuckle slipped from his lips. "Good to know you actually speak."

Charli's cheeks heated up quicker than an oyster in boiling water. "Yeah. Sorry about yesterday. I'm not usually so rude. I was in kind of a hurry." The lame excuse did little to alleviate her embarrassment.

The man nodded, then stuck out his hand. His knuckles were bruised and full of cuts, making Charli frown, but she hurried to reach out so as not to be rude again."

"Bronson Ramsay," he said, gripping her fingers firmly.

Charli's jaw snapped shut. *You've got to be kidding me. THIS is my client? What was the good Lord thinking?* She took her hand back and straightened her shoulders and back. "Well, it's a good thing we ran into each other, then. I'm Charlize Mendez."

BRONSON PAUSED. "YOU know I'm supposed to meet..." His eyes narrowed as she looked at him expectantly. *Charlize...no!* "Are you Charlie?"

She gave him a rueful grin. "Are you spelling that with an 'i'? Because Charli is what I go by, but it's not spelled the same as the boy name."

Bronson shook his head and pushed a hand through his hair, knocking dust into the air. He fought the temptation to wave it away. He was a mess from being in the house this morning. But he'd figured another manual laborer would give him a break for being this way. He hadn't planned to run into the beautiful woman from the candy shop, and he'd planned even less for her to be the man he was looking for. "I think maybe there's been some kind of mistake..."

One beautifully shaped eyebrow slowly rose high. "Really? Is this the time when you tell me that I can't be a handyman because I'm a woman? That I can't get the job done because of my gender?" She huffed and folded her arms over her chest. "Wow. I didn't expect you to be misogynist."

Bronson leaned back, his temper flaring. "I didn't say any of those things. Don't put words in my mouth."

"I didn't need to," Charli snapped. "Your face said it all." She backed up a couple of steps, putting her hands in the air. "That's okay. I don't need your job. Good luck finding anyone within an hour who can give you the level of work you'll want." She spun on her sandal heel and began to storm toward the old truck Bronson recognized.

Bronson felt shell-shocked for a minute after her little performance. Yes, he didn't think she could do the job, but it wasn't anything personal, and had little to do with her gender. A man the same size as her probably wouldn't be able to handle some of the projects his house needed. In his mind, he'd pictured someone as large as himself. Then and only then would he have a chance at getting this house ready in time. Those eight weeks were sitting heavily on his shoulders and Bronson needed every advantage he could get.

Her comment about not finding anyone else close by, however, had him panicking. Before he could think better about it, he lunged after her. "Charli...wait."

The look she gave him when she turned around should have stopped him in his tracks, but apparently he was a glutton for punishment, because he couldn't leave things like this. It bothered him that she thought so lowly of him. The fact that in a few weeks he'd never see her again didn't matter. He didn't want her thinking he was a jerk. "Let's work this out like adults, huh?"

She snorted, her dark bangs coming down to cover one eye. "I think we're already past that, don't you?"

Bronson shook his head, finding himself strangely intrigued by her spicy attitude. "Let me at least buy you lunch. You came all the way here and even though the job isn't going to work out, the least I can do is feed you."

"All the way here?" She made a face. "Have you driven around yet? There is no 'all the way here'. I literally live less than five minutes away."

Bronson chuckled. "You can tell me all about it," he urged, "over lunch."

Charli gave him a reluctant grin. "Sorry. I guess I sort of jumped all over you." She sighed and her shoulders relaxed. "Okay, lunch is fine. But I'll pay my own way, thank you."

This time it was Bronson's eyebrows that went up. He'd never had a woman refuse a meal before. "Okay…if that's the way you want it."

She nodded. "Yep."

Bronson waved a hand toward the door and they squeezed their way inside.

"Hey, Charli!" the young hostess chirped. "Two of you today?"

Charli nodded. "Yeah." She looked around and leaned forward. "Do you have any room out back? This is more business meeting stuff and it'd be nice to hear ourselves think."

"Sure thing." The young woman wrote something down. "I think two of the tables are filled with employees taking breaks, but the third is open." She looked up with a grin. "That work?"

"Perfect. Thanks, Sarah."

The girl nodded, motioned to a nearby waitress and handed off some menus. "Have a good meal."

"Thanks!" Charli called again as they followed the waitress into the employee area and out a back door. On the small alleyway, behind the buildings, sat three small bistro tables. Just as the hostess had said, employees were sitting at two of them, but a third was open.

"Can I get you two something to drink?" the waitress, whose name tag said *Madison*, asked.

"Water," Charli immediately responded.

"You have all the usual sodas?" Bronson asked. When the waitress nodded in affirmation, he gave his order and then settled into his seat. Looking around, he noticed how peaceful and clean the alley was. "Wow. This certainly isn't what I expected."

Charli nodded, looking at ease in her seat. "Yeah. The tourists don't know this is back here, which is nice. Usually it's reserved for workers, so we got lucky today." Her dark eyes leveled on him. "So tell me about this job."

Bronson frowned. "I don't know if that's a good idea." He didn't want to discuss things that wouldn't work out.

Charli's eye roll was impressive with how much disgust she portrayed through it. Leaning onto the table, she folded her hands together. "Listen, Mr. Ramsay—"

"Bronson. Just Bronson."

She nodded. "Fine. Bronson. I meant what I said about there not being anyone else who would be able to handle your needs close by. I get calls for the next two towns north and south of us. If you're looking to fix something up, then I'm your woman."

Bronson matched her stance. "But see, that's the problem. As capable as you probably are, I need something built practically from the ground up, and I need it done quickly." He shook his head and forced himself to relax in his seat again. Leaning forward had felt too intimate with a woman he was attracted to, but trying to let down gently. "It's nothing personal. I need someone who can do the big jobs."

"Try me."

He sighed. *Fine. What'll it hurt? After she sees the house, she'll probably run for the hills and it'll all be over.* "Okay. You think you can handle it? After we eat, I'll take you there and tell you exactly what I'm looking to do. Then you can make up your mind yourself."

Charli nodded firmly. "I appreciate the vote of confidence." She leaned back and a small, seductive smirk played on her lips. "You're expecting me to run, aren't you?"

Bronson met her stare, but didn't respond. This woman was too clever for her own good. *It's probably why she's in such demand around here.* Her attitude was fierce but playful at the same time and he could only imagine how enticing that was to the residents.

Charli's grin turned into a full-fledged smile and then she began to laugh. The sound was low and husky, stirring more unwanted feelings in Bronson's chest. He hadn't come here to be attracted to a local. He'd come here to earn his inheritance, something that was rightfully his. And he wasn't going to let anyone, not even the oh-so-tempting handyman that wasn't really a man, ruin that for him.

CHAPTER 5

Charli almost laughed out loud as she followed Bronson to the house he was renovating. Mrs. Miller has been the resident cat lady of Seaside Bay. If Bronson had been inside, he would've already figured that out. Between the smell and the shredded…everything…there was no way to deny what had gone on in that place.

Mrs. Miller had been almost blind by the time she'd passed away and the cats had begun to multiply at an alarming rate as her eyesight disintegrated. When a person couldn't tell the difference between male and female anymore, things tended to get tricky.

Charli hopped down from her seat and put her hands on her hips. "She's a beaut, isn't she?"

Bronson looked like he might choke. "Excuse me?"

"This is a Queen Anne-style home," Charli said, looking at the weary building with a sharp eye. "It was popular with the early settlers between, oh…1840 and 1965. Part of the Classic Revival." Charli slammed her door shut and walked up to the front porch. "There were several styles that came into being during that time, but Queen Anne was one of the prettiest." She looked over her shoulder at a shocked Bronson. "Funny thing was, they began building homes like this because they were looking for styles that had nothing to do with English influences at all. The inhabitants of the coast wanted to show they were Americans, completely unaffected by the traditions of the country who had once ruled over them."

Bronson's mouth opened and closed a few times before he laughed and shook his head. "You know your history."

Charli smiled proudly back. "Yep. My favorite subject." She ran a hand lovingly over the splintered handrail of the porch stairs. "Every object has a story to tell. My job is to make it easier to see."

There was a moment of quiet and Charli realized she'd probably shared too much. Feeling embarrassed, she turned to say something, but Bronson's look stopped her cold. His eyes were a steely gray at the moment, the blue having fled at the intensity of his gaze. She swallowed, not sure how to act under his scrutiny.

"It's nice to see someone who's so passionate about their work," he finally said, his voice lower than normal. "I think everyone should find something they're passionate about."

Charli's eyebrows pulled together. The words seemed a little strange, but didn't truly reveal anything. She cocked her head. "Just why did you buy this place?"

His stare dropped to the ground and Bronson cleared his throat. "I planned to flip it."

"Really?" Charli frowned. "That seems a little odd. If you're looking for rundown homes, we've got those in spades, but our little haven is a far cry from a real estate hot spot." She folded her arms over her chest. "Why do I get the feeling you're hiding something?"

Bronson looked up and glared at her. "I don't have to spill my life secrets to you."

"Never said you did." Charli fought her rising frustration. No matter how good-looking this guy was, she wasn't about to deal with someone who was playing things on the shady side. "But if I'm going to be working on this home, then you'd better tell me the real story."

Bronson's look turned cool. "I didn't say I was hiring you. In fact, I believe you got mad because I didn't think you could do the job." He waved toward the house. "Do you see why I feel the way I do?"

Charli glanced at the house, then back. "There's nothing that needs fixing in this house that I can't do. All you need is the right budget and we'll put together a plan and schedule."

Bronson snorted. "And when heavy lumber needs to be moved in? Or what about putting up the sheetrock or installing granite countertops?" He gave her a pointed look. "It's obvious you're fit, Charli, but how do you propose to manage those things?"

"How did you figure you would do it before?"

"Between me and another large man, we should have enough muscle power to move almost anything," Bronson said.

Charli laughed incredulously. "First off, there shouldn't be any sheetrock lifting unless you're planning to change the floorplan. And even if there was, there are machines to do that for you." She flexed. "My lack of muscles shouldn't be an issue."

"And the countertops?" Bronson challenged.

She shrugged. "Again, there are plenty of ways to rig things up, but I want to know the truth behind your work here." She looked at him intently. "Have you ever flipped a home before?"

Some of Bronson's defensiveness disappeared, his shoulders dropping and tension visibly shedding from his face. "No," he admitted softly. "This will be my first."

"Do you plan to do this for a living?" He paused and Charli knew more than ever that he was holding something back.

"Not necessarily."

Charli shook her head. "That's not good enough. I need the truth here or I'm out, whether you want me or not."

Bronson pushed a hand through his hair. "It all sounds so dumb," he grumbled.

Charli waited. She'd learned that trick with her brother. Stay quiet and the other person would inevitably spill everything. Silence was sometimes the best form of torture.

"I want to enter a competition, okay?" Bronson finally shouted. "I need to—" He snapped his mouth shut and stormed toward her. "I need this, okay? I need to renovate this house in the next eight weeks, win the Homeowner's Renovation award, and then return to California."

"Eight weeks?" Charli laughed incredulously. "You're kidding, right? If you really want to fix this house from top to bottom, you're gonna need at least three to four months."

Bronson shook his head. "I don't have that."

She groaned. "You need an entire crew, Bronson. Why didn't you bring a construction crew with you?" She scrunched her nose. "Though, it's always harder to keep the integrity of the home when you have a bunch of men tramping around like Neanderthals, but still, at least you'd have enough manpower to make the deadline."

"I can't."

"Why not?"

Bronson gave her a tired look. "Because the rules specifically state that it has to be work you do yourself. Hiring a single helper is fine, hiring a company to do it for you is not." He ticked his head to the side. "Unless they were your own company, I suppose. Then you could probably play with the rules a bit."

Charli shook her head and stepped back from his alluring presence. She was going to be sad to see this job go, but there were too many red flags. "I'm sorry. But you were right. I'm not your gal."

He looked surprised. "What? Why say that now?"

"Because I don't work with partners unless I need an extra set of hands for just one or two things. I work alone."

"Always?"

"Always."

His eyes went gray again as he looked at her. "I find that hard to believe." His eyes dropped to her hand and Charli scowled. "Does that mean no husband or boyfriend either?"

"What business is that of yours?" She backed up even more.

Bronson smirked. "It's not. But you were so adamant you do everything yourself, it makes me think you probably don't let men into your life at all."

She folded her arms over her chest, suddenly feeling attacked. "I live with my brother." She leaned forward. "My protective brother," she emphasized, to Bronson's apparent amusement. "That's enough for me."

He was still grinning. "Good to know. But that doesn't help us here. I need someone to work *with* me, not over me."

"Then good luck, because it's not going to be me."

"NAME YOUR PRICE." THE words were out of his mouth before Bronson could think better of it. *Wait...I thought I didn't want to hire her?* He hadn't. Or he didn't. Right now Bronson wasn't sure what he wanted. The spitfire in front of him had his head spinning.

She obviously knew her stuff and had answers to almost all his construction worries, but she thought his timeline was crazy and didn't want to work with him.

The challenge of her shutting him down was proving too intriguing to ignore. The more she said she didn't work with a partner, the more he wanted to be the partner. *But that's not going to help us make the deadline or help me win my inheritance.*

"Price?" Charli scoffed and those bangs slid into her eyes again.

Her hair was cut short, at chin level in front, but shorter in the back. The strands were straight and silky looking, but styled with a little more punk than Bronson would have expected. Long and blonde was the order of fashion in the area he lived in in California and Charli was the exact opposite, which might explain why he found himself so drawn to her.

"Yes. Your price. Everyone has a price." It was an ugly truth, but one nonetheless. Growing up with a wealthy lawyer for a father had shown Bronson that everyone could be bought.

She shook her head. "We're not in California anymore, Mr. Ramsay."

Her formal words didn't go unnoticed.

He made a point of looking around. "I think I'm aware of that."

"Then you should know better than to think you can buy me off."

Bronson shrugged and put his hands in his pockets, feigning a nonchalance he didn't feel. If Charli didn't agree to his terms, he wasn't sure what he would do. He believed her assertion that no one else was close enough to do what he needed done. But Bronson didn't know enough about construction to do it himself and he didn't think online videos would be enough. Without Charli, he was well and truly sunk. "Are you telling me you don't have any use for a lucrative paying gig?"

Charli's brown skin had a pink tinge to it and her jaw was clenched tighter than a bank vault. "You wouldn't be able to convince me to work for you if you were the last man on earth," she spat. "I'm out of here."

Bronson felt a wave of sadness mixed with relief flood him as she stomped to her truck. While he was in a major pickle now that she'd turned him down for good, he was also extremely glad to see her stand up for herself and not give in just because a few dollar signs were flashed in her direction.

In fact, if he wasn't in such a bad situation with the house and his inheritance, Bronson could see himself trying to start a relationship with the spunky handywoman. The physical attraction had been immediate, and now that he was seeing her inner strength and fire, his interest had grown tenfold.

Her truck sputtered a little before roaring to life and Bronson watched her spit gravel and pine needles in her hurry to get onto the road and away from him.

"Now what?" he asked the remaining silence once her truck had disappeared. He sighed and turned to the house, but couldn't quite make himself go inside. He'd slept in his car last night, so he could leave the windows and doors open in order to relieve the ammonia smell enough to be able to walk inside the home. It had helped, but the very foundation of the home seemed to reek with the odor.

He'd walked through this morning, gagging and inspecting every part of the house, coming away with a sense of foreboding plus a layer of dust and dirt that he hadn't had time to scrub off.

"Time to call for reinforcements." Bronson grabbed his cell and sat down on the front step. For the next half-hour, he Googled every form of the word handyman that he could think of. After writing down all the names he found, he spent another almost two hours calling around and looking for someone with availability.

When the sun began to slip behind the trees and the heat of the day started to wave, so did Bronson's hopes and plans. He'd called dozens of contractors and laborers, and no one, not a single one, would be able to help him in his situation.

His only option was Charli, or losing his inheritance, which ultimately meant losing Fathers and Sons.

Bronson dropped his phone on the step next to him and put his head in his hands. The sensation of failure felt extra heavy tonight. Sometimes he wondered why he couldn't be more like his brother and sister. They always seemed to have their act together, knew where they were going in life, and the death of Janine, their father's girlfriend, hadn't even been a blip on their radar.

Bronson's sigh was long and loud. While he might have inherited a similar temper to his siblings, he had somehow also received a desire for something beyond the shallow emotions the rest of his family had in spades. He just couldn't imagine going through life so cold and hard as they seemed to be.

It had been Janine who had shown him what it was like to build others up, rather than cut down the competition. She'd shown him kindness and it made him want to reciprocate to others, while that same kindness gave Canon indigestion. Janine's motherly affection had given Bronson the desire for a home filled with laughter and love, rather than granite and steel.

Now he wanted to keep open a charity that did just that for struggling kids, but how was he to accomplish that if he couldn't get his inheritance? The lease for the building the nonprofit was in was almost up and they were about to be kicked out, which left Bronson with only one option. He had to find a way to buy the building. But land prices in California were astronomical and he didn't have enough. His inheritance did.

All of that was simply a pipe dream, however, if he couldn't prove to the courts that he could hold down a job and have something tangible to show for it in eight weeks.

Bronson's lips twisted to the side as he picked up his phone again. The odds were completely against him, but the thought of those children who desperately needed a good adult influence in their lives tugged at him too strongly for Bronson to ignore.

No matter what Charli said, Bronson had to try. He might go down in flames, but at least he would be able to walk away saying he'd done his best.

Pulling up the internet, he searched for home renovation videos. The first order of business was going to be figuring out what needed to actually be fixed. There wasn't time to rebuild the entire house. He'd have to prioritize projects, though a few were obvious.

The floor would have to be replaced to get rid of the smell. He'd need a new roof and new paint on the outside and inside. As for the things behind the walls, he'd have to rely on whatever he could find online. Bronson had no idea how to take care of plumbing or electrical and he wasn't about to sell a home that wasn't in good enough shape to live in.

"Here's hoping those parts have been updated at least some time in the last twenty years," he muttered as the first video began to play.

It was going to be a long eight weeks.

CHAPTER 6

The situation with Bronson wouldn't leave Charli's mind. Two days sped past and every minute of it had been spent trying to push handsome Bronson and his impossible task out of her head.

How in the world does he think he's going to renovate that place from top to bottom in eight weeks? He would need a full crew or a miracle. She snorted. *He has no experience at all. It really would be a miracle.*

"Ouch." She put her finger in her mouth, trying to ease the sting of a pinch from her wrench. "Stupid Bronson who keeps distracting me."

"Everything okay in here?" Mr. Smithers asked, shuffling to the bathroom door.

"Just fine," Charli automatically answered.

"I thought I heard you say, 'Ouch.'" The elderly man bent down a little in order to see Charli's face under his sink where she'd been working on a leak.

Charli forced a soft laugh. "I did. The wrench slipped and nicked my knuckle. But I'm fine. It's just a little pinch."

He straightened, taking him out of sight. "If you say so. I'll just be grateful to have this leak gone. Last week it soaked my towel before I could even use it."

Charli grinned. She adored the elderly widower. Most of the town did. "I'm almost done. The leak was coming from the water supply. Your compression fitting has started to erode, which I'm working on replacing. That's why your towel was wet, because these types of leaks will drip even when the water's not running."

Mr. Smithers chuckled. "How you hold so much knowledge in that head of yours is a mystery, Ms. Charli."

Charli grinned into the dark cabinet space. "Eh...I just have too much time on my hands, Mr. Smithers."

Still chuckling, he shuffled out of the bathroom and all became quiet again.

Charli sighed and put her finger in her mouth for another second before pulling her brain back to the task at hand. It was harder than it should have been. She could still hear Bronson telling her about the project.

Despite the craziness of the situation, Charli was a little bit intrigued by the proposition. No, she didn't want to take on a newbie as a partner, but the idea of winning a competition had never occurred to her and was a cool idea.

Winning that kind of award would probably be a big boost in her work, which could make a difference in when she'd be able to open that storefront. If she had enough of a social media following, she might be able to sell a few extra pieces and put away the reserves she was going to need in order to pay the bills.

A grunt escaped Charli as she gave a last tug on the fitting. "Time to test this puppy out," she muttered, crawling out from under the sink.

She headed to the small utility room, reached around the water heater and turned the main water line back on before heading back to the bathroom.

"Gotcha," she said with a smile when no water leaked from the pipes. Standing up, she stretched and cracked her neck. Sometimes she wondered how a big man could handle doing this type of work. It gave her kinks all over her body and she wasn't even close to being tall.

An image of Bronson trying to fold his body under a sink came to mind and at first it caused Charli to laugh, but it was quickly followed by a scowl. "Get out of my head," she demanded.

"What was that?" Mr. Smithers called from the sitting room.

"The water's on!" Charli answered. "Leak looks like it's gone and your house has water again." She gathered her tools and walked to where the homeowner was reading a book.

"You're a miracle worker," Mr. Smithers said with a crooked grin.

Charli smiled in return, though the words were eerily reminiscent of her earlier thoughts. "No biggie, Mr. Smithers. Just doing my duty by keeping your towels dry."

He chuckled.

"Have a great rest of the day!" Charli let herself out and dumped everything in the back of her truck. Her stomach growled and after glancing at her cell, she figured she had time to go home for lunch before her next appointment.

Deciding to take it slow, Charli cruised down Main at an easy pace, enjoying watching the tourists and colorful seaside shops that made up her place of residence. She loved Seaside Bay. Living in a bigger town would have made it easier to build up her restoration business, but she just couldn't seem to drag herself away from the quaint area she lived in. It was beautiful with the ocean so close and clean, and neat in a way the bigger cities could never achieve.

Her eyes caught on a large, new sign to her right and Charli nearly hit her brakes when she read what it said.

FOR SALE

"No..." she breathed. She quickly pulled off to the side of the road so as not to block traffic and jumped from the cab of her truck. It was sheer luck that the road was empty as she darted across, because she hadn't bothered to look at all before walking up to the sign.

The warehouse she had been eyeing for years was finally for sale. Charli swallowed hard as she grabbed one of the fliers with information. She skimmed through all the statistics on the building, she had those memorized. What she wanted to know was the price and who was selling it.

Her heart fell when she realized the price wasn't on the flier. That was never a good sign. With shaking fingers, Charli punched in the Realtor number.

"Hello. Seaside Realty. This is Jonathon speaking."

"Hi, this is Charlize...Charli Mendez," she rasped, then cleared her throat.

"Hey, Charli. What can I do for you?"

"So...I saw that you're selling that warehouse off Main."

"Oh, yeah! The owner isn't local, so they haven't paid a lot of attention to it since it went empty. I finally convinced them it was a good idea to sell it." Charli could hear the smile in Jonathon's voice. Big commission opportunities like this one didn't come along every day.

"Well, I was wondering what the owner is asking for it," Charli managed to get out. The words were sticking to her dry throat and she felt like she might throw up. She'd been waiting so long for an opportunity like this, but her savings wasn't where she wanted it, which meant her chance might come too soon. And with the positioning on Main Street, she was terrified that if she didn't act, someone else would grab it before she could.

"Really? I didn't know you were interested in real estate."

"It's mostly curiosity," she lied. Her dreams were just that. Hers. It wasn't common knowledge that she wanted to do restoration full-time and she wasn't ready to share it with the public. If it happened, then wonderful. If not, then no one would be able to talk about her failure.

"Sure. Let me grab it..." His voice trailed off and she could hear papers being shuffled. When he came back and quoted her the price, Charli almost fell to the pavement.

It was far more than she'd expected and planned for. In order to act now, she'd need a much heftier loan than she'd thought. "Is that a good price?" she asked, hoping he would say the owner was asking too much, but had been stubborn or something.

"Yeah...it's fair market value," Jonathan said, not knowing that every word felt like a knife stab.

"Great." Charli choked on the word. "I appreciate you answering my question."

"Anytime," Jonathan said cheerily. "Talk to you later."

Charli hung up and her vision blurred. She rarely cried, but right now felt like the perfect time for a sob fest.

A STRING OF EXPLETIVES poured from Bronson's mouth as he held his throbbing thumb. Who knew a hammer was such a weapon? The scenes in movies where people hit themselves had always been funny, but laughing was the farthest thing from Bronson's mind at the moment.

Everything was falling apart. He'd slept less than two hours each of the past two nights, knowing that unless he utilized every moment of every day, he wouldn't stand a chance at finishing.

But his lack of slumber was hitting him. His mind drifted and he found himself nodding off at odd times. Like when he was swinging a hammer. The upside was that he wasn't the least bit sleepy at the moment, not while every drop of blood in his body tried to push its way into the small extremity.

He sucked on his thumb, knowing he must look ridiculous, but not caring. He groaned. This was never going to work. He just didn't have the skills necessary to do this by himself. Forbidden thoughts of a strong, beautiful woman passed through his head and for the first time in forty-eight hours, Bronson let her stay. He'd worked hard not to think of the dark-haired handywoman. She'd shut him down so cleanly that he had no hope of recourse.

He'd jumped the gun on the situation, a mix of eagerness and anticipation fueling his actions. Bronson and the other volunteers at the children's shelter had been looking for a miracle, and as sad as he was to lose his father, Bronson thought the solution had fallen in his lap. Instead, it was proving to be a curse.

The hoops he was having to jump through made no sense and went against everything he'd ever known about his father. Conrad Ramsay was a strict man, yes. He was self-disciplined and more intelligent than the majority of the population. He had to be in his line of work. But he wasn't cruel. Having the will say that Bronson had to prove himself like this before receiving his inheritance was exactly that…cruel.

Bronson's eyes stayed glued to the hardwood floor. He'd felt completely lost after Janine died, then again with his father, and now life was throwing him another curveball that he wasn't prepared to swing at.

Dust filtered through the sunlight streaming in the window. "I've got no hope of anything at this point," he muttered to himself as he stared into the light. He thought of the kids he wouldn't be able to help and his heart sank even further. He wanted to offer so much and right now his hands were tied. He needed that inheritance.

Deciding to swallow his own pride, Bronson stood up and walked outside, grabbing his phone on the way. The time had come to start begging.

His brother picked up on the first ring. "What do you need, Bron?"

Bronson grimaced. He didn't want to do this, but the kids were more important. "Hey, Canon. How are things going?" Maybe buttering up his stoic brother would help.

"I don't have time for chitchat. Why are you calling?" There was a slight pause and then Canon continued on without waiting for an answer. "You're not calling to tell me you're quitting, are you?"

There was an odd tone to Canon's voice, but since he couldn't see his brother's face, Bronson didn't worry about it. "N-no," he assured Canon. "I, uh, was hoping maybe you'd found something that would help with the stipulations though. I really need that money."

A long sigh came through the line. "For what?" Canon snapped. "So you can buy a house in Miami? Or sail around the world in a yacht? Some of us have worked for what we have, you know. Maybe you should try it."

Bronson's jaw clenched. He'd had this argument with his brother too many times. Why no one was willing to see his work with the nonprofit as actual work was beyond him.

"Oh, wait, I forgot. You spend all your time at that charity house, right? How come you don't ask them to pay your bills?"

"That's the whole point of a charity, Canon," Bronson said tightly. "People volunteer so the money can go toward helping others."

"Others who should look at getting a job themselves," Canon shot back. "The will is what it is, Bron. Either abide by its rules or lose it. I don't really care. But you should know that your eight weeks started as soon as you left home, so if you botch things with that house, or whatever it is you're doing, you're done. The judge will rule against you."

Bronson didn't respond. He had no idea what to say. Any hopes of finding a loophole or getting sympathy from his brother had fluttered out the window like the robin he'd found nesting in a back room earlier this morning. The fact that the two of them were brothers and yet so polar opposite in their personalities still baffled Bronson. He knew Canon had learned his people skills from their mother, but the man was intelligent enough to realize the behavior was wrong. Or at least he should have been. *If only Janine had been able to get through to him,* Bronson thought regretfully.

His head began to pound and he squeezed his eyes shut.

"Did you hear me?" Canon asked curtly.

"Loud and clear," Bronson said. He pinched the bridge of his nose. "Guess I better get back to work, then."

"You had to learn sometime," Canon grumbled. The line went dead before Bronson could respond at all.

Growling slightly, he shoved the phone in his back pocket, then winced when he pushed against his still hurting thumb.

"Now what?"

Bronson went to his cooler, grabbed a soda and headed out to the front porch. He sat on the top step and popped the top of the can, taking a long, refreshing swallow. He began to go through his options. Changing directions wasn't going to work. His eight weeks had started, so he either finished this project, or let go of the inheritance.

"But I can't do this alone. The rules say I can't hire a crew, so I have to simply find a partner." His lips pinched into a thin white line.

It always seemed to come back to Charli. She was his only option. Bronson pushed a hand through his hair. "The question is…how much groveling is it going to take to get her on my side?"

He'd admired her values when she'd turned down his money, but now he wished she wasn't quite so morally strong. She had to have a price. It might not be money, but everyone had a breaking point. Bronson slumped on the stoop. He didn't like thinking of someone like that, especially someone as intriguing as Charli. It was a technique his mother had excelled at.

Study a person, find their weakness, then squeeze it until you get what you want.

He felt sick. His stomach churned at the thought of doing that to her. "I can't," he rasped. "I just can't. Charli doesn't deserve that, and I refuse to be that person."

Janine had taught him a better way, and it had brought more fulfillment to his existence than anything his mother had ever given him.

"I'll just have to use logic," he decided. "She seemed like a reasonable woman, if you don't get on her bad side. Surely she can be convinced to help."

Determination building in his chest, Bronson chugged the rest of his drink, then rose and threw the can away. He grabbed his gear and headed for his car. The first order of business would be to get a hotel, and get cleaned up. Convincing Charli to help him was going to take his best effort, and his filthy appearance was not it.

CHAPTER 7

Charli's foot wouldn't stop tapping on the floor. *Why are banks always so cold and austere? You'd think they'd want people to feel welcome, not terrified.*

With no other options before her, Charli had decided the best thing she could do was see about a loan. It wasn't the ideal situation, not even close. It was far more debt than she wanted to take on, but with time ticking away and the warehouse available for anyone and everyone to purchase, she felt trapped.

You could have taken that job with Bronson. He said to name your price.

"No," she murmured to herself.

"What was that?" Gladys, one of the tellers, looked up from her computer screen.

"Nothing," Charli said, pasting a smile on. "Just talking to myself."

Gladys gave her a weird look, but didn't ask questions, thankfully.

You work alone. Taking Bronson's offer would mean having a partner and that just wouldn't work.

She deflated a little in her seat. She knew all the facts, but somehow the idea still taunted her. What she really wanted in life was just out of reach and the easiest path of resistance was Bronson's offer. The problem was...it was also the worst path. His looks were distracting enough, Charli didn't need to work alongside a man who had no idea what he was doing and was simply playing around for a lark. That wasn't who she was.

"Ms. Mendez?" Tim Flannagan called from his office door. He smiled politely and waited for her to walk his way.

Charli's knees were shaking and she prayed it couldn't be seen through her slacks. "Mr. Flannagan," she said, reaching out to shake his hand.

Tim reciprocated. "I think we've known each other too long for that," he said kindly. "Just Tim will do."

Charli nodded. "Thanks. Then be sure to call me Charli."

"Sounds good." He waved her inside his office and they both got settled in their seats. "So." Tim folded his hands on top of his desk. "It says on my notes that you're interested in a loan?" His dark brown eyebrows rose up high, accenting the beginning of wrinkles on his forehead.

Charli nodded. "Yeah...I, um, am interested in buying a piece of real estate."

"Ah." Tim straightened and went back through the papers on his desk. "Do you know what piece of property you're looking to buy?" He frowned. "I'm assuming we're looking at a commercial loan, not a home loan?" His brown eyes met hers, seeking confirmation.

Charli nodded. "Right. I'm interested in that warehouse down on Main."

Those eyebrows shot up again. "Really? What exactly are you planning on doing with it?"

Charli paused. She wasn't quite ready to share her ideas. Not even her friends knew she wanted to open a storefront. "Is that something you have to know?" she finally asked.

Tim gave her a small smile. "Not always, but it helps. Truth be told, the amount of money you're asking for is quite high for us. We don't do a lot of large commercial loans. And against your income...well..."

Charli squirmed in her seat. "What about if Felix and I split the loan? Does that make a difference?"

Tim pursed his lips. "It might. Does he make more than you do?"

Charli shrugged. "We have fairly similar incomes. His is high during the summer, but almost dead during the winter."

"Understandable," Tim muttered, still looking through the papers. "But I think one of the biggest problems is the fact that you have so little collateral."

Charli held in her sigh. She knew this wasn't going to work. "Mr. Flannagan...Tim...what exactly would I need in order to make this loan work? That warehouse hasn't been up for sale in years and I don't know when it'll be up again. I'd like to jump on it now before my chance is gone. So what exactly does your bank need to see in order to make that happen?"

Tim sighed, his look sympathetic, which sent Charli's heart plummeting. "I can't give you an exact number you'd have to have in your bank account or anything like that, Charli, but...why don't I show you some numbers and then you can see why we're concerned, okay?"

Charli nodded eagerly. Numbers were facts and those she could work with. If she knew exactly what they were seeing, she had a better chance of reaching whatever level they wanted in order to get the loan.

A half-hour later, she was back out in the mostly overcast weather, trying to hide her tears from those passing her on the street. Keeping her head down, she wound through the tourists until she reached her parking spot. After she was closed inside her truck, all bets were off.

Between the down payment she would need in order to buy the building and the high interest rate because it was a commercial loan rather than residential...well, Charli stood no chance, whatsoever. She'd have to use her entire savings just for the down payment and that would leave her with nothing to live on while she tried to build the restoration business.

Tears streamed down her cheeks and she didn't even bother to wipe them away. It had been a difficult few days, which had tugged her normally controllable emotions all over the place. She felt like a dramatic teenage girl, who had no control over herself and broke down on a daily basis.

"Get a hold of yourself!" she scolded, wiping harshly at her cheeks. She forced herself to take deep breaths, until it felt like her heart was calming back down to normal. Closing her eyes, she focused on bringing her mind and body back under control.

A knock on her window caused Charli to scream and all her hard work disappeared as her heart nearly jumped out of her chest.

"Oh my gosh," she breathed as she looked into Bronson's concerned blue gaze. Her chest heaved as they stared at each other, neither moving for several seconds. Finally, Bronson put up his hand and made a rolling motion with his arm. Charli almost laughed as she turned the key in the ignition so she could get the window down. "I don't think anyone actually rolls down their window by hand anymore," she said, feeling a little lighter from the change in topic.

Bronson gave her a sheepish grin. "Maybe not, but I think we all still know what it means."

Charli shrugged. "True enough." She cleared her throat. "What can I do for you, Bronson?"

Bronson studied her. "Are you okay?"

Charli turned away. He was seeing too much. She should have gone home before breaking down. It was no one else's business what was going on with her life. "I'm fine," she said curtly.

"Are you sure?"

Charli snapped her head to look at him. "I'm *fine*, Mr. Ramsay. Now...did you have something else you wanted? If not, I have a schedule to keep."

Bronson pinched his lips together, then nodded. "All right. If that's how you want to play it." He scratched his chin. "I actually was hoping to run into you. I know you're busy, but do you have like ten minutes for a..." He looked around. "A smoothie?" His smile was dazzling and Charli had to wonder how many yachts his orthodontist had gotten out of that deal. "My treat?"

Charli frowned. "Why are you wanting to buy me a smoothie?"

Bronson's smile lost some of its genuine note, but to his credit, it stayed in place. "I need some help, and I'm afraid you're my only hope."

※

BRONSON WANTED TO GROAN at his words. *Nothing like sounding like a desperate idiot. Works every time.*

"I'm your only hope?" A smile played with the edge of her beautiful lips. "Are you going to take me to a galaxy far far away?"

Bronson chuckled. "Not this time. But I'm sure we could work something out in the future."

Charli's answering laugh was exactly what Bronson needed to hear. The huskiness to her tone caused warmth to hit him right in the sternum and made him wish their situation was different. In another time and place, Charli would be exactly the type of woman Bronson would ask out. As it was, he needed her help. Mixing emotions into the situation wouldn't be a good choice. Maybe after everything was over and done he could see about taking her to a dinner that had nothing to do with business.

"Okay," she said, rolling up her window, then stepping out of the truck. "But only because I'm a sucker for Mel's new smoothie bowls."

Bronson frowned. "Mel? Smoothie bowl?"

Charli tilted her head toward the shop. "Mel, or Melody, owns the shop. She added smoothie bowls to it a few months ago and they're amazing. I pull on our friendship wayyy too often and end up eating my weight in Kiwasome Granola whenever I get the chance."

"I have no idea what you just said, but I'm game." Bronson stepped back, so Charli could move past him, and they headed to the restaurant. They walked in companionable silence to Smooth Moves, or it at least appeared that way on the outside. Inside, Bronson was running through every possible scenario he could think of that would convince Charli to help him. At this point, he was the desperate idiot he sounded like earlier.

"Charli!" A tall, willowy blonde waved eagerly at Charli as she and Bronson came inside the store.

"Hey, Mel!" Charli said, waving back.

The blonde's eyes darted to Bronson, widened, then went back to Charli. Those bright blue orbs spoke volumes and Bronson held back a chuckle at Charli's discomfort.

Charli shook her head at her friend, then stepped up to the counter. "A Kiwasome bowl with granola," Charli said quickly, still darting glances at Mel, who looked ready to bounce out of her spot behind the counter.

Bronson leaned down close to Charli. "What do you recommend?"

She glanced up, then paused, looking surprised at his nearness. "Uh...I thought I already made that clear."

"Yeah, but I'm allergic to kiwi."

Charli leaned back, frowning. "Really?"

Bronson shrugged. "It makes my throat itch."

"Huh." Her deep gaze went back to the menu board. "Then I'd try Sweet Citrus. It's almost like a dessert."

Bronson nodded and straightened. "I'll take your word for it." He smiled at the girl waiting for his order. Her cheeks pinked up and Bronson smiled wider until an elbow hit his side.

"You keep on like that and she'll faint soon," Charli hissed.

Bronson looked over at her, his eyebrow raising. "Whatever do you mean?"

Charli rolled her eyes and leaned in front of him. "Hey, Megan. Can we get a Sweet Citrus...large."

Megan nodded jerkily and kept her eyes down as she gave them their total. Bronson took out his card and got them paid for before they turned to grab a table.

"Wonder Woman!" a voice called out, startling Bronson.

He spun and noticed the woman named Mel smiling at Charli again. She held up a bowl, reading the side.

"Sorry!" Mel chirped. "That's...Wonder Woman who can run a mile in less than five minutes and is totally amazing and gorgeous and deserves—"

"Okay, okay!" Charli shouted, lunging across the linoleum to grab the bowl. She whispered something to Mel that made the shopkeeper laugh, even as Charli remained disgruntled.

Mel looked up and winked at Bronson, who felt like he was in some kind of alternate universe. He had no idea what was going on at the moment.

The boy next to Mel handed her a cup and she glanced at it before meeting Bronson's gaze again. "Wonder Woman's hot friend! Your Sweet Citrus is ready."

Bronson couldn't help but smile as Charli groaned and banged her forehead on the stainless steel counter. "Thanks...I think?" he said to Mel.

Mel preened. "No problem. Enjoy!"

"Come on." Charli grabbed his forearm and pulled him out the doors before Bronson could respond to anyone. Once outside, she let go of him and began to storm down the sidewalk. "I'm never eating there again," she muttered.

Bronson laughed as he caught up with her. "I feel like I just left the twilight zone. Do they call out names like that for everybody?"

"Yes," Charli said with a sigh. She aimed for a bench and sat down with a plop. "But normally Mel is a little more...subtle about it."

Bronson sat down and took a tentative sip of his drink. "Wow," he said, his mouth puckering just a little, in a pleasant way. "This is delicious."

"Everything she makes is awesome," Charli said proudly. "Even if she is a little over-eager sometimes."

Bronson nodded thoughtfully. Now that they were talking, the reason for this meeting was weighing heavily on him. He needed to bring it up, but he didn't want to ruin the camaraderie they were experiencing. He liked Charli. A lot.

Think of the kids.

"Now...you said you needed something?" Charli asked before scooping a green mixture into her mouth.

Bronson eyed her choice, but shrugged off how odd it looked. It must be good by the way Charli was devouring it. "Yeah." He pumped his straw up and down a few times. "I've come begging again for your help."

Surprisingly, Charli didn't immediately shut him down and Bronson decided to run with it.

"I've tried every other contractor or handyman...and woman..." he corrected, "that I can find online. No one is free or able to do all the things I need." Bronson turned himself on the bench so he was facing her more fully. All the humor from their encounter in the smoothie shop was gone. This was all business. "I need someone with a passion for history who can help me restore this house in a short amount of time. The rules won't let me use a full crew and this competition is really important to me. I can pay you really well, much more than you'd make on your other jobs during the weeks that we'd work together."

Charli peered sideways at him. "Why?"

Bronson pinched his lips together. "I don't really want to get into it all, but suffice it to say that if I fail at this, a lot of people will be hurt."

Charli frowned into her bowl. It was clear from the silence that she was thinking hard and Bronson left her to her thoughts. He'd laid it out on the table. Now it was up to Charli to pick it up. The silence went on much longer than Bronson was comfortable with, but he forced his impatience into submission.

"How much?"

He blinked, surprised by the question. She hadn't seemed interested in money before, so he hadn't been expecting that question. "How much do you want?"

Her lips rolled in and out as she waited for a moment more before naming a number.

Bronson leaned back. She was asking a fairly decent amount.

At his response, Charli deflated. "Sorry. I shouldn't ask for so much, but..."

"But?"

She sighed through her nose then turned. "*Suffice it to say,*" she said wryly, repeating his earlier words, "that without the money, my plans for the future will be impossible."

Bronson nodded. "Okay. I can respect that." He scratched his chin. "That's pretty steep though."

"That price will get you access to me twenty-four-seven for the next eight weeks," Charli added. "I'll teach you everything I know and will make sure you win the competition."

"You can guarantee a win?" Bronson gave her a skeptical look.

Charli smirked. "I won't put that in a contract, but yeah...I'll stake my reputation on it."

Bronson smiled. That was good enough for him. He put out a hand, shaking her calloused palm firmly. "Deal." Life was going to get very interesting for the next couple of months.

CHAPTER 8

Charli was already dreading arriving at work the next morning. She had told Bronson she needed the day to change her schedule and take care of the urgent jobs on her list. She'd worked extra late last night in order to clear up enough of her schedule to truly be open for Bronson's every need during the next two months.

Now I just have to hope no one breaks a pipe for the next little while.

Luckily, it was warm rather than during the winter. Not only would that make her job with Bronson easier, but it meant less things around the house usually broke down.

She pulled into the driveway at Mrs. Miller's old home. Charli had come prepared with masks and fans in order to help with the smell that was sure to be sticking around. Charli might not have been in the house since Mrs. Miller died, but she'd been in it a few times when the elderly widow was alive, and it wasn't a joy to any of the senses.

Bronson came out the front door as she turned off her truck. His T-shirt was already dirty and his dark hair disheveled. He looked absolutely delicious. Charli clenched the steering wheel. "Not here for that," she reminded herself.

Bronson raised his eyebrows at her, obviously wondering why she hadn't gotten out of the truck yet.

Taking a fortifying breath, she grabbed her tool belt and opened the door. "Good morning," she said, wrapping her belt around her waist. "Ready to do some demo?"

Bronson put his hands on his hips and looked at the pile of garbage off to the side of the porch. "I think I started before you."

"Well, you've already been at it three days. I'd hope you had something to show for it." She squinted up at him with a grin.

"Ooh, we haven't even gotten going yet and the smack talk is moving." He laughed. "I'll have to be on my toes with you."

Charli slapped a mask into place and arrived at the bottom of the steps. "I'm ready!"

Bronson raised a single eyebrow. "I should have thought of that." Turning to go inside, he muttered, "That would have saved me some sleep."

Charli grinned behind her mask and marched up the steps. The interior of the home was dark, with only the sun coming through the windows lighting up the space. The darkness made the home appear forbidding and Charli almost hesitated in the doorway. Instead, however, she walked in and let her eyes adjust while she took in her surroundings.

"What do you think?" Bronson asked.

"I think we'd better hope that the bones of the home are in good shape," she said, her voice slightly muffled behind her face covering. "We absolutely do not have time to do the inside of the walls as well as the outside."

Bronson nodded and rubbed the back of his neck. "Yeah. I thought of that. But I don't have enough know-how to understand what, if anything, is wrong."

"Right." Charli headed to the kitchen and turned on the sink. She made sure the water heated and cooled, then looked under the sink to look for leaks. "Looks good in here," she muttered. "Bathroom?"

Bronson led the way down a hallway to a half bath. It also appeared to be in good shape and the upstairs bathroom was free of leaks as well.

"Okay, whew," Charli said. "That would have been some of the worst stuff to happen, so plumbing looks good." She looked at the dark lights. "Did you turn off the electricity?"

Bronson shook his head. "Nope. I think the city turned that off and I haven't bothered to have it fixed yet."

"That's your first order of business," she ordered. "I need to know if things have to be rewired. It'll have to happen before I paint the walls or anything because otherwise I'll waste my time and have to redo work, which I don't have time for."

"We," he corrected.

"What?" Charli frowned.

"We'll paint the walls," Bronson said. That eyebrow went up again. "I have to be involved per the rules of the competition. You don't get to do it all."

"Right," she snapped. Her lips were pursed tightly behind her mask. This was the part that was going to kill her. She'd been fighting to do things herself her whole life. Too many people had said she'd never make it in her "man's profession" and Charli was constantly proving them all wrong. Letting someone work with her was going to drive her crazy.

"I'll be right back," Bronson said, stepping toward the front door and pulling his cell out of his pocket. "Take a look around while I call the electric company."

Charli nodded and began to wander the house. Even through her mask, there were places she could smell the ammonia from the house's ex-inhabitants. Her eyes watered and she shook her head. "Hopefully I'll never be a cat lady," she muttered to herself.

"Find anything?"

Bronson's voice startled her and Charli spun around. "Nothing crazy, thank goodness. From my quick assessment, and it was quick," she emphasized, "it looks like this will mostly be an aesthetic remodel. Which is fantastic. But even with that caveat, we'll be dead by the end of the eight weeks."

"I hope not," Bronson said with a grin. "I'd like to enjoy the fruits of our labors."

"Good luck with that," Charli retorted. "I'll be sleeping for a week before I enjoy anything."

Bronson's grin slowly spread and Charli had to look away. He was much too movie-starish for her womanly hormones. "Big sleeper, huh?'

"I can be," she said primly, still not looking at him. "My line of work can really make you tired."

"I hear ya," he said softly.

Charli frowned and turned to finally meet his eyes again. "You do? I thought you had no experience in this?"

"I don't in this." Bronson indicated the house. "But I've spent a few days pulling long hours and working myself into the ground."

Charli nodded, not sure if she really believed him, but not willing to argue. They had too much work to do. "First things first," she said, grabbing her gloves out of her back pocket. "It's time to clean this place up." She pointed down the hall. "Let's start in one corner of the house, cleaning out everything. I seriously doubt there is anything from Mrs. Miller's stuff that will be salvageable, so I'm not going to waste time trying to go through individual stuff. Pull it, then dump it. That's the motto of the day."

Bronson shrugged. "Let's do this."

Charli led the way and immediately began grabbing drapes off the window.

"What all is being dumped?"

"Anything on the floors, the trim and anything on the walls," Charli called over her shoulder.

"Pull it and dump it. Right."

Charli threw herself into the work, doing her best to ignore the sounds of the handsome hunk behind her. Bronson was proving to be fun and friendly, and normally she would be interested in seeing where their chemistry would go, but right now she was fighting for her future, making him only a means to an end. She simply didn't have the time, and soon wouldn't have the energy, to add another project on the side.

Bronson might be the most attractive man she'd ever seen in person, but it was the ugly house that she was going to keep her focus on. That was the only thing between her and that warehouse, which would help all her dreams come true.

IT WAS CLEAR TO SEE where Charli got her good reputation from. She worked with the energy of two men and Bronson could hardly keep up with her. He knew what it was like to be active with kids from sun up to sun down, but this was a whole new level of tired. Muscles he didn't even know he had ached and there was dust in places that were unmentionable in public.

After throwing yet another disgusting piece of carpet onto the outside pile, he wiped his dirty forehead and sighed.

"Ready for a break?" Charli asked from behind him.

Bronson turned. "Did my girly moan give it away?"

Charli let out one of those husky chuckles Bronson enjoyed. "There is nothing girly about you, Bronson Ramsay." Her eyes widened after she spoke as if she hadn't meant to say those words and he found himself struggling not to puff up like a stupid peacock.

It was nice to have confirmation that the attraction he was nursing back went both ways. "I think that's the first nice thing you've said about me," he teased. "I'm gonna have to write it in my journal."

Charli's cheeks were slightly pink even with her darker skin, but she smiled at his joke anyway. "Don't get used to it. You wanted to work with me? You'll have to keep up."

Another truck pulled into the driveway and Bronson frowned. "Who's that?" he asked more to himself.

"My brother," Charli said. She began walking to the driveway. "I asked him to bring us dinner so we wouldn't have to waste time getting it ourselves." She grinned over her shoulder. "Hope you like fish!"

Bronson huffed a quiet laugh and shook his head. This woman just kept getting better and better. When her brother got out of the vehicle, Bronson hurried to go over. He definitely wanted to meet this guy. Maybe it would help him crack open the mystery that was Charlize Mendez.

Her brother was taller than Charli, but definitely shorter than Bronson's six-foot-two. He was stocky with dark hair and eyes that matched his sister's. Considering how stunning Bronson thought Charli was, he figured her brother had no problem getting dates. "Bronson Ramsay," he said, holding out his hand as he approached.

The brother eyed him carefully. "Captain Felix Mendez." He shook Bronson's hand with a tight grip. Felix's hands were just as calloused as his sister's, and his grip extra tight.

Bronson tried to press back, but he wasn't sure he succeeded very well. He did manage to hold in a grimace, however. "Nice to meet you, Felix. Are you part of the police force?"

Charli chuckled and shook her head. "He wishes. No, Felix captains the *Morwenna*."

Bronson nodded. "Oh, a boat. I love boats."

Felix's eyes were still narrowed. "Boats or yachts?" His eyes went over Bronson from head to toe. "There's a difference."

Charli whacked her brother's chest. "Be nice," she hissed.

Felix ignored her.

Wow. Skepticism obviously runs in the family. Guess I'm not getting any bro talk with this guy. "Boats," Bronson clarified. "My brother owns the yacht." He waited, hoping his message had been clear. Canon was the one who showed off the wealth. After holding his breath, Bronson wasn't disappointed as Felix gave him a slow smile.

"Good to know."

"So, you're a fisherman, then?" Bronson asked, taking the Tupperware that Charli handed him. He could feel its heat, but didn't dare drop Felix's gaze yet. Their man-staring contest was still going.

"You could say that," Felix answered.

"Oh my gosh, would you stop?" Charli demanded, slugging her brother's shoulder this time.

Bronson did wince that time. Charli's arms showed off very nice muscles and he imagined that punch hadn't felt very good.

Felix finally looked down at his sister. "I brought you dinner. Why are you hitting me?"

"Because you're treating Bronson as if he's some boy I brought home for a date. This is a business transaction. Are you going to start vetting all my clients like this?"

"If all your clients are young, single men, then I just might," Felix shot back.

Bronson pressed his lips together when Charli's cheeks turned pink again. *Guess I don't have to ask if she has a boyfriend.* He shook his head at himself. *Nope. Project first. Then you can think about other stuff. The kids are depending on you.*

"I can take care of myself," she argued with Felix.

"She's right," Bronson added, earning Felix's glare. "I've seen her heft wood and cat-stained carpets three times her size today. I don't think I'll be crossing any boundaries."

"Thank you!" Charli said, nodding her head toward Bronson. The flash of disappointment in her eye, however, had Bronson's heart picking up pace.

This is getting dangerous.

"I'll hold you to that," Felix said, pointing a finger at Bronson.

Bronson met Felix's gaze and did his best not to hide anything. "Your sister is a very attractive woman, Felix. But right now I have a pressing deadline that comes first."

Felix nodded as Charli turned back to the truck.

"Please tell me you brought silverware," she muttered, her back to the men.

Bronson didn't know if she was embarrassed or honestly worried about forks and spoons, but either way, at least they had everything out in the open. It was stupid to say he didn't like the way she looked or that he wasn't enjoying her personality. It had to be obvious every time they locked eyes. But he really did need to help save his kids. Their well-being was definitely top priority.

"It's on top of the dash," Felix shouted over his shoulder.

"The dash? Felix!" Charli grumbled under her breath as she climbed up the step and grabbed what she needed.

Felix growled...actually growled, at Bronson, who immediately snapped his eyes away from the curves and extremely nice-shaped calves that Charli was putting on display.

Bronson busied himself with opening the container in his hands. The smell of fried fish hit him in the face along with a wave of heat after he pried off the top. "This is great," he said, chancing a glance up at Felix. "Thanks."

Felix nodded again, his shoulders relaxing.

"Your dash is a dusty, disgusting mess," Charli grumbled when she came back. She handed a fork to Bronson. "You might want to wipe it off. Who knows what diseases he carries in there."

Felix rolled his eyes. "You should be grateful I brought you anything at all, instead of complaining."

"Maybe if you cooked something other than fish, I would," Charli retorted. Her smile told Bronson that this was a common practice for them, and it fit. Both siblings seemed to have a slight edge to their personalities, but despite that, Charli was extremely likable. Bronson assumed Felix would be too, if he hadn't caught Bronson ogling his sister.

"I'm trying to utilize our food storage," Felix said with a sniff. "It's not my fault you don't know how to put the freezer to good use."

"I'm thinking my question about you being a fisherman was right on the money," Bronson stated before taking a bite. The fish was cooked well, surprisingly enough. "And this is really good, by the way."

Felix smirked and folded his arms over his chest. "Glad someone appreciates it." He ignored Charli's snort. "And I own a fishing charter." He tilted his chin at Bronson. "You should come out sometime. I'll help you reel in the big one."

Bronson barked a laugh. "With the look you gave me a minute ago, I'm pretty sure you'll put me in cement shoes and use me for bait."

There was a second of silence before Felix burst out laughing.

It had been a risk to tease that way, but Bronson was glad it paid off. He was usually a pretty good judge of character. It had come from working with so many teenagers with a chip on their shoulder. Most were simply trying to protect themselves or someone else. It was a human trait that Bronson saw a lot of.

Felix held out his hand again. "I think you and I are going to get along just fine," he said, grinning even wider as he squeezed Bronson's hand into oblivion once more.

CHAPTER 9

The sun was barely up by the time Charli arrived at the house a couple mornings later. She groaned as she dropped from her truck. She hadn't done a big project like this in a long time, and even as fit as she was from her training for Ironmans, she was using muscles she didn't usually use.

Straightening her shoulders, she marched up the steps and headed inside. "Bronson?"

A groan came to her from the kitchen area.

Frowning, Charli followed the noise and came to a stop in the entrance of the room. She couldn't help but smile as she saw Bronson sitting on the floor with his back against the wall. His hair stood on end and his eyes were closed. A glass was next to him on the floor, but his hand was simply laying around it, not actually gripping.

"Don't make me move," he moaned, peering through tight lids.

Charli snorted as she tried to keep her laughter in. "Are you telling me that a big guy like you can't keep up with little old me?"

Bronson opened his eyes and glared. "I do believe that your friend, Mel, made it clear yesterday that you do more than fix up houses. You compete in Ironmans." He raised his eyebrows though the sentence had been more of a statement than question.

Charli nodded.

"Then I think your endurance is way ahead of someone like myself."

Charli gave him a look. "I can tell you spend time in the gym, Bronson. Now quit being a baby and come on."

Making all sorts of weird noises, he climbed to his feet, finished the protein shake and slapped the cup on the counter. "A weight room doesn't do the same thing as cardio. I think I need to shake up my routine if how much I hurt is anything to go by."

Charli continued to chuckle as she pulled a notebook out of her back pocket. "You ready to get going?"

"Nope. But we're gonna do it anyway." Bronson put his hands on his hips. "I was thinking we should start with replacing the lights and stuff."

Charli rolled her eyes. *Rookies.* "No way. We need to tape everything off for a paint job. Once we do the walls, then we can do the extras. It's much harder to paint after you hang up new lights and switch fixtures."

Bronson yawned and scratched the back of his head. The move was so boyish that Charli felt her heart skip a beat. Why was it so attractive to see a big, muscled man act like a little kid? "I can see the logic in that," he said. "Guess we need to hit the store."

Charli stared. "You don't already have paint?"

Bronson shook his head. "Nope."

"Great," she muttered, stuffing her notebook in her pocket again. "We're gonna lose the whole morning to go get it."

"We can't just run into town? It's less than ten minutes," Bronson pointed out.

Charli shook her head. "The best hardware store is a town over. It'll take us close to an hour to get there."

"Guess I should have looked into that," Bronson grumbled. He sighed and straightened. "Should we split up?"

Charli pondered the question. "That might work, but do you know what and how much paint to get?"

Bronson shook his head. "Something that looks good?"

Charli hung her head backward. "Okay, that means I should go get the paint. Can I trust you to stay here and tape things up?"

"I've never done it before, but I'm sure I can manage it," he snapped.

Charli felt a pinch in her chest. She really wasn't being quite fair. It wasn't Bronson's fault he was new. "Look," she said, putting her hands up. "We might as well go together. If you did things wrong while I was gone, it would take longer to fix it than it would for us to just work together." She paused after saying that. Never in a million years would she have expected those words to come out of her mouth.

Bronson rubbed his hands together. "Sounds good. Let me run and brush my teeth and we'll take off."

"I'm driving!" Charli called out as he disappeared down the hall. She grinned as he huffed. As much as she enjoyed poking at his manliness, it really was just a better choice. Her truck could fit all the buckets and wouldn't be ruined if anything spilled.

Charli waited in the driver's seat for Bronson to join her. They were on the road within five minutes and she might have been pressing the gas a little more than usual. Time was of the essence at the moment.

"So...tell me about yourself," Bronson said, leaning his elbow onto the window.

Charli felt a bolt of alarm hit her squarely in the chest. "Uh...what?"

"You said we're going to have like an hour each way. Might as well use the time wisely," Bronson said with a wicked grin.

"Do you really think it's wise to ask me about myself? What if I have a dangerous past or something? Or may I'm on the run from the mafia?"

"I love a good bit of danger," Bronson said, chuckling. "Lay it on me."

Charli sighed and fought the desire to smile. They'd only worked together a couple of days, but she found it incredibly easy to talk to Bronson and that made her attraction all the more worrisome. This guy wasn't sticking around. When all was said and done, he would go back to California and Charli would go back to trying to build her business. It didn't seem smart to test their boundaries. But after his admission the other day about finding her beautiful, she had to admit that she was secretly struggling to keep her thoughts in check.

Bronson was not only incredibly attractive, but she enjoyed his personality. He was easy-going, a hard worker, liked to tease and held up well to her demanding personality. She'd already learned that if his tone changed when they were speaking, she had gone too far. *Not that I would ever admit that to him though.* She wasn't one to back down, but she did try to read the signals.

"So?"

Charli scrunched her nose. "Okay...you asked for it. Brace yourself." Charli glanced at him for a second. "I've lived in Seaside Bay my whole life. My dad was a fisherman like my brother. I, however, prefer the beach, not the sea. But I was a really active kid. Always taking things apart and putting them back together. So my mom got me started in fixing things around the house." She shrugged. "It stuck."

"And the history?"

Charli huffed a laugh. "You can't really live in a coastal Oregon town and not know some history. It's part of the lifestyle here."

Bronson's eyebrows were high on his forehead. "Really? I don't remember filling out that application."

Charli's smile grew. "Okay, so I'm a bit of a nerd. When I wasn't running around, destroying and building, I was reading about how the older generations destroyed and built. It's all part of the same passion really."

Bronson nodded. "I can see that, but I'll admit I never thought about it that way."

Charli took a deep breath. "Your turn."

Bronson was quiet for a few minutes. "I think my *dangerous* lifestyle is about like yours."

"Yeah? How's that?" Charli asked, truly curious to know more about this guy.

"Short and to the point."

Charli gave him a look. "Fair is fair, so you better share."

BRONSON SNORTED. "NICE rhyme."

"Come on," Charli pressed. "I had to spill. It's your turn."

Bronson nodded. "You're right. That's only right." He debated how much to tell her. While telling her about his volunteer work seemed fine, Bronson wasn't sure if he wanted her to know about his dysfunctional family, nor about the weird requirements to his father's will. Since nobody else was being put through the wringer, Bronson felt as if his dad was using the opportunity to make Bronson look like the black sheep of the family. Something he already struggled with. *Now I just wish I'd known that when he was alive.*

"Bronson?"

He shook his head. "Sorry. I got lost in thought for a minute."

"Maybe it's not quite as easy as you make it out to be, huh?" She was grinning, so Bronson knew she was teasing, but the words were too close to the truth for comfort.

"Maybe not," he said, forcing a cheerful tone into his voice. "You just might be changed forever by what I'm about to tell you. Are you sure you want that on your shoulders?"

That fantastic chuckle escaped her and Bronson found himself smiling without even thinking about it. That husky tone to her voice was so compelling, he wanted to just sit and listen to her all day. It was a miracle she hadn't been snatched up by some guy yet, but he supposed that small-town life made it hard to find a significant other. *And thank you for that,* he thought before opening his mouth to spill his life story. Sort of.

"Like you, I still live in the town I was born in. My mom was a model, my father a lawyer—"

"Wait...who's your mom?" Charli interrupted.

"Clarisse Rhodes." Bronson held his breath. This was the time when people either had no idea who he was talking about, or they decided he was their best friend because he was related to famous people. He actually wasn't quite sure which one Charli would turn out to be.

"Clarisse..." Charli's eyes narrowed behind the sunglasses she'd put on. Her eyebrows shot up and Bronson's heart sank. "The lady who used to be on all the Merther's commercials!" she cried, referring to a clothing store his mother was contracted with.

Bronson nodded and turned away to look out the window. Everything was going to change now and it disappointed him. He'd been enjoying Charli.

"I *knew* you looked familiar," Charli said triumphantly, hitting the steering wheel with her fist. "And now I can see it." She smiled over at him. "You have her eyes."

Bronson nodded again.

"Well, I'd say that's really cool to have her for a mother, but I'll bet that was actually kind of hard." Her voice dropped. "Especially since she's...gone."

Bronson had to give her credit. That was a kind way of talking about suicide, but it wasn't the sympathy that caught his attention. "You don't want to hear all about her?"

Charli frowned. "Do you want to tell me all about her?"

"No." His answer was too quick, but right now Bronson was too shocked to care.

"Then, no." Charli shrugged. "I thought you were telling me about you, not her. So I'm happy to leave it and move on."

Bronson clenched his fists. He had a sudden, overwhelming urge to grab Charli's face and lay one on her. *Not appropriate!* he scolded himself. *And not worth the car crash.* He could honestly say that Charli was the first woman he'd ever met who wasn't going googly-eyed over his parentage. That knowledge made her attractiveness skyrocket and it had already been on the border of uncontrollable.

"So, your father was a lawyer..." Charli urged.

Bronson smiled and relaxed. "Yep. My older brother followed Dad's footsteps, little sister is following Mom. And you're sitting with the oddball." He hoped she didn't detect the bitterness in his tone. Bronson didn't want to be like his siblings, but he didn't want to be pointed out as the weirdo all the time either.

"So what led you to Oregon for a house competition?"

Now they were reaching information Bronson didn't want to share. Maybe he could give her a half-truth and it would be enough. "I work with Fathers and Sons," he hedged. "It's a nonprofit that helps kids in dysfunctional families find a steady adult influence in their lives. They specialize in boys without fathers, but anyone is welcome. Our chapter in L.A. is hurting for money and this competition is a way to help us out."

Charli's feminine brows were pushed together. "How in the world does winning this help your charity? Which is cool by the way, but I don't get it."

Bronson's mind worked furiously. "If I win, I get a prize that'll help them be able to purchase the building they're in." He decided not to mention how their contract was almost up and they were about to be evicted or that the prize wasn't coming from the housing commission.

"I didn't realize there was a monetary prize," Charli mused. She pulled into the parking lot of a big box supply store. "Well, I guess since we're working for such a good cause, we'll have to make sure we win."

"I thought you already told me we were going to."

Charli grinned as she jumped down from her truck. "I did. But helping out a bunch of kids might give me an added boost." She pumped her eyebrows, then closed the door and took off, leaving Bronson scrambling in her wake.

He was beginning to adore her sassy streak. It kept him on his toes and made him excited to spend time with her. The fact that he had so many weeks left with Charli almost was enough to push his anger over the will to the back of his mind...almost.

"Hold on there," he called, rushing to her side just as she grabbed a cart. "Should we get anything else while we're here?"

Charli nodded. "Yeah. We'll need some trim and you can probably pick out light fixtures as well."

"How many do we need?"

Charli stopped pushing the cart and pulled out her notebook. "I've got it all written down right here."

This time Bronson couldn't help himself. He leaned down and left a soft kiss on her cheek. "You're amazing. Let's go pick out paint colors." He quickly began to walk farther into the store. A small part of him was worried she would sneak up and smack him upside the head, but the other side hoped she had enjoyed the little touch. It had been bold. They'd only known each other a few days, but it seemed right at the moment. Saying thank you for being such a good partner just hadn't seemed like enough.

"Paint is this way," Charli said from just behind his shoulder.

Bronson didn't say a word about how her voice was slightly lower than normal, but when he turned to follow her, he couldn't quite contain his smirk. She might be willing to act like it never happened, but the clues were all there that she'd been just as affected as him.

Two hours later, they pulled back into the driveway. Things had gone pretty smoothly at the store, and luckily, almost everything they'd wanted was in stock. The few supplies being ordered were things they didn't need right away, so it wasn't a big deal to wait for them.

"I should have the guy pick out the fixtures every time I do a remodel," Charli said as she got out of the truck and headed toward the bed. "You were way faster than my normal clients."

Bronson laughed. "Are you saying women have a hard time making up their minds?"

"Unfortunately...that's exactly what I'm saying," Charli huffed. She climbed up the back tire and into the bed before handing him a couple of five-gallon buckets of paint. "Take those in and I'll start unloading things here."

Bronson didn't argue, just saluted, took the buckets and headed inside. When he crossed the threshold, he paused. Something sounded off. His ears tuned into a sound that shouldn't be there. Setting the buckets down, he walked through the family room and stood in the entrance to the kitchen. "CHARLI!" he bellowed.

Her rushing footsteps came up from behind. "What's wrong?" she panted, then skidded to a halt at his side. "Ah, crap!" she cried as soon as she spotted the water pouring out from underneath the sink. "Quick! Go turn off the water main!"

"I don't know where it's at!" Bronson said, turning in a circle.

Charli growled. "You grab towels, I'll get the water." With that she was gone and Bronson ran to his bedroom. He only had a couple of towels, but he did have a basket of dirty clothes that needed to be taken to the laundromat. That would have to do.

CHAPTER 10

Charli blew a chunk of hair out of her face and fell onto her backside.

"What in the world was that?" Bronson asked. He was finishing wringing out the last of his T-shirts into a bucket.

"I don't know," Charli admitted, shaking her head.

"I thought you checked everything the first day you got here."

"I did!" she snapped, then immediately felt guilty. This was obviously on her head. She should've detected the problem when she came through a few days ago, but she'd obviously missed something. She didn't get to be mad at Bronson for asking about it. "Sorry," she said, rubbing her forehead. "I promise I checked it the way I always do when we went through the house, and I didn't see any sign of a leak. How this one sprung up, I can't quite figure out."

She got onto all fours and crawled over to the open cupboard. The wood had been soaked, but looked like it would dry out just fine. Luckily, they hadn't been gone long enough for the wood to warp from the water, though a few more hours would have done it.

"How far behind is this going to put us?" Bronson asked softly.

Charli glanced over her shoulder. "I'm not sure." She rolled onto her back and began to slide under the sink. "Give me a minute to really see what's going on." She could hear him shuffling around as she shined a flashlight around the pipes. "What?" she asked no one in particular as she realized the supply hose was almost completely hanging loose.

"What did you find?" Bronson squatted in front of her and ducked his head.

"The water supply line is loose," Charli grumbled. She crawled out, waiting for Bronson to move first before getting to her feet. "Let me get my wrench and I'll have this fixed easy." She headed out, not waiting for his reply. She was so frustrated. How could she have missed something so simple? It wasn't like her.

And right now I can't afford to make these kinds of mistakes! What if Bronson decides to dock my pay because I can't cut it?

Charli shook her head as she grabbed what she needed from the bed of the truck. "He wouldn't do that," she reassured herself. "You have a contract."

But I don't want him to feel stuck with me. I want to do this right.

She'd been so touched about how he was doing this in order to help that charity group. She'd never heard of the particular nonprofit, but that didn't matter. Anything that helped kids was totally awesome in her book. In fact, everything about Bronson was proving to be awesome. His personality was turning out to be just as amazing as his looks. And that kiss he gave her in the store?

Charli had thought she would melt into a puddle right then and there. Her cheek warmed just thinking about his touch. The jolt of electricity she'd felt had not been in proportion to the touch of his lips, and it made her think too hard about what it would be like to have him kiss her mouth instead.

"He's probably regretting having done it at all since you're totally inept at being a plumber," she grumbled. Charli stormed back into the house and went straight to the sink. Within ten minutes, she had the problem fixed.

Finishing up, she scooted out from under the sink and sat up with a sigh. "I'm sorry, Bronson. I have no idea how I missed that." She waved behind her. "A rookie would have caught that. The line was barely connected."

Bronson stood off to the side, his arms folded over his large chest. He narrowed his eyes and studied her.

Charli dropped his gaze and squirmed. She didn't like being wrong.

"As long as we can still finish on time, I'm not worried about it," Bronson finally responded. "But is there anything else we need to check before we get back to our regular schedule?"

Charli shrugged. "Not that I can think of, but I'm going to go around to check all the other sinks. If I was dumb enough to miss this, I want to double check everything else."

"Don't say that," Bronson said firmly.

Charli jerked her head up at his tone. "What?"

"Don't call yourself dumb," he scolded. "No one's perfect and it would've been incredibly naive to go into this project thinking it would all go smoothly." He gave her a crooked smile. "Things have gone too well for us since we got started, so we were due for a disaster, right?"

Charli laughed softly. "I suppose you're right." They stayed in their positions, smiling at each other without speaking. The moment sparked their chemistry to life and Charli could have sworn she could see flashes of light out of the corner of her eye.

"I suppose we ought to get going, huh?" Bronson kicked the basket of clothes sitting at his feet. "I think I need to do laundry tonight."

"Bring them to the house," Charli said, climbing to her feet. "It's the least I can do since this is my fault."

Bronson raised his eyebrows at her. "Are you offering to do my laundry?"

Charli's laugh was loud. "Not a chance," she called over her shoulder as she headed to the bathroom. "I'm just offering the use of our machine."

"A guy can dream!"

Charli's smile didn't leave her face the whole time she checked all the other sinks in the house. Every other supply line was nice and tight and showed no signs of erosion, which she was grateful for. It was time to get this painting show on the road.

By the time she got back downstairs, Bronson had finished unloading the truck and the middle of the family room looked like a real construction zone.

"Grab the tape and I'll show you what we're going to do," Charli said, indicating the large plastic bag at his feet.

Bronson bent over and dug through the bag until he held up some blue tape. "This?"

"That." Charli held out her hand and Bronson tossed it her way. She tore off the wrapping and waved her arm. "Okay, I'm going to get you started, then I'll go grab some of the tarps and get to work on the bigger tape jobs."

Bronson picked his way out of the middle of the supplies and followed her to the bedroom.

"Crud, I forgot the paper. Hang on." Charli ran past him and grabbed the brown paper they'd purchased as well. She had to admit that it was really nice to be able to use all the right supplies for this job, since Bronson had said money was no object. Usually, she dug around and made due with whatever she could find because her clients needed her to and Charli couldn't afford to simply eat all her profit margins.

I wonder how true the no budget thing is.

She'd never had a client who had easy money to spend.

Since his mom was Clarisse Rhodes, he probably grew up with money.

It made sense, now that she thought of it. His clothes were dirty, but well made. His boots were a brand Charli would never be able to afford. And when he'd told her about himself, Bronson hadn't mentioned a job, only that he volunteered with Fathers and Sons.

What would it be like to not have to save every penny?

She'd grown up solid middle class and had never worried about it. Seaside Bay had wealthy tourists, but not a lot of wealthy residents. She'd never felt like she might be missing something...until now. If she had Bronson's money, she would be able to purchase that building and start her business and not worry about paying the bills on the side. There was a part of that that was really enticing, but she wasn't naive enough to think it didn't come with its own problems.

The fact that Bronson's mom had committed suicide and he hadn't wanted to speak about his family at all told her more than he probably intended. Not that Charli would push him about it, but she decided she probably wasn't going to envy him his monetary status. She had enough problems of her own. She didn't need to borrow his.

"THIS IS DEFINITELY not what I imagined when I thought about remodeling a house," Bronson grumbled, tearing the thousandth piece of tape off yet another blue roll. He'd thought Charli was crazy when she'd made him buy so many rolls, but she had proved to be right on the money. He paused and frowned. She'd been right on for everything they'd done...until the sink disaster.

The more he thought about it, the more the moment seemed so out of place. Charli knew her stuff, really well, but had somehow missed something she said a rookie would catch. He shook his head. It just didn't fit. *Must have been having an off day,* he mused.

"No one ever thinks about the tedious jobs," Charli said as she walked by the doorway yet again. "Everyone wants to see the big jobs get done so they can see the big reveal, but no one wants to help prep for those big jobs."

"Yeah, well, that's because they're smart," he grumbled. He smiled when he heard her soft laughter. If acting like a whiny brat meant she would grace him with her amusement, then Bronson would be more than happy to comply.

A soft strain of music filtered down the hallway and into his room, causing Bronson to pause. The beat began to get to him and he found himself bobbing his head. Some of his earlier dreariness lightened with the addition of music to their work day.

It was late afternoon at this point and Bronson's body was screaming for a break. He was only about a third of the way through the house at this point and he wasn't looking forward to another full day of prep, though Charli assured him that spraying the house would make a huge difference for their timeline. Apparently, taking longer to prep still gained them time in the long run.

The song changed and Bronson began to mouth the words of a popular pop song, but when he heard Charli singing along, he stopped. The temptation was too much. He set down the tape and snuck down the hallway. His stealth was definitely rewarded.

Charli was bopping to the beat as she covered the window in brown paper. Her hips were swinging and her voice, though kept light, bounced off the walls, making it easily audible.

Folding his arms over his chest, Bronson rested his shoulder against the hallway wall. The show was well worth the few minutes he would lose in their progress. His eyes devoured her as she moved. She really was a beautiful woman. She was fairly average in height, maybe around five-foot-four, but the rest of her was anything but mainstream.

Tight muscles were visible everywhere, though not overly bulky as if she were some kind of body builder. Visible, but attractive. Very attractive. The way she moved to music showed off her athleticism as well. She was in perfect control of every part of herself and the results were mesmerizing.

A small voice in the back of Bronson's mind told him that he shouldn't be staring, but he wasn't willing to listen. Charli was fierce and didn't seem to ever let down her guard. At least until now, and Bronson was totally going to take advantage.

She spun unexpectedly and their eyes clashed. Charli screamed so loudly that Bronson actually winced, then fell back against the wall when a roll of tape hit him in the head. "What the heck, Charli?" he shouted, holding a hand to the spot she'd managed to hit. "What team do you play for?" he grumbled, rubbing the rising bump.

"What were you doing?" she demanded, a hand on her chest as if her heart were beating rapidly.

"I was enjoying your dancing and singing," Bronson said, a slow smile spreading across his face.

"Oh great," she snapped. "As if that's not creepy at all."

Bronson rolled his eyes. "If I was a creeper, I wouldn't have been out in the open. They hide while they're watching."

"Doesn't make it better," she retorted.

Bronson chuckled and stepped in her direction. "I'm only human, Char," he said calmly. "There isn't a man on this earth who wouldn't enjoy watching a gorgeous woman have fun."

She glared at him and put a hand out. "Stop right there," she demanded, though her voice shook slightly.

Bronson paused for only a second. "Why?" he asked, slowing his pace, but still moving.

"You're supposed to be taping the bedroom," she said, her eyes wide as he came within a couple feet of her.

"Why are you so freaked out about being called beautiful?" he asked softly. His eyes roved over her pink cheeks and the worried look in her eyes.

Those dark brown pools darted back and forth between his. She seemed to be looking for something, but Bronson wasn't sure what. All he knew was that every time he mentioned her looks, she seemed to get defensive. "I don't," she denied, but the lie was easily heard in her voice.

"You do." Bronson took one more step. He was now only about a foot away. The hand she had out was lightly pressed against his chest and he could feel her shaking. "Tell me you don't feel that," he whispered.

Her fingers curled into his shirt ever so slightly. "Feel what?"

He raised an eyebrow. "You're better than that." Fire flashed through her eyes and Bronson wanted to move closer. Being burned had never appealed to him before, but it did now.

A few breaths passed between them. "Being called beautiful isn't what scares me," she finally admitted.

"Then what does?"

Charli swallowed hard enough to be audible. "Not being in control."

He leaned into her hand. "Do I make you feel out of control?" Bronson knew he was pushing boundaries. He'd told himself he wouldn't cross that line until after they were done with the remodel, but now he wasn't sure he'd be able to keep that promise. The more time he spent with her, the more he was pulled in.

"Yes." Her voice was small and contained a hint of fear that brought Bronson out of his haze.

He blinked and leaned away, breaking their touch. He would never want to scare a woman, no matter how much he was drawn to her. "I should get back to that tape," he said, forcing a stiff smile. "The harder I work, the faster this part of it will be done, right?"

Charli took in a long breath through her nose and the tension eased on her face. "Right."

Nodding, Bronson turned on his booted heel and headed back to his part of the house. He worked in silence for a few minutes, but his mind refused to calm down. All he could think about was the nearly tangible pull he felt toward Charli and how she'd looked afraid of him. A shiver ran down his back. He never wanted to see that look in her eyes again.

He knew he'd pushed the boundary a little, but surely Charli wasn't really afraid of him. They'd gotten to know each other the past few days and she had to know he would never do anything to hurt her.

His hand tightened on the tape and the piece in his hands ripped at an odd angle. The only thing that made sense was that at some point in her life, another man had put that fear into her. The thought made easy-going Bronson want to throttle somebody.

Forcing himself to breathe until his body calmed down, Bronson put himself back to work. When music finally began to filter down the hallway again, he felt himself relax. Charli must have calmed down as well if she was turning on the music again. He decided to take the cue from her and not worry about other things right now.

It was time to go back to his original promise. No breaking the partnership boundaries until the job was done. That would not only make life easier, but it would give Charli enough time to feel like she could trust him. And Bronson found that that was something he desperately wanted.

CHAPTER 11

He was walking behind her. It didn't matter that Charli could hear his boots. She would have known anyway. Every day that they worked together, which had been close to two weeks at this point, Charli had grown more and more aware of Bronson.

Ever since he'd cornered her during their first few days together, she had felt something shift between them. Truthfully, he'd never hidden his attraction to her. Bronson had said too many things and given her too many unsaid signals for Charli to deny it. Charli, however, had tried hard to hide hers in return. Despite the fact that his actions gave her a little thrill and heady feeling of power, she did all she could to keep from giving into the chemistry between them.

She had no desire to get attached to someone who wouldn't be staying. And Bronson definitely wouldn't be staying. His family and life were down in California and a long-distance relationship was at the very bottom of her priority list.

She grit her teeth, fighting her awareness of his nearness, as she touched up some of the corners that hadn't gotten quite all they needed when they sprayed the house.

"Doing okay over there?"

Charli turned her head, but didn't look at him. "Yep."

"Need any help?"

This time his voice was right next to her ear and Charli just about hit the ceiling. "Oh my gosh, Bronson." She turned and pushed against his chest. She definitely didn't notice the firmness of his muscles or how his laughter vibrated through her, making butterflies take off in her stomach. "You've got to stop doing that." He seemed to enjoy catching her off guard and it drove Charli crazy...mostly. She would never admit how much she enjoyed the attention.

Bronson's smile was slightly crooked, which was made more visible since his looks were nearly perfect. It was absolutely charming. "Sorry," he said, not looking the least bit sorry. "I couldn't resist."

"I think you say that every time," Charli muttered. She did her best to glare at him, but it was hard with him still chuckling.

"What can I say?" He shrugged. "You're beautiful when you pretend to be angry."

"I'm not pretending!" Charli cried, even knowing that her cheeks were pink. It had always ticked her off that even with her darker skin tone, her blushes were still visible. It was a curse.

"You're better than that!" he called over his shoulder as he headed back to his job. That was his favorite line every time she tried to tell a fib. He was annoyingly good at knowing when she was pushing the truth.

"Has it ever occurred to you that I'm exactly who I want to be? Maybe I don't want to be better!" She scrunched her nose in his direction, then schooled her face when he poked his head back out the bedroom door.

He gave her a wry look, obviously having caught her face. "Again...you're better than that."

Charli huffed and turned around. She was all set to ignore him when her phone buzzed on the counter behind her. She set her paintbrush down and walked over, wiping any wet paint on her already stained pants.

Charli pressed the button to accept the call, then put it on speaker phone. "Hey, Caro!" she said, making sure not to give away the fact that she'd just been flirting on the job. "What's up?

"Hey, girl," Caro said, her sweet, Southern twang echoing through the empty room. "How goes the reno?"

"Pretty good," Charli replied. She found her attention already waning from the conversation and began to look around for more spots she had missed around the kitchen. Even though all the cabinets had been taken out of the small space, there were still lots of corners to keep track of.

"I just wanted to check in and make sure you were coming to the bonfire tonight."

Charli froze. "There's one tonight?" She slapped her forehead. "I completely forgot."

"How in this great green earth could you forget such a thing?" Caro scolded. "It's tradition!"

Charli chuckled. "We only started doing this like two years ago, Caro. I don't think that's long enough to create a tradition."

"It's tradition to me!" Caro shouted.

Charli winced away from the phone. "Geez, princess, ease up. I'm sorry I forgot."

Caro sighed long and loud. "Charli, I swear you'd forget your head if it wasn't attached to your neck."

"Caro," Charli growled. "You're being dramatic."

Caro sniffed. "Fine. Be that way. I guess we'll all just go have a good time without you."

Charli rolled her eyes. "Give it a rest. I said I forgot, I didn't say I wouldn't come." She paused and looked around the construction mess. "Well...maybe. I've still got so much to do here. We've been working late every night."

"Surely you can take one night off?"

Charli tilted her head back and forth as she considered. "Maybe. It's hard to tell. We're making good progress, but I'm not sure taking a night off this early in the game is a good idea."

"Honey, if you don't come and bring that handsome hunk you're working with, I'm gonna come out there and tell him that you've got a crush on him."

Charli's jaw dropped and she scrambled for the phone, turning off the speaker phone. "Caro," Charli hissed once she had the phone on her ear. "You can't say things like that!"

"Why not? It's true."

"I had you on speaker phone." Charli enunciated each word very carefully.

"Oh, good. So now he already knows." The smugness of Caro's tone was easy to hear. "Bring him along."

"What?" Charli screeched.

"Honey, if I lose my hearing from this conversation, I'm coming back to haunt you forever."

Charli made a face. "What in the world does hearing have to do with haunting? That's for when you're dead and a ghost."

"If I lose my hearing, I might as well be dead," Caro snapped. "I mean, who wouldn't feel that way if they couldn't hear Mr. Handsome's deep voice, amiright?"

Charli hung her head. "Caro, you're killing me here."

Caro laughed, completely unconcerned that she was driving Charli up the wall. "Just come and bring the hunk. If you don't want him, at least let the rest of us have a crack at it."

"I don't think..." Charli's voice trailed off when she looked up and her gaze clashed with a stunning sapphire blue.

"Charli? Hello?" Caro's voice carried through the phone and into the room. The woman had a set of lungs, Charli had to give her credit.

"I'll talk to you later," Charli quickly said, hanging up the phone and stuffing it back in her pocket. "Hey," she said with a small wave. The movement was followed by a wave of humiliation. *How much did he hear? Please don't let him have heard anything.*

Bronson's lips twisted in amusement. It looked like he was trying to keep from smiling as he stuffed his hands in his pockets.

"Hey...whatcha been up to?" He twitched an eyebrow at her. "Got any plans this evening?"

Charli let her head fall forward and groaned. He'd heard it all.

BRONSON MANAGED TO hold back his laughter, but he couldn't seem to completely contain his smile. Charli, with her tough exterior and in-control attitude, had absolutely no control over her friend Caro. Bronson had met her at the candy store when he was new in town and he could understand why. Caro had appeared to be a pint-sized cup of fire. There was no way she'd fall in line with Charli's rules.

The house was so empty of furniture and appliances that it had been easy to hear the girls' conversation all the way down the hall. The part that had been particularly interesting was when Caro said Charli had a crush and Charli didn't deny it. She'd tried to shut the candymaker up, but not once had Charli denied the accusation.

"Cheer up, Charli," Bronson said, still smiling. He paused. "I think that's a song or something," he muttered.

Charli finally looked up and glared. "It is. It's from *Willy Wonka and the Chocolate Factory*. And if you think I haven't heard it a million times...you're wrong."

Bronson smirked. "Well, now you've heard it a million and one." He rocked back on his heels. "But what I was *going* to say was that at least you have friends who want what's best for you. It must be nice."

"Sometimes it's a little too much," Charli grumbled, pushing a hand through her hair. She left a little streak of paint that stood out starkly against her rich, dark strands.

Bronson put his hand up and pointed to his head. "You've got something..." He motioned with his finger.

Charli frowned and raised her hand again, only to stop. "Like it really matters," she snapped. "I'm sure I'll be covered with stuff by the time we're done here."

"You'll have to take a shower before you go to that bonfire."

"Did you really hear the whole thing?" she asked, wincing slightly in anticipation.

Bronson's lips twitched again as he nodded slowly.

"Ooh." Charli put her face in her hands, then snapped upright again. "Look, you have to know that she wasn't—"

Bronson put up a hand. "Don't do it," he warned.

Charli snapped her mouth shut. "Don't do what?" She turned her head to the side and eyed him carefully.

Bronson shook his head. "You're always trying to fib," he said, tsking his tongue. "I can't decide if you're a pathological liar, or just too scared to tell the truth."

Her eyes widened and her mouth opened and shut several times. "I... You don't... You're calling me a liar?" Her voice rose really high at the end.

Bronson nodded cheerily. "Yep."

She stared again, as if she were shocked by his response. "How dare you!" she finally said, seeming to come back in control of herself.

Bronson shook his head. "Have you or have you not fibbed to me dozens of times over the last two weeks?"

Her cheeks turned pink, giving her away even as Charli tried to shake her head.

"You're doing it again," Bronson pointed out. He stepped closer to her. He couldn't help it. The draw was just too strong. "Every time the topic of your feelings or...me," the word came out deeper than he meant it to, "comes up, you clam up and run for the hills."

"That doesn't make me a liar," she said, her voice weaker than normal. She was beginning to resemble that deer in the headlights again and Bronson knew he needed to tread carefully.

"What are you so afraid of?" he asked, taking another step. "Do you really believe that I'll hurt you?"

Charli blinked and finally dropped his gaze. "I don't know what you want from me," she finally whispered.

"All I want is for you to admit that you feel the same pull I do," Bronson said, matching her volume. "Even your friends are shouting it from the rooftops, so why are you so dead set on denying it?"

Charli had been surprising Bronson since they'd first met and her reaction now was no different. Her face crumpled and she turned away from him. "It would never work," she said through her sniffles.

"Char..." Bronson breathed. He dared to reach out and rub a hand along her arm. "Just tell me what's going on."

She spun and he pulled his hand back, almost afraid she would snap it off. "What would be the point?" she asked, though her tone lacked any bite. "You live in California, Bronson. You want me to tell the truth?"

He nodded.

"Okay. I think you're attractive, though I have no doubt you already know that. Every woman probably finds you attractive."

"Well...not *every* woman," Bronson teased. He smiled when Charli let out a barking laugh.

"It doesn't really matter though," she said, sobering slightly. "I'm not interested in a fling or a long-distance relationship." Her glassy eyes met his. "I love my town. I have no intentions of leaving it. All my hopes and dreams are focused on things here." She shook her head. "So I don't see what giving into a little crush would do."

"Little crush?" Bronson scoffed. "I think we can both agree the draw is more than little."

"Still doesn't matter," she said, wiping the corner of her eyes.

"Charli, Charli, Charli," Bronson crooned. He cupped her cheek and let his thumb explore the soft skin there. He'd been careful to touch her as little as possible. His attraction was too strong to play with and touching her would have made it nearly impossible to keep his distance. "First of all, we have no idea where a relationship between us would go. You're jumping to conclusions." He held up a hand to stop her rebuttal. "But I agree that it isn't the kind of situation for a short-term romance. That isn't my style either."

He let his eyes roam lazily over her face, a masterpiece of lines and curves. "But don't you think we'd always regret not testing it out?"

"You told my brother the kids came first," she rasped. When her body swayed toward his, Bronson could tell he was wearing her down.

He nodded. "They do. Saving Fathers and Sons is my first priority. But that doesn't mean I can't find happiness along the way." He smiled softly. "Truth be told, there's been too little of it in my life."

Charli's brow furrowed and he reached his other hand out to force the wrinkles away. "You don't really mean that, do you?" she asked. "You didn't have a good childhood?"

Brons gave a noncommittal grunt. His childhood had been recorded by the media as his mother went through the last few years of her career. His adolescence had been spent watching out for her manic moods and depressions. As a youth, he hadn't understood it all, but he did now. Any resentment he'd had from her death had turned into remorse. His mother had been ill and he was truly sad she hadn't gotten the help she needed.

But now he was an adult, he'd found a good purpose in life, and he was doing everything he could to save that dream. His plan might not be perfect. He was just hoping it was enough.

Charli sighed and closed her eyes for a second before turning back to him. "Bronson?"

"Hmm?"

"Would you like to go to a bonfire tonight?"

His smile hurt with how much it stretched across his face. Daring to lean forward, he kissed the tip of her nose. "I'd love to," he whispered. *Next time, I'm aiming straight for the mouth. And I'm thinking tonight might provide the perfect opportunity.*

CHAPTER 12

Be there in five.

Charli took a deep breath as she waited for Bronson to pull into the parking lot. She'd agreed to meet and walk him down to the bonfire so he wasn't showing up all alone. She knew her friends would make him feel welcome. *Especially Caro,* Charli thought wryly.

She had a weird possessive streak when it came to Bronson. While they might have admitted they liked each other, a relationship was still mostly up in the air, leaving Charli with no real reason to be jealous, but the emotion was there anyway.

Bronson's car pulled in, sleek and quiet until he hit the gravel. "You clean up nice," he teased as he stepped out of the driver's seat.

"I thought I was supposed to say that to you!" Charli called back. She smiled as he sauntered her way. The man was too attractive for his own good.

"You can say it," Bronson said as he approached. "I don't mind."

Charli laughed. She was equal parts nervous and excited for tonight. Bringing him tonight was probably making a statement, even if she didn't mean for it to. But she'd also never brought a man with her to a friend gathering. It was akin to meeting the parents and she was slightly worried what everyone would think of him.

Bending over, she grabbed the cooler she'd brought with her. "Come on." She jerked her head toward the sand. "I'll introduce you."

Bronson grabbed the cooler. "While I've been admiring your muscles enough to know that you have them, my nanny taught me better manners than to let you do so."

"You had a nanny growing up?" Charli asked, surprised. She'd never met anyone who had a nanny. It had always seemed like one of those rich people quirks that you only saw in movies. *But now I'm hanging out with one of those rich people.*

"Several, in fact," Bronson said easily. "Mom was always busy, so someone had to take care of us."

Charli nodded. She folded her arms over her chest, unsure what to do with them now that he was carrying the supplies. "They're over there." She pointed out a group of people who were clearly having a good time around a roaring fire.

Bronson nodded. "Looks like a good group."

"Yep." Charli picked up the pace. "I'll introduce you." She slowed as they drew near to the group.

"You made it!" Caro called out. She was almost always the first one to greet a newcomer and tonight Charli was grateful for it.

"Hey, guys," Charli said, her nerves acting up again. All eyes were on her and her guest. She turned and took the cooler from Bronson, buying herself more time to be brave. It was a new experience for Charli. She wasn't afraid of much, but introducing a man to her friends had her shaking in her sandals. After setting it down by the food table, she turned back to everyone. "This is Bronson Ramsay," she said, putting a hand on his forearm in a light touch. "He's the one who hired me to remodel the old Miller home."

"Heya, Bronson," Caro said with a wide smile. "Enjoy those truffles?"

Bronson chuckled. "They were amazing," he answered. "Thanks for forcing me to buy them."

"Really, Caro?" Rose asked, giving Caro a look. "You *made* him buy something?"

"Rose!" Charli said with a more relaxed smile. "I didn't see you there." Rose didn't always make it to the bonfires. She had a young daughter at home that required special care and who often monopolized Rose's time. Lilly was an absolute doll, but being deaf meant she was a little more needy than the usual child.

"Hey, Charli," Rose replied in her smooth soprano. She was the epitome of elegance and beauty. Red hair that stood out in the firelight, porcelain skin and cornflower blue eyes.

She could have been a model right alongside Bronson's mom.

To Charli's surprise, Ken, or Captain Kenneth Wamsley, as he was known to the town of Seaside Bay, was sitting next to Rose. Charli had always suspected there were some feelings between the two, who happened to be the oldest of their friend group, but in all the years Rose had been living in Seaside, neither had ever made a move.

"Good to see you, Bronson," Felix said, stepping out of the shadows. He came over and shook Bronson's hand. "How's the house coming? Charli said something about a competition?"

Bronson nodded. "Yeah. I'm planning to enter the home in the Oregon Homeowner's Renovation Competition."

"What made you pick the Miller home?" Bennett called out. "Just getting the cat smell out of there is going to be a miracle in and of itself."

Charli grinned as Melody, Benny's sister, smacked him upside the head. "Lay off, Bennett." Mel's other hand was clutching Jensen's, her soon-to-be husband.

"Well, it will," Benny whined, rubbing his head. "You guys are all going to give me a concussion if you don't knock it off." He leaned around Mel to speak to Jensen. "You wouldn't want your best man to fall down at the wedding, would you?"

"Of course he wouldn't," Felix shot out. "But I feel fine."

Everyone laughed and the chatting picked back up again.

"Okay, I'm ready for the rundown," Bronson said in an aside.

"I won't say there'll be a quiz on this later...but there'll be a quiz on this later," Charli teased.

"If it's a private quiz, I think I can handle that." His eyes twinkled in the fire's glow and Charli couldn't help but laugh as she tucked a piece of hair behind her ear. They were standing very close to each other, closer than casual friends would, and it made her fingers itch to reach out and touch him again. Each of the few times they'd come in contact with each other had lit her skin on fire...in a good way, and she wanted more of it.

"Okay. You've met Caro, Felix and Mel, right?"

"The woman at the smoothie shop," Bronson nodded, all business.

"Right. So holding Mel's hand is her fiancé, Jensen. He's a school teacher and budding guitar player. He plays in the smoothie shop and his online videos do pretty good. They're getting married at the end of the summer."

Bronson nodded.

"Bennett is Mel's sister, he's the guy on her other side. Then we have Ken, or Captain Ken, if you want. He's the police captain." Charli began pointing her way around the circle. "Rose owns the flower shop in town and has a picture-perfect four-year-old, Lilly, who's too beautiful to look real."

Bronson glanced down. "Are she and Ken married?"

Charli shook her head quickly but softly. "No. We don't know what happened to Lilly's father. Rose showed up in town four years ago with a newborn and a stunningly sad smile. She opened the shop a few months later and the rest, as they say, is history."

Bronson nodded. "Wonder what her story is," he mused.

Charli shrugged. "I don't know, but we all love her too much to press."

"Right."

"Next to Rose is Brooklynn. She owns a clothing boutique on Main and is our resident Hollywood expert." Charli grinned. "From the way she's eyeing you, I'm guessing she's figuring out your parentage."

Bronson's humor seemed to disappear. "Brooklynn, huh?"

Giving into temptation, Charli touched his arm again. "But don't worry. She's not a big gossip, she just loves fashion."

Bronson looked down and the intensity in his gaze had her backing up. His hand landed on hers before she could fully let go of him and Charli froze. Slowly, he twisted their hold until he could pass her into his other hand and intertwined their fingers. The weight of the moment made Charli forget all about introducing him to the rest of the group. And the heat she was feeling had absolutely nothing to do with the fire.

"I SHOULD HELP SET UP the food," Charli whispered, her eyes never leaving his.

Bronson ran a thumb over the back of her hand. Her skin was warm and smooth. He glanced over her shoulder then back. "Looks done to me." He gave her a slow smile. The one Janine had always told him was dangerous. "Come sit with me." He leaned closer. "I'm afraid to sit by myself."

Charli's inviting lips pulled into an answering grin. "I don't believe that for a minute."

"Then at least save me from Caro," Bronson teased. "She'll eat me alive if you leave my side."

"That's probably true," Charli said with a quiet laugh. She started to walk, tugging him with her. "Come on. Felix brought us chairs earlier."

Bronson followed behind like an obedient puppy and this time, it didn't bother him a bit. As long as he got to be close to Charli, he'd trip along in her wake anywhere.

"Thanks," Charli said to Felix as she plopped into the seat next to him.

Bronson quickly sat as well, in order to keep their hands connected.

"Didn't answer my question about the house," Felix said, though his eyes darted to their interconnected digits and back up. A cool eyebrow rose high and Bronson met Charli's brother's stare.

"It's coming along," Bronson said, shifting so he was facing the siblings a little better. "Your sister is amazing at what she does."

Felix nodded. "She is," he agreed. He narrowed his gaze. "I thought you were focused on some people who were relying on you?"

"Felix, stop," Charli said wearily. "This isn't the time or place."

Bronson squeezed her hand. "It's fine. When my sister shows up with a guy, you'd better be sure I'm gonna be quizzing him." *If we ever got together anyway. I can't remember the last time we had a family dinner.* He turned to Felix. "They're still relying on me. I need to win this house competition in order to help keep a charity afloat. I haven't forgotten that."

"But?" Felix pressed.

"But that doesn't mean I can ignore how wonderful your sister is forever."

"And when you go back to California?"

Bronson could feel Charli stiffen and he almost cursed at Felix's question. Asking the exact excuse that Charli had expressed earlier wasn't helping any. "We'll cross that bridge when and if we get to it."

"If?" Felix scratched his jaw. "That sounds ominous."

"Enough," Charli said firmly. "You've done your interview. Not to mention I'm an adult and can make my own choices."

Felix gave a chin tilt to Bronson. "Looks like we're done for now."

Bronson smiled. "She's hard to argue with, isn't she?"

Felix laughed and relaxed into his seat. "If you've already learned that, then I think my work here is done."

Charli was scowling when Bronson looked at her and his laugh intensified. He brought her hand up and kissed the back of it. "Cheer up, Charli. We both know when we're beat."

"What's that from? It sounds so familiar."

Bronson turned and realized that there were still more people he hadn't met. "*Charlie and the Chocolate Factory,*" he said, glancing at Charli just as she rolled her eyes.

"Genni, this is Bronson. Bronson, that's Genni and her fiance Cooper."

"Wassup?" Cooper nodded at Bronson, who returned the greeting. The couple were sitting slightly behind everyone else, just barely into the shadows of the beach, and Bronson thought it looked like a perfect way to be a part of the group, but still have some privacy. Obviously where they were sitting now hadn't kept their conversation to themselves at all.

"I knew I'd heard it before," Genni said with a smile. She gave a fake shiver. "I hated that movie as a kid."

"What?" Caro screeched. "It was perfect!"

"Only someone as obsessed with candy as you would think that," Bennett added. He pointed to Genni. "Those Oompa Loompa guys were the stuff of nightmares."

"Actually, it was the face of the kid being sucked up the pipe that creeped me out the most," Genni said, leaning her head on Cooper's shoulder. His arm tightened around her.

The group broke into a loud argument about the movie that lasted for several minutes before most of them got up to start eating.

Bronson waited until Felix left, then pushed his chair back a little. "The fire's a little too warm," he said, helping Charli do the same.

"Yeah, but out here it's chilly," she complained.

Grinning, he tugged her chair closer to him and wrapped an arm around her back. "Exactly."

Charli looked startled momentarily, then began to laugh. "That was the lamest pick-up ever."

"It couldn't be," Bronson retorted.

"Why not?"

"Because it worked."

Charli laughed again, then settled her shoulder against his, leaning ever so slightly into his hold.

It was a little awkward, since their chairs weren't made for cuddling, but that didn't matter at the moment. The newness of being able to touch and be close was more exciting than worrying about an armrest poking his ribcage.

The party went on another hour before Jensen pulled out his guitar and everyone quieted down. From the first strum of the strings, Bronson could see why the schoolteacher had a following. He was good. Really good.

The music floated through the salty sea air and gave their little spot on the beach a romantic atmosphere. Even though most of the friends were single, they all seemed to settle into their seats, looks of contentment on their faces.

Bronson was back to holding Charli's hand and he brought it to his lap, playing and teasing her with his touch. He trailed his fingertips around her palm, enjoying the catch in her breath at his ministrations. Slowly, he brought her hand up and began to kiss her knuckles one by one. He could hear her breathing grow faster and it matched his pulse, which was currently trying to win the Kentucky Derby.

Grabbing her hand fully again, he brought the back of it to his mouth and let his lips simply sit against her skin, then turned and met her stare head-on. Her chocolatey eyes were fathomless pools in the firelight, looking more warm and tender than he'd ever seen them.

Letting their hands fall down to the arm rest, Bronson leaned in, waiting at the halfway mark for her to meet him, giving her own permission for what he craved more than anything else at the moment.

She began to lean forward, paused for what seemed eternity, then closed the small gap between them.

As soon as her soft lips touched his, Bronson knew he was a goner. Every bit of electrical charge that had been building up during their weeks of working together exploded, slamming into him with more force than a Mac truck on a freeway. He had to fight and tighten his body to keep from grabbing her and pulling her into his lap. A very small part of him recognized that they were still in public, and he was grateful he hadn't lost his head completely, even though he sincerely wanted to.

He still had a job to do in Seaside Bay. But as of this moment, everything had changed. Bronson would earn his inheritance, and he'd save Fathers and Sons down in California, but never again would that place be his home. The rest of his money would go toward building himself a new life somewhere else. Somewhere where bonfires and friends were the norm, instead of traffic and schmoozing.

"Ooohhh." The sound grew louder and eventually Bronson realized the group was teasing him and Charli. He pulled back, breathing heavily, and smiled at her dazed expression.

"Charli and Bronson sitting in a tree..." Caro sang out before Rose shushed her.

"Oh my gosh," Charli moaned, putting her face in her hands.

"Way to go, bro!" Bennett shouted, putting a fist in the air.

Felix grunted, but didn't say anything else.

Bronson was just as embarrassed as Charli at being caught, but he refused to give into it. Instead, he squeezed her hand, smiled for the crowd and took all the teasing with good grace. If he was going to be friends with this group, he figured he'd better get used to it. Because he wasn't going anywhere anytime soon.

CHAPTER 13

Charli's heart began to pound harder and harder as she pulled into the house's driveway. Things had not gone as she had expected last night. She knew bringing Bronson to the bonfire was sort of an announcement, but she had still been fighting within herself as to whether or not to open herself up to a relationship. Bronson had obviously taken things into his own hands and moved ahead full steam.

Not that she was exactly complaining. Their kiss had been fairly tame as far as kisses went, but it had felt as if the sands were shifting under her feet. The sparks between them had been building for weeks and last night had finally come to a head. His touch had made her skin flush and her heart flutter in a way Charli had never experienced before. The biggest problem was how much she wanted more of it.

Charli had always assumed she'd eventually get married and have a family of her own, but it hadn't even been on her radar for the near future. She figured she would build her business, then worry about finding someone to spend her life with. Not that Bronson was close to proposing, but the way he made her feel was noticeably different than her past relationship experiences. Whether it was age, attraction or something else, Charli didn't know, but she did know that it was just a little frightening to look ahead, knowing that this could possibly be *it*.

Bronson crept out of the front door, probably wondering why she was staying in the truck for so long, and at the sight of him, Charli felt her breathing grow shallow. *This is why,* she thought. *This is why I'm worried. Am I ready for something more serious than casual dating? Do I truly want to let someone into my life like that?*

When she looked closer, Charli realized that Bronson didn't look very happy. He waved her in, his eyes darting back inside. Charli frowned, suddenly feeling worried for a whole different reason. The thought of Bronson changing his mind or regretting their kiss last night made her nauseous.

Bronson waved harder and again looked into the house.

"Better just get it over with," Charli grumbled, slipping from her seat. "Hey..." She called out with a fake smile. "What's up?"

"Shhh!" Bronson put a finger to his lips. "Come here."

Oookay... Now Charli was growing more curious than worried. She pursed her lips, but walked up to the door. When she got close, Bronson grabbed her hand and kissed her cheek quickly.

"I think something is in the house," he whispered in her ear.

Charli's fears had fled at his sweet touch, but when his words penetrated, she stiffened. "What?"

"Shhh!" Bronson waved down her volume. "Follow me," he mouthed.

Charli shook her head in disbelief, but did as he asked. The house was quiet, so she wasn't sure why he was acting so weird, but she figured for now she'd play along. Careful not to step on anything that would make noise, she followed him to the stairs.

"It's up there," he whispered.

Her lips pinched together as she watched this large, muscled man try to quietly climb the stairs of an old, creaky house. He winced every time he hit a noisy board and Charli did her best to move around the spots he pointed out.

Once they were upstairs, he tiptoed to the middle of the hallway, his eyes on the ceiling.

"What now?" Charli asked in a low voice.

Bronson pressed his finger to his lips again, then pointed upward.

Charli made a face, but tuned into the ceiling. They waited for what seemed like forever. Nothing but the sounds of a breeze rustling the trees outside could be heard, but Charli continued to wait. Bronson's eyes never left the ceiling, so she humored him.

Several minutes later, she put her hands on her hips and opened her mouth, only to snap it shut as a shuffling noise moved from behind her to the other side of Bronson. Charli felt her eyes widen and she blinked several times. "What *is* that?" she asked.

Bronson relaxed and then shook his head. "I don't know," he said. "I heard it this morning while I was getting dressed and have been trying to pinpoint it ever since."

Charli's eyes drifted to the open bedroom door and she cringed at the sleeping bag she found on the hard floor. "Your back has got to be killing you by now," she said, looking at Bronson with sympathy.

Bronson gave her that crooked grin he loved. "I can't say it's happy, but I'll live. I don't sleep here every night, just the really late ones." He leaned close. "Want to kiss me and make it better?"

Her cheeks immediately went into blazing fire mode and Charli shook her head. "I thought that didn't work past the age of like, eight."

Bronson closed the distance between them. "I don't think I've ever paid attention. Should we do an experiment and find out?"

She couldn't stop the smile from spreading across her face, but she also couldn't just give in and kiss him...could she? "I don't—"

Bronson cut off her words with a firm kiss that had Charli forgetting why she was protesting in the first place. He pulled back, pausing only a second before going back for more. His arms grabbed Charli's waist and she stumbled into his chest, her hands automatically landing on his shoulders as he brought their bodies together.

One large hand slid to her back and spread wide, creating heat throughout her entire upper body. She gripped his T-shirt in her fists, then forced them open and let her hands begin to roam. When her hand ran into his soft hair, things shifted.

Bronson groaned and changed his angle in order to deepen the kiss and Charli felt her knees begin to shake. She gripped him harder and kept herself upright, unwilling to cut the exchange short.

This was the kiss that had been kept on hold last night. The soft touch of lips at the bonfire had, apparently, only unlocked the door, and with this morning, the floodgates had been slammed open.

It wasn't until the scrambling above their heads lasted for more than a few seconds that Charli pulled back with a loud gasp. She was breathing as if she'd finished one of her long training runs and felt overheated everywhere.

"I'll never look at mornings the same way again," Bronson whispered, his voice deep and raspy.

Charli shook her head. "Me either."

The scrambling once again echoed down the hall and Charli found herself finally pulling away from Bronson's steely gaze. "It appears you have a rodent in the house."

Bronson finally pulled back from her, running a hand through his hair. "Good thing my back is feeling much better." He winked at her, causing Charli to laugh. "So...a mouse or something?"

A crash came from above their heads and the sounds of hissing.

Charli's eyebrows almost hit her hairline as she tried to see through the drywall. "Uh...negative, Ghost Rider. That's much bigger than a mouse."

"CRAP," BRONSON MUTTERED. He was frustrated, for more reasons than one. The last thing they needed was to deal with pests in the attic, but the bigger reason for his emotions was the fact that his time with Charli had been cut short. That kiss was the kind of kiss other kisses only dreamed of being.

He could still feel her against his mouth and he wanted nothing more than to put the real thing back into action. Charli, however, looked like she had lost interest as the noises in the attic continued. He sighed. She was always looking to fix the problem and he probably wouldn't be able to get her attention again until it was taken care of.

"So what should we do?" he asked.

Charli pursed those delectable lips and began to move around, scanning the ceiling. "We need to find the attic entrance."

"We have to go up there?" Bronson asked with a grimace. "What if it's got rabies?"

Charli laughed, the sound deliciously low. He could listen to it all day. "Are you afraid of a little woodland creature?" she teased.

"How do you know it's little?" he shot back. "You already said it was bigger than a mouse."

Charli shrugged. "That still doesn't make it large." More screeches came from above them and she ducked in response.

This time it was Bronson who chuckled.

"Okay, so it sounds big," she admitted. Her eyes twinkled when she met his. "But you're definitely going up there."

"Me?" Bronson folded his arms over his chest. "I'm not the one getting paid to be here."

"We didn't include insurance in my contract," Charli argued, poking him in the chest. "I can't afford a trip to the hospital."

Bronson grabbed her hand and stole a quick kiss. He couldn't help it. She was perfect when she was being feisty. "With what I'm paying you, you should be able to afford a dozen trips to the hospital," he muttered.

"Nope. The money—" Charli snapped her lips together and turned away from him. "I'll search for the entrance," she said, walking away.

Bronson grabbed her arm. "Hold on a minute," he said, his mind running in circles. "What's going on with you and the money I'm paying you?"

Charli opened her eyes wide. "What do you mean?"

"Don't play innocent," Bronson snapped a little more harshly than he meant to. "You sounded like you were about to say you had no money or that it had gone somewhere. Where would it go? I'm paying you as we go, so why would you have no money?" His brows furrowed. "Are you in trouble or something? Some kind of heavy debt?"

"No!" Charli shouted, pulling out of his hold. She rubbed her arm, though Bronson knew he couldn't have hurt her. "It's nothing like that." She straightened her shirt and stuck her chin in the air. "But what I do with *my* money is none of your business."

"It is if we're in a relationship," Bronson argued.

"No, it's not," Charli said, shaking her head. "We're not married."

"No, but if you're running something shady, then I think I should know about it." Bronson didn't really believe she was doing something against the law, but at the moment he couldn't think of anything else that would cause her to hide whatever she was doing.

"You think I'm running some kind of scam?" Charli's jaw dropped and hurt flashed through her eyes, hitting Bronson right in the chest.

He sighed and hung his head. "No...I don't really think that. I'm sorry it ever came out of my mouth." He'd been spending too much time with his brother. Canon always had a pulse on the crime in L.A. *Probably because he represents the wealthiest of them,* Bronson thought angrily. It didn't matter to Canon whether he was in the right or wrong, all that mattered was winning.

"Then why would you say it?" Charli asked, her voice shaky.

"Charli," Bronson groaned. "I'm sorry. I was just getting frustrated and it slipped out. I don't think you're some kind of scam artist. If you were, then I'd have to be blind to all the work you've already done here," he said, struggling to get his foot out of his mouth. "You're amazing and you prove it every day."

That weird screech came from the attic again and they both looked up.

"And you're about to be more amazing by figuring out what the heck has taken up residence in the attic."

Charli scowled at him. "Whatever." She sniffed. "Go back to your project. I'll take care of it." She turned and stormed off, leaving Bronson to follow like the whipped pup he was.

If he was that dog he kept comparing himself to, then his tail would be between his legs. He shouldn't have said what he did, but right now Charli was too angry and hurt to listen. Hopefully if he just let her breathe, she would calm down enough to forgive him.

When she finally found the cut out of the ceiling in the back corner of one of the bedrooms, Bronson offered to go get the ladder. He was careful bringing it upstairs, trying not to punch a hole in their newly painted walls.

The hinges squeaked as he set it down and straightened the locks.

Charli put her foot on the bottom rung and Bronson dared to stop her. "I've got it," he said, gently urging her to the side.

"It's my job," she argued, putting her hands on her hips.

"Nope." Bronson winked. "I didn't insure you, remember?"

Charli huffed and shook her head, but a small smile played on her lips, giving Bronson hope that he'd be ending his day the same way it started.

He climbed up and carefully lifted the door up and off to the side. A heavy wave of musty sea air hit him in the face. "Nasty," he muttered under his breath.

"It's not like there's air-conditioning up there," Charli said, the smile in her voice audible.

"The least the attic could do is brush her teeth," Bronson called over his shoulder. "It smells like ten-year-old morning breath."

Charli laughed softly and Bronson relaxed even more.

He stepped up another couple of rungs and cautiously poked his head around. It was too dark to see anything and all the noises from the animal had stopped. He ducked his head back down. "I think I need a..." His voice trailed off as he took her offered flashlight. Saluting her with it, Bronson quipped, "This is why you're paid the big bucks."

Charli shook her head. "I think I deserve a raise."

He put his head back up the hole. "I think I deserve a raise after this." Cobwebs and insulation met his gaze as he looked around. Nothing looked out of the ordinary and Bronson pinched his lips together. "I can't see anything."

"Just stay quiet," Charli said, her voice almost a whisper. "Shine the light into all the corners."

Bronson clamped his jaw shut and turned his body in as much of a circle as he could, trying to aim for every nook and cranny. Nothing was forthcoming, but they'd heard too many noises to think there wasn't something up there.

He slowly stepped up another rung, wiggling his shoulders to get more of his body through the opening. This way he was able to angle himself better, and when he heard a slight rustling, he immediately turned the light toward the area. A curse word slipped from between his lips. Two eyes, red from the flashlight, glowed back at him. "Charli?"

"Find something?"

"We're going to need some help with this one."

CHAPTER 14

"What?" Charli felt panic begin to build in her chest. "What is it?"

Another curse word echoed through the attic and Bronson jumped to the ground, covering his head. "It's a raccoon!" he shouted, looking up from under his arms.

Charli yanked the ladder away from the opening as if the creature would crawl down and attack them. She could hear the animal chattering and screaming at them and Charli kept a close eye on the opening. The last thing they needed was for it to jump down.

"Hang on," Bronson said, grabbing the ladder and moving it under the opening. "We have to close it up." Just as he started to climb again, the raccoon leapt through the opening onto the top of the ladder. "ABORT!" Bronson shouted, jumping to the ground and running out the door, grabbing Charli's hand and dragging him.

Once in the hall, they slammed the door behind them. "What the heck...was that?" she asked between pants. Bronson was standing with his forehead leaning on the door, his breathing coming out in great heaving movements.

"A rabid raccoon," he managed.

"I didn't see it foaming at the mouth." Slowly, her heart rate was coming back under control and she turned to put her back against the door. A scratching sound from behind her had Charli leaping forward. "What are we going to do?" she asked, not really directing the question at anyone in particular.

Bronson shook his head, his hands on his hips. "Maybe call Animal Control?" He turned to look at her. "Do you have one of those around here?"

"Considering how many wild animals you get in a town like this, we definitely have an Animal Control." Charli headed toward the stairs. "I'll have to grab my phone."

"Don't leave me up here alone!" Bronson shouted, chasing her down the stairs, his steps thundering behind her.

Charli couldn't help but laugh. "You afraid it might get you? I don't think it can open the door."

Bronson scowled at her. "Have you seen those hands? All those videos of them stealing food from dog bowls?" He widened his eyes and leaned close. "They're eerily human."

Charli laughed harder. "Come on, then, little boy. I'll protect you." Bronson grumbled behind her the whole way, but Charli ignored him. The whole situation was tickling her funny bone and pushing away the anger she'd been experiencing from their earlier fight. Thinking about his claims that she was hiding something gave a burst to that tiny flame of anger, but it didn't grab hold. She could address that with him later...maybe.

She was hiding something, so she wasn't sure it was wise to bring it up. It might not be anything illegal, but that didn't mean she wanted to spill all of her dreams to him. The relationship they were testing out was still brand new and it was too early for that. Charli would have to be pretty attached to a man to share that with him, as in...we're going to get married. Her dreams were private and precious, and she held them close to her chest.

She scrolled through her phone until she found the number she needed and pressed the call. For the next ten minutes, Charli argued with the woman on the other end of the line and when the call was over, Charli's anger had flared once again, and it had nothing to do with Bronson.

"When will they be here?" he asked, although by his voice, he could tell something was off.

"They're not coming," Charli snapped. She put the phone down on the cardboard box and rested her hands on it, leaning her weight forward.

"Why not?"

Charli shook her head, not yet ready to turn around. This day had started off so promising and now she was losing time for something as stupid as a wild animal. "Because the entire office is off looking for a cougar that was spotted about a half-hour from here."

Bronson grunted. "Well, that's annoying."

"You're telling me," Charli snapped. She jumped when a warm body came up behind hers. Bronson's arm came under hers, caging her in.

"I'm sorry," he whispered against her ear.

"For what?" Charli asked, closing her eyes. This man had way too much power over her emotions. He was already pressing against her walls, and Charli wasn't sure how to handle it. She didn't let people in this close, but Bronson had managed to get her to agree to be partners in the house, and now he was pushing himself even further into her life. She felt out of control, scrambling to catch up with how quickly he was moving. The most frightening part, however, was that she wasn't sure she wanted him to slow down.

"For saying you were hiding something." He kissed the edge of her ear. "It was wrong and was a defensive action rather than a true thought."

Charli sighed and let her head fall forward. "It's fine," she said. "I get it." She turned just enough to see his eyes. "I have a little experience with saying things in anger, if you can't tell."

Bronson grinned and kissed her temple. "You're beautiful when you get all feisty."

"Feisty." She laughed breathlessly. "That's a nice way of saying I'm a shrew."

Bronson turned her around. "You're not a shrew, Char," he said firmly. "If you want a less cute word, then I'd say you're bossy."

She glared at his smile.

"You're confident, capable of being in charge and know what you want. There's nothing wrong with that. I have yet to see you be cruel about it, or run over others to do it. That's what a shrew would do."

Charli reluctantly smiled back. "Well, thanks. But as long as we're offering our true feelings here, then I might as well let you know that I think you're very touchy-feely." She looked pointedly down at his hands which were on her waist. "I don't usually let someone touch me this much."

"I have made no secret of the fact that I think you're stunning," he said easily. "What guy wouldn't want to be hands-on with you?"

Charli rolled her eyes. "Yeah, well...right now we need to be hands-on with the raccoon."

"What do they want us to do with it?" Bronson asked warily.

"We're supposed to catch it and bring it in."

"What?"

Charli stifled a laugh, covering her mouth with her hand. "Why do I get the feeling that you're more afraid of the animal than you are about losing time for the renovation?"

Bronson gave an exaggerated shiver. "Can you blame me? Who knows what kind of diseases he carries?"

"He?" Charli leaned back and gave him a look. "You got close enough to know it was a male?"

Bronson scoffed. "No way. But no female would ever attack me that way."

Charli scrunched her nose. "What? You totally lost me."

Bronson tilted his head and shook it slowly. "Charli, Charli, Charli, don't you know by now that you're dating a hot commodity?

No girl ever comes at me with murder in her eyes. This guy was definitely afraid I was going to steal his girlfriend."

A barking laugh came out of Charli and she shook with it. "Did you want to be touchy-feely with her too?"

Bronson grimaced. "Not that I'd ever tell the dude that, but no way. Raccoons creep me out." His mouth slowly spread into a smile. "You, on the other hand...don't creep me out at all."

"Ooooh!" Charli said in an exaggerated tone. "Good to know."

"In fact..." Bronson re-grabbed her waist and pulled her in close. "If we didn't have to go save our lives..." He dropped his voice and let his lips brush her ear. "I'd like to get touchy-feely with you again."

Charli patted his chest. "Good thing we have to go save ourselves, then."

Bronson turned and headed toward the front door. "You say that now, but you'll be begging for it later!"

Charli laughed softly and followed him out, her body still humming. *He's probably not wrong...darn him.*

"ARE YOU SURE THIS IS going to work?" Bronson asked, frowning at the cardboard box in his hands. "That thing has nails a mile long. It'll probably shred this to pieces."

Charli rolled her eyes. "If I'd known you were this big of a baby, I'd have never let you kiss me yesterday."

"Is it my fault that I don't want my hands taken off?" Bronson asked. He was hard-pressed to hold back his laughter and grin. Getting Charli worked up was turning out to be one of his favorite things. Her reactions were fantastic. He probably shouldn't egg her on so much, but it was just too tempting. She took the bait every time. "How else am I supposed to get touchy-feely with you if I don't have hands?"

Charli snorted and smiled widely. Bronson reciprocated. His work here was done for the moment.

"Okay, are you ready?" Charli had on her work gloves and held a broom in her hands.

"In all seriousness, I'm not sure this is going to work," he whispered.

Charli pinched her lips together. "Me either, but I don't have anything else. Unless we want to waste even *more* time going into town to get supplies, we're going to have to deal with what we have." She looked pointedly at the box, then back up to him. "And that's it."

Bronson sighed. "Right."

"On three. One...two...three!" Charli threw open the door and they rushed inside before slamming it behind them. There was no way they wanted the critter to have free reign of the house.

Bronson came to a standstill, only his head moving around. "Where the heck is he?"

Charli pointed above their heads. It wasn't until then that Bronson realized the scratching noise was once again occurring.

"Crap," he muttered. "We can't go after him in there. We won't even be able to stand up, let alone chase him down."

Charli squished her lips to the side. She finally handed him the broom. "Hang onto this."

"What are you planning?" Bronson asked, not even trying to be quiet. Who cared if the raccoon heard them at this point? Maybe the little guy would come out and they could catch him. Glancing at the ceiling, he knew they'd have no such luck. The noise had stopped as soon as he and Charli had started speaking.

"I'm gonna close up the attic entrance," Charli said, stepping toward the ladder.

"Whoa, whoa," Bronson dropped the gear he was holding and stepped forward. "Why are you doing that? We can't just leave him in the attic."

Charli shook off his hand. "I know that, but we're not really prepared to face him right now anyway, so it's better to hold this off until we can do better."

Bronson frowned but stepped to the ladder. "Well, at least let me do it." He wanted to smack himself as soon as he said it. He might like to tease Charli, but Bronson knew the woman was anything but a fragile female who needed to be taken care of. Charli was a doer. She was independent and fierce, and any hint of thinking otherwise was going to get him put in the dog house...no matter how good his intentions.

"I think I can handle it," she said through clenched teeth. Pushing him out of the way, Charli quickly scaled the ladder and had the hole closed up before Bronson could respond. Coming back down, she dusted off her hands. "There. See? Even a *woman* can handle it." Putting her nose in the air, Charli began to leave the room, but Bronson stopped her.

"Before you go, we need to get one thing straight."

Charli's dark eyes were piercing, but she stilled.

All the previous humor and teasing was gone and while Bronson mourned its loss, he needed to be sure she understood his thoughts on the matter. "I was not intending to insult you when I offered to do it," he said, raising a quick eyebrow when she tried to retort. "It wouldn't have mattered who was standing next to me. If I thought there was any kind of possible danger, I would have offered to go. You could have been the world's strongest man, or the high school's best defensive lineman. I still would have offered." Bronson leaned down so they were nose to nose. The fire hadn't dissipated from her eyes yet, letting him know they'd probably be working on separate projects today.

He sighed, hating it. All he wanted was to spend time with her, but Charli held her independence so tightly that there were times she went too far. "An offer from someone who cares about you is because they care, not because they think you're incapable."

Finally, she softened and Bronson felt the sweetness of relief trickle through his veins. "Thank you for explaining," she said, her voice a little lower than normal. "I think maybe we should set food out in a trap on the back steps." She swallowed and stepped back, putting a little distance between them.

Well, that's better than nothing, I guess.

"He has to be eating, which means he has a way of getting in and out. If we can catch him in a trap, then we won't have to do battle and we can turn him into Animal Control."

Bronson glanced down at the cardboard box, his eyebrows high. "You know how to set a trap with a cardboard box?"

Charli's lip pulled up into a small grin. "No. But with the attic closed, we're not in any hurry. I can pick something up in town later that will do the trick. And we don't have to waste any more time on it today."

Bronson nodded. "It's a good plan."

Charli gave a curt nod in return. "Good. I'll get that taken care of later, then. Right now, let's get to work. We're way behind."

Bronson followed her downstairs. "What project are we doing today?"

Charli grabbed something off a work table and turned around to hand him a small roller. "You're going to paint the trim."

Bronson's shoulders fell. He knew it.

"Be careful not to leave any streaks. And we'll have to set you up with the work horse, outside."

A soft moan began, building louder and louder as the wind picked up speed. Both of them glanced outside and Bronson noticed the tree branches whipping around as if they were being shaken by a two-year-old. "Uh...I don't think that's a good idea."

Charli groaned. "A storm. Great. That's all we need." She sighed. "Guess you're setting up shop inside." She scrunched her nose. "I hate the smell of paint."

"Then why in the world do you do what you do for a living?" Bronson asked.

Charli shrugged. "It's not like I..." She trailed off and cleared her throat. "It doesn't matter. I'm not the kind of person to let something deter me if I want to do it."

Bronson dared to step forward and kissed the top of her head. "You're not," he agreed. "It's part of what I admire about you." Leaving that hanging between them, Bronson walked away to gather his supplies. He figured the best thing to do was to let Charli have her space, then hopefully he could wiggle his way back into her good graces after she'd had enough time to order him around for a while. Hopefully soon, she'd recognize he wanted to be an equal partner in more than just the house.

CHAPTER 15

Rain beat against the windows and Charli winced when a branch slapped the side of the house. The storm was turning out to be much stronger than she'd expected. She made a face. It was a good thing a lot of their work was inside, but still...not being able to go in and out made things much more difficult and they couldn't afford to waste any more time.

She'd already taken off last night for the bonfire and now they'd lost half the morning to that stupid raccoon! If they didn't get this house done in time, Charli wasn't sure she'd be able to live with the guilt of how that would affect Bronson's charity.

With one last growl at the uncooperative weather, Charli went back to screwing in the electrical cover plate, making sure to line up the screws in the proper order. It always drove her crazy when the screws were turned every which way.

"Next," she said sarcastically as she looked at the pile of cover plates. It was going to take her a long time to get the house done. There seemed to be hundreds of them, although Charli was fully aware that in a modern home there would have been twice as many.

Grabbing her stuff, she moved to the next wall and started wiring in the new outlet. A scrambling sound over her head had her ducking, like the raccoon would somehow come crashing through the ceiling. "So ridiculous," Charli scolded herself. She mentally reminded herself again to buy that trap when she went back to town. The sooner they got rid of that pest, the better. She just hoped the animal didn't cause too much damage before they could be taken care of.

"Charli?"

She paused. "Yeah?"

"I think I need help."

Charli's shoulders fell. This was the problem with having a partner. They were often needy and she didn't want to deal with needy. She wanted someone who would just do the work and leave her to do her own. Squeezing her eyes tight, Charli pinched the bridge of her nose.

That's not fair. He hasn't been needy at all and Bronson has done everything you've asked him to do. "Not to mention you've gotten some amazing kisses out of the deal," she reminded herself under her breath.

Climbing to her feet, Charli headed to the hallway and stairs. "What's up?" she asked as she walked into the family room. Seeing the streaks of white on Bronson's face made Charli pinch her lips shut to keep from laughing. He looked like a small boy who had been playing in his dad's stuff.

Bronson glared at her. "You said no streaks. You didn't say it would take a magician to make that happen."

She lost it. The pouty look on Bronson's face, the paint...the stress of the morning all came bubbling out of her in incessant giggling that she felt helpless to control. "I'm sorry," she said, trying to cover her mouth."But you've..." She wiped at her whole face. "Got something..."

Bronson's glare got even more ferocious, which only added to Charli's amusement. "You think this is funny?" he asked, his voice calm. Too calm.

"Nope." Charli clasped her hands in front of her and tried to school her face. "Zero fun, sir."

Whether or not he recognized the quote, Charli couldn't tell, especially as the large man sauntered her way, looking pleased with himself. He bent down to meet her face to face. "I think I need to show you what fun is."

"I don't think—" Charli gasped and cut off her sentence when a paint-coated finger drew a line down her nose. Her eyes felt like they would bug out of her head as he proceeded to draw lines over her cheeks and polka dots on her forehead.

"There." Bronson smirked, apparently pleased with his art. "Now that's fun."

"You didn't," she said breathlessly, running for the bathroom. *Please say he was teasing.* But even as she thought it, Charli could feel the wetness drying on her skin. She studied her face, noting that her eyes were bright, looking alive and passionate, even with all the ridiculous white paint all over her skin. The realization that Bronson had put that there shook her to the core. Charli had been very content with her life before he showed up. So content, she was afraid of risking it in order to try for more.

But something had shifted ever since the tall, greek god of a man had come into Caro's candy shop. Her skin looked flush with good health and her dark eyes seemed to dance, while energy zipped through her body in a way it never had before. And all because the dork in the other room liked to tease and force her to step outside her normal comfort zone. He was breaking through every boundary she had, one inch at a time.

She turned to leave the bathroom, forcing the too-wide smile into submission. Right now was not the time to tell Bronson that he was coming to mean something wonderful to her. Right now was the time for revenge.

She narrowed her eyes and stormed into the front room. Her anger must have been palpable because Bronson had the good sense to put the table between them.

"Hey...you look good in war paint," he teased. "Uh..." His eyes darted around when she continued to slowly stalk his way. "Maybe we can talk this over?"

Charli didn't say a word. He liked teasing, right? Well, now it was time for him to have a taste of his own medicine.

HE WAS DEAD. BRONSON could see in Charli's eyes that he'd finally gone too far and she was going to strangle him with his own tongue or something else equally as frightening.

The problem was, there was nowhere to run. The house wasn't very large and there was a storm raging outside. All of which explained why he found himself stuck in the corner with nowhere else to go. "Now, hold on, Char," he said, trying to soothe her anger. "It was just a bit of teasing." He forced an awkward laugh. "You can take a joke, right?"

A single eyebrow went up as she continued her advance. She was like a sleek predator and her approach was as beautiful as it was terrifying. Part of Bronson just wanted to stand still and watch the show. The other part knew he wouldn't like the end result.

"Charli," he said, this time putting a warning in his tone. If begging didn't work, maybe being in charge would. "You need to stop this right now. I'm your boss after all."

"My boss, huh?" Charli pursed her lips and drew closer until Bronson was as folded into the corner as his large body would allow him to be. She put one hand on his chest and leaned in. "And as my boss, what is it you want me to do?"

It's a trap. Bronson almost laughed at the immediate thought. It was obvious to all and sundry that Charli was baiting him, but he couldn't stop now. She was finally doing something other than ordering him around and focusing on her work. "I want you to go back upstairs and get back to work." There. Reverse psychology at its best.

"Okay," she said, her voice smooth. "But first..." The hand she had been hiding came up and she began dragging her finger around his face.

Bronson relaxed, knowing he would live for another day, and gave her a dry look while she finished up. The glee in her eyes was addicting and he wished he could get her to play like this more often. However, when she dragged her finger over his lips, leaving a wet streak in its wake, Bronson had had enough of playing the victim.

"There." Charli brushed her hands together with a loud clapping sound. "All finished. *Now* I'll get back to work." She spun, but Bronson grabbed her hips.

"Not so fast." He spun them around, this time pinning her in the corner. "I think we need to make things a little more even," he whispered.

"Oh? I thought we just did." Charli challenged him with her defiant gaze.

"Nope. But don't worry, I know just the way to fix it." Bronson leaned in and took Charli's mouth in a searing kiss. He didn't bother working up to the intensity he was craving. Charli had started all this with her stalking, he was just finishing it. He knew she liked being in charge, but Bronson wasn't going to let her run him over.

Charli sighed against his mouth and wrapped her arms around his neck, letting him know she didn't mind when he took charge at all, and he grinned against her mouth.

"You're cute when you're angry," he said, letting his mouth trail to her cheeks and jawline.

"You wait until I really have reason to take you out," Charli said breathlessly. "You'll be singing a different tune."

"I look forward to it," Bronson joked as he kissed her racing pulse.

Before they could say anything else, the room was suddenly plunged into darkness. The storm outside kept much light from filtering through the windows, and though there was enough light to see, it looked far from midday.

"What happened?" Charli asked as they straightened from the corner.

"Must be the storm," Bronson said, looking around as his eyes adjusted to the dimness. "Guess I'll have to go check the breaker."

"I'll come with you," Charli said with a frown. "This is a good storm, but not enough that I'd expect the electricity to go out. We have storms like this all the time."

"Come on, then," he said, grabbing her hand. He fumbled for his phone, turning on the flashlight feature, all while holding her hand. "I'm guessing we'll find the breaker in that utility closet?"

"Probably," Charli replied. "Although...the water heater is in there, so I don't know for sure." She huffed. "I guess I should have checked for that when we first got started."

Bronson gave her hand a squeeze. "It's not a big deal. We'll figure it out."

They picked their way carefully through the room, stepping over all the construction materials which were mere shadows on the floor, looking eerily menacing, especially with the wind and rain still howling outside.

"Okay," Bronson muttered under his breath as they got to the closet. "Let's see what we've got here." He let go of Charli and opened the small door. The room was tucked against the kitchen and under the stairs, which made it barely big enough for the water heater and vacuum cleaner it contained.

"Let me," Charli said. She patted Bronson's chest. "I'm smaller, so it'll be easier for me to get around."

"Okay, but be careful," Bronson said. He handed her the light and she stepped inside the dark space, leaning around to get a good look at the walls.

"Got it," Charli responded.

A squeaking noise hit Bronson's ears as she opened the panel. Bronson waited, but Charli looked to be frowning. "What's up?"

"None of the breakers are flipped," she grumbled, her fingers dancing along the switches. She turned to him, the flashlight giving just enough light to see her face. "It really must have been the storm." Her nose scrunched up. "Huh. I know they went through these neighborhoods not too many years ago and did a massive update for all the wires, especially since some were still fuses at that point, so I would have expected it to be a little more sturdy."

Bronson shrugged. "Maybe a line went down closer to town or something?"

"Maybe..." Charli agreed, though Bronson could tell she didn't believe it.

Truthfully, neither did he. The storm was a solid summer storm, with decent wind, but it wasn't destruction-worthy. The odds of it taking out a powerline seemed small.

"Well, if we can't fix it, we might as well learn to live with it," Bronson said. He held out a hand, helping Charli step over a bucket of supplies on the floor. "Let's grab lunch and then we'll get back to work as best we can."

"I suppose that's all we can do," Charli agreed. "We can't waste any more time." Her eyes flashed to his as she crossed in front of him coming out of the closet. "Someone likes to play instead of work, so it makes it hard to stay on schedule."

Bronson chuckled and kissed her nose. "Someone else likes to work and never play at all." He wrapped his arms around her shoulders. "Maybe if we're lucky, between the two of us, we'll find a happy medium."

She pushed playfully at his hold. "At least wait until after the competition is over, huh? That deadline is approaching like a tidal wave."

Bronson sobered at the reminder of why he was here in the first place. "True enough," he said, stepping back and taking her hand once more. "Lunch and then work. It's the best kind of day."

Charli laughed softly, obviously seeing right through his lie, and Bronson smiled as they made their way back to the kitchen. This was always Canon's complaint about him as well. Bronson's brother seemed to love to tell others about how Bronson preferred play over work, but it wasn't the real story.

Bronson preferred life over work. It was why he adored volunteering so much. He could settle down and work when it was necessary, but he also got to get up and move with the kids. They needed a mix of work and play and so did adults... They just seemed to forget. As usual, it was Janine who had taken the time to help Bronson see just how much he'd been missing by keeping his nose in dusty old books all the time instead of recognizing what was right in front of him.

And hopefully, Bronson could help give the same gift to Charli, no matter where they ended up finding themselves in the future.

CHAPTER 16

Two days later, Charli was ready to throw a fit. Their electricity was still off and she thought she had been more than patient. "This is ridiculous," she said, slapping her hand on the table.

Bronson grimaced. "Yeah, but what are we supposed to do about it? It's not like we can force them to fix it faster."

"Did you call the electric company?" Charli asked. When Bronson didn't answer, she turned to look at him. "Bronson?"

He scrunched up one cheek. "No?"

Charli threw her empty hand in the air. "Not even once?"

"No," he said, rubbing the back of his head. "You said it was the storm, it seemed logical, so I figured we'd wait it out."

Charli slapped a hand to her forehead and groaned. "I'm so stupid."

"Charli," Bronson warned.

"This is exactly why I don't do partners," she muttered under breath, setting down the screwdriver and grabbing her phone. Bronson was quiet, so she didn't bother looking at him while she was transferred to a tech man.

"We don't have any lines down anywhere," the guy, whose name was Gary, said.

"Nothing at all?" Charli asked. "We've been without electricity for two days."

"Well, why didn't you call in sooner?" Gary asked.

Charli sighed. "Doesn't matter. Can you come help figure out what's going on? I checked the breaker box and everything looked fine, but I'll be the first to admit that electrical wiring isn't my strongest point."

"Something the great Charli Mendez can't handle?" Gary crowed.

"Shut up," Charli muttered. "Can you come out or not, Gary?"

"Yeah, yeah. I'll be there in an hour."

"Thanks. I appreciate it." Charli hung up and turned to speak to Bronson, but he wasn't there. Frowning, Charli walked around looking for him. "Bronson?" He wasn't in the house, so she finally went out to the front porch. "Bronson? What are you doing out here?"

His large shoulders were hunched forward as he leaned his elbows on his knees. Blue eyes peeked over his shoulder before he went back to studying the ground.

"Is everything okay?" Charli gingerly sat down next to him, wanting to reach out to comfort, but feeling apprehensive about doing so.

"Fine," Bronson said, though his tone said it was anything but. "Just realizing a few things, I guess." He stood and dusted off his pants. "Thanks for calling the company. I better get back to work."

Charli watched him go, feeling as if she had lost something precious, but not quite sure what it was. Bronson was obviously upset about something, but what? It wasn't her fault he hadn't called the electricity company. It was his house, so wasn't that his responsibility?

Unsure what else to do, Charli finally pushed the problem to the back of her mind. He was right. They had work to do and things were only getting farther and farther behind schedule.

An hour later, a horn in the driveway caught her attention and Charli set her tools down to walk outside. She held up a hand. "Hey, Gary."

"Heya, Charli," the older man said with a grunt as he pulled a tool kit out of the back of the truck. "Why don't you show me the breaker first, eh?"

"Come on in." Charli stepped back and nearly tripped on Bronson standing silently behind her. "Sorry," she said, expecting him to grin and tease her about her clumsiness, but his face remained stoic as he nodded.

"You must be Mr. Ramsay," Gary said as he came up the steps. He held out his gnarled hand. "Pleased to meet you. I'm Gary Mathews."

"Nice to meet you, Gary. Thanks for coming on such short notice."

Gary nodded. "I retired a few years back, but still show up at the office most days and help out." He grinned. "Those young guys just don't know what they're doing yet."

"Well, we appreciate it."

Gary bobbed his head again and they all headed inside.

Charli gave Bronson an inquisitive glance, but he wasn't paying any attention to her. While Gary fiddled away inside the closet, Bronson stood at the wall, leaning his shoulders back and folding his arms over his chest. His playful, smiling demeanor was nowhere to be found.

"What's up with you?" Charli asked, a little frustrated at his behavior.

Bronson finally looked at her. "I don't know what you mean."

"This." Charli waved a hand at him. "You're not being yourself."

Several heartbeats went by as Gary muttered under his breath inside the small room. "Maybe I finally decided to be the partner you want," Bronson said quietly.

Charli jerked back as if she'd been slapped. Her mind whirled and her chest felt as if it had been stabbed. "What?" she said breathlessly. She didn't quite understand what he was talking about, but they weren't able to converse more before Gary came stumbling out.

"Cursed bucket," he grumbled, glaring back at the innocuous object holding the mop.

"You okay?" Charli asked, though her concern was for the giant behind her, not the small man in front.

"Fine." Gary wiped his hands on his pants. "There's nothing wrong in there. I'd like to go outside to the entrance point. Some of these homes have an outside switch that might have gotten jostled somehow."

Charli nodded, feeling slightly foolish she hadn't thought to look for that first. "Of course."

"It should be just outside that." Gary pointed back to the closet. "It'll be close to the breaker."

"There's a screen door in the kitchen." Charli nodded her head in that direction and led the way. Sure enough, a switch box was on the corner of the house and Gary worked his way to his knees to check it out.

Charli stayed back, not only to give Gary room but because she was struggling to concentrate on the situation at hand. Bronson was several feet back, his presence dark and heavy. Her mind whirled as she tried to figure out where his statement had come from, when suddenly it came to her.

She swayed as the blood rushed from her head as her words, grumbled in anger, came back to her. *This is why I don't do partners.* The pain in her chest intensified and her vision grew blurry. She hadn't meant it as a direct comment about Bronson, but it would have been easy to take it that way. She'd already snapped at him about not calling the electricity company and then she had to go and say make that statement.

No wonder he wasn't speaking.

I'm giving you the partner you wanted.

She turned just enough to see his form in her periphery. The weighted silence between them hurt more than she would have expected. This was definitely not what she wanted. Working with someone else had proved challenging, but it hadn't been all bad. She secretly adored his playfulness and how he kept the hours moving quickly with his laughter, teasing and moments of passion.

Secretly. That's the problem. He's done nothing but give and you've done nothing but take.

Gary looked over his shoulder. "I think I found yer problem."

"Oh, good." Charli sniffed and tried to cover up her emotions. "Is it an easy fix?"

"Easy enough." Gary shrugged. "But I think the bigger question is...why would someone want to cut yer wires?"

BRONSON LURCHED FORWARD. "What did you say?" he rasped. He forgot about his fight with Charli for a split second as they both descended on Gary.

Gary leaned back a bit, giving Bronson the stink eye. "I said it looks like someone cut the wire to the house."

"Let me see," Charli said softly, kneeling down.

Bronson stared at the top of her dark head, waiting for her reaction. She finally looked up at Gary. "Is it possible a raccoon could have done this?"

Gary scratched his stubbled chin. "They could, I suppose, but the break looks cleaner than a bite to me. Plus the little guy would have received a nasty shock."

Charli glanced over her shoulder, met Bronson's gaze, then turned back to Gary.

Bronson couldn't read what message she was trying to send, but he figured they'd have to talk it out later. In a professional and completely non-attracted way.

"We have a raccoon in the attic that we haven't been able to capture yet," Charli said softly.

Gary nodded. "That could be it. Seems more likely than someone coming out and cutting the power." He groaned and rose to his feet. "I can't think of anyone around here that would want to do such a thing." He peered at Bronson. "And with you being new in town, it's not like you would have any enemies to speak of."

Bronson shook his head, though it wasn't a question. He had no idea why someone would want to cut their power. It made absolutely no sense. Bronson took a deep breath. Charli had to be correct. It had to be the raccoon.

Bronson backed up and let Charli continue chatting with Gary. Hopefully they were figuring out a way to fix the wire, because Bronson didn't know the first thing about electricity. He'd probably get himself killed if he tried messing with anything.

His ringtone sang from his back pocket and Bronson pulled it out, then made a face. "Hey, Canon. What's up?"

"Have you finished the house yet?"

Bronson sighed and walked away from the others. He headed to the front of the property so they wouldn't be able to hear his conversation. It rarely went smoothly with Canon on the line. "No. I have eight weeks, remember? There are still four left."

Canon snorted. "I'm afraid, dear brother, that the rules have changed."

"What do you mean, they changed?" Bronson growled. He forced himself to calm down. His brother was too good at pushing his emotions and since Bronson was already on edge with the situation with Charli, he wasn't controlling himself as well as normal.

"It means that I had my friend, Judge Simmons, look at the will. He interpreted it differently than me and said you're down to just two weeks left. The eight weeks started when Dad passed."

"You can't change the rules in the middle," Bronson insisted, holding his panic at bay. "The will said eight weeks. That can't be changed."

"Actually...it doesn't," Canon said softly. He almost sounded sad about the situation, but Bronson wasn't sure he believed it. Canon was beyond mundane emotions. He didn't cry for anyone, not even himself.

"You *told* me it said eight weeks."

"I told you a layman's version of the will," Canon corrected. "The exact words were open to a little interpretation and a judge has now interpreted them."

"Why is Judge Simmon's word law?" Bronson argued. "You're a lawyer and a member of the family, and you told me eight weeks from when I started. They shouldn't be able to change that."

"His word is law because he's the judge who will hear the case when you present for your share."

Bronson was struck into silence. He felt like his entire world was being swept away with a rogue wave. He had been depending on that time. He *needed* that time. The competition wasn't until the end of the eight weeks and that award would be his ticket to saving Fathers and Sons. Even if he and Charli somehow managed to finish the house in the weeks provided, which was debatable, he wouldn't have anything to show for it. The reward was supposed to be tangible enough to prove his worth. A fixed-up house would never make it.

"I want a copy of that will," Bronson said through clenched teeth.

"Bron, you don't need—"

"A copy, Canon! Or I'll call in another lawyer and fight you about it. I have every right to see it."

Canon sighed. "Fine. I'll email it soon. Look, I don't like what Jedediah did any more than you, but—"

"Save it," Bronson interrupted. "I don't need your sympathy. But if you think I'm going quietly into the night, you're wrong. I'm going to fight this. Dad was proud of my work and I'm not giving up on my rightful inheritance like this." By the time he finished his rant, Bronson's hand holding the phone was shaking. He was flushed and overly warm and had the insane desire to beat something to a pulp. Any kind of activity that would help alleviate the building pressure inside of him would be a welcome retreat.

Canon's sigh was even longer than the last one. "Do what you need to do, Bron, but you won't be able to fight this. In fact, I think at this point, rather than embarrass yourself, you should just let it go. No matter what the old man told you while you were alive, it's clear that he thought your *work*, and I use the term lightly," Canon drawled, the weight of his sarcasm tangible to Bronson's listening ear, "was a waste of time and money. If he hadn't kept that Janine woman around so long, we wouldn't be having this fight."

"Don't you say a word about her," Bronson snapped. "She was the best thing that ever happened to Dad and changed our lives." Bronson shook his head even though Canon couldn't see it. "Don't you ever get tired of being the mean guy? Don't you wish people were around you because they actually liked you, instead of just fearing you?"

"Enough!" Canon bellowed through the phone. His voice dropped to a dark, steely tone. "That woman made you both weak. She tricked Dad into giving up everything that he had worked so hard for and you followed along like the obedient lamb you were." His laugh was harsh, nothing amusing about it. "You might as well walk away with your tail between your legs, Bronson, because you can't win this. The terms are nearly impossible and it was Dad's way of telling you that you meant nothing to him. He didn't care about you or your stupid charity. And even though he might have put on a good face while Janine was alive, his will made his true thoughts clear enough."

Bronson had no words. Canon's insults struck deeper than ever before and the malevolent tone in his brother's voice was strong, even for Canon. Bronson's brother didn't like to lose control. He was a master of manipulation and aloofness, so to hear him so wild was more frightening than his usual coldness.

"What's it going to be, Bron?" Canon taunted. "Give up and run, like you always do? Or beat your head against a wall? Neither one will end up helping you, but at least one will be less painful."

Bronson's voice was completely emotionless as he responded. "Send the will." Without saying anything further, he turned his phone all the way off and stuffed it in his pocket. He had no idea what he was going to do, but too many people were counting on him. So what if it was a painful experience? If he could handle his brother's verbal tortures without dying, he could handle anything.

CHAPTER 17

Charli stood frozen as she listened to the last part of Bronson's conversation. From the very beginning, she had known Bronson wasn't sharing everything with her, and this proved it. It also proved, however, that Bronson was fighting for something...and losing. Now that Gary was gone and the electricity was fixed, it was the perfect time to bring it all into the light.

"I think we need to talk."

Bronson spun, his mouth open, only to snap shut. He stared at her, then nodded firmly and turned, walking toward the house.

Charli expected him to go inside, but instead, he sat on the front porch steps, his shoulders sagging with an unseen weight. She approached tentatively, unsure what to say to get the conversation started. She had secrets of her own that she wasn't quite ready to give away, but hers didn't affect Bronson.

"How much did you hear?"

Her eyes were on the dirt as she kicked her boot into a small hole. "Enough."

Bronson snorted and shoved a hand through his hair. "I guess I need to tell you everything, huh?"

Charli shrugged. "I guess that's up to you." She dared to look up. She wasn't going to force anything out of him, but she also wasn't sure what to make of the situation. She'd never seen Bronson...playful, teasing, light-hearted Bronson...speak to somebody the way he did a moment ago. Even his silent treatment from that morning was preferable to seeing him look so angry and then so broken. "But I'd be lying if I said I wasn't curious and that I felt like whatever is going on inadvertently affects me."

Bronson shrugged. "I guess it does in a way, but only because you're helping me with the house. The end result is mine alone to bear."

When he didn't speak more, Charli perched gingerly on the edge of the step just below him. She reached up and took one of his hands, cradling it in her own and studying the calluses. She didn't think they had all been formed during their few weeks together, though probably some had. His hands were rough and in some places, the calluses too thick to be new. They told silent stories of hard labor and sweat. He was such a conundrum. He threw his money around like it would never run out, but his hands didn't speak of a life of privilege. Having grown up with the mother he did, he probably wanted for nothing. Nothing material anyway.

"I mentioned before that my family doesn't get along all that well," he said, his voice low and rough.

Charli nodded, but continued to wait.

"When my mom died, as much as we mourned the loss, there was also a sense of…relief in the home. She and her demands were a burden that had grown almost too heavy to bear over the years. Demanding and volatile. She was always looking for a way to get back in the spotlight." He sighed. "It shouldn't have surprised any of us when she finally took her life. Her moods swung from one extreme to another and I think she should have been on some kind of medication, but she wouldn't hear of getting help. That was definitely beneath her."

He paused and Charli wondered if she should offer some kind of platitude, but even before she spoke, it fell flat. Words weren't going to help right now. She'd already thrown around words carelessly this morning and they'd hurt Bronson. Right now he needed something more. She shifted their hands until they were gripping each other's thumbs. It was a strength hold, one that she hoped would give him the courage to finish what he was starting.

His eyes never met hers, but when he straightened his shoulders, she silently cheered him on. "A few years went by, Canon left the house and I was just about to do so myself when Dad brought Janine home." A small smile played on his lips. "She was the sweetest thing I'd ever met and still to this day, I wonder how my dad convinced her to go out with him. We'd been zombies, moving through life without emotion or desire, just...existing." He snorted. "Existing in the lap of luxury. We had everything money could buy, but life was cold." His hand went to his hair again. "Anyway...Janine was like a burst of sunshine. She brought love and warmth to a family who'd never experienced it before." His face grew tight. "Canon never cared for her. He says she made Dad and I weak."

"And your sister?" Charli dared ask.

Bronson shook his head. "Aria was too entrenched in the power of being Mom's daughter. She wasn't vocally cruel, but she kept her distance."

"I'm sorry." The words had been automatic, but they were just as useless as Charli had known they would be.

"It's not your fault."

Another automatic response, Charli was sure.

"Anyway, Janine showed me a new way of doing things. I stayed close to home while I studied at college. I just couldn't quite bring myself to let go of everything she had brought into our lives. And it was Janine who introduced me to Fathers and Sons." His breathing grew shallow and a drop of sweat slid down his temple.

Charli tracked its progress with her eyes, recognizing how difficult this was for him. Dread filled her as she realized that she was about to hear the worst part of the story.

"After graduating from college, I began working with the charity full-time. I had money of my own." His eyes darted to hers, then dropped again. "My mom left all of us trust funds. And I invested my money wisely, so I'm never hurting for what I want or need. It also allows me to help others." He blew a ragged breath out of his lips. "After I'd been working there a couple of years, Janine grew sick and eventually died."

"Oh, Bronson." Charli's eyes filled with tears. His grief was still palpable and it hurt Charli to watch him. Her own struggles and dreams seemed less important now that she understood where he was coming from.

"I continued working, knowing she would be proud of me." He sniffed and squinted at the sun. "After losing a woman for the second time, Dad needed something to fill his time and I convinced him to volunteer with me...in Janine's name." Bronson shook his head, his hair falling over his eyes. "I thought he enjoyed himself. I mean, he smiled and seemed to look forward to everything we were doing. Got to know the kids, listened to them, offered advice and help." Bronson's shaking head grew more fierce. "But it was all a lie." The words were short and clipped, nothing like the sweet reminiscing he'd been doing a moment ago.

"I'm lost," Charli whispered. "What do you mean, it was a lie?" She bent her head to catch his eye and lost her breath at the intensity of his stare.

"My dad died a couple months ago. It was an auto accident. His will was mostly as you would expect. The estate was split three ways between us kids."

When he stopped, Charli raised her eyebrows, asking silently for him to finish.

"Let me preface this by saying that Fathers and Sons are just about to be kicked out of the building they rent. They've had a few tough quarters as far as fundraising goes and are nearly at the end of their lease. The landlord has already told them they won't be renewing without a big hike in rent." He took in a long breath. "Anyway, I have enough to share with my investments, but not to save them, and the trust won't let me give them what they need. So when Dad died, I thought I'd be able to use my inheritance for something good. I wanted to save the charity."

Again he paused and Charli almost screamed at him. She knew he was about to drop a bomb because this story should have a happy ending, but his behavior told her elsewise.

"So back to the will...Dad gave everyone their share...except me." His blue eyes looked like a frozen lake in their coldness. "I was given a bunch of hoops to jump through and no way to accomplish it. If I don't fulfill it all in the next two weeks...I lose it all and Fathers and Sons will fall apart."

BRONSON KNEW HE SOUNDED melodramatic, but the situation was exactly how he'd described. The only thing he hadn't told her was why the charity meant so much to him, though he figured that would come out sooner or later.

His father had been distant, though not as much as his mother, during his growing up years. Now, working with this nonprofit, Bronson had a chance to give to other boys what Janine gave to him. An adult influence to help guide them on their path into adulthood.

But his sob story was enough without spilling every part of him that wasn't quite up to snuff. He didn't need Charli's pity. He needed her help and her expertise.

"What hoops do you have to jump through?" she asked, looking slightly wary.

"I haven't actually read the will," Bronson muttered, feeling foolish for even saying the words, especially after the electricity fiasco. "My brother is a lawyer with a specialty in inheritance law, and he told me that Dad said I had to hold down a job for a minimum of eight weeks and have something to show at the end of it."

She frowned and her eyes dropped from his, looking unfocused as she considered his words. Finally, Charli shook her head. "I'm still lost."

Bronson ran his hand through his hair again. He was going to be bald by the time this was all over. "Canon didn't say it specified that I had to work for someone else, so I took on the job of a house remodeler, but I needed someone with an actual license to help me do it. My job at the charity wasn't considered enough to fulfill the requirements. Dad said I had to be in the real world."

"I'm not sure I agree with that, but go on."

"In order to have something to show at the end, I assumed that meant I have to show that my efforts amounted to something tangible, so when I saw the Homeowner's competition, I thought winning the award might be a way to have something in hand to give the courts."

"You have to take this to court?" Charli's eyes flared. "It's that big of a deal?"

Bronson's cheeks heated and he went back to studying the wooden step. "It's a fairly large estate. My dad was a shrewd businessman."

She whistled low under her breath. "So what were you fighting about?"

The reminder of his recently ended phone call slapped Bronson in the face, reminding him of the imminent failure of his mission. He pulled away from Charli's grip and put his face in his hands. "Canon was telling me that a judge looked at the will last night and said the timing was wrong. I have two weeks left instead of four."

"What!" Charli shouted, jumping to her feet. "How can they change the rules like that? What about the competition?"

Bronson shrugged. "I don't know. Canon said this is the same judge that will ultimately decide if I win my inheritance."

Charli began to pace in front of him and if Bronson weren't so worn down and worried, the sight would be amusing. Every muscle was tight with tension and she looked ready to pummel the first person who looked at her wrong. "You can't change the rules mid-game, It's not right." She paused to look at him. "You need to get a copy of that will."

"I told Canon that."

She opened her mouth, then stopped whatever she was going to say as sorrow took over her features. "Bronson, I'm sorry."

He nodded. "I know, but again...this isn't your fault. I'm sorry I dragged you into it." He huffed. "I'll still pay you what I owe, but I think the house is probably the least of my worries at this point, so I'm gonna let it go for now."

Charli shook her head and came to kneel at his feet. "No. I mean I'm *really* sorry. I shouldn't have made that comment this morning," she whispered. She swallowed hard, never letting his gaze go. "The one about partners."

Bronson nodded. "Yeah. I remember."

Charli's eyes began to fill with tears and it tugged at his heart. "I didn't mean it."

Bronson nodded. "It's fine. I get it." He pulled away and put some distance between them. It had been a bad idea to start anything with Charli anyway. In another time, she would have been exactly what he was looking for, but not right now.

"No. You don't." Charli stood, her hands clenched at her sides. "I've spent my entire life trying to keep up with the men." She took a couple of steps in his direction. "First it was my brother, but as I got older..." She took a deep breath. "Since we're having confession time, I suppose it's my turn, huh?" She laughed bitterly and put her hands on her hips. "I worked construction straight out of high school," she began.

Bronson stiffened. He already didn't like where this was going to go.

"I know everyone always screams about women's rights and stuff, but hiring a woman didn't mean the environment was good for one." She huffed, her glassy eyes meeting his. "I spent four years being treated like an object. Like a plaything for their amusement." She rolled her eyes. "They all told me how I couldn't keep up, and exactly what I was good for."

"They're wrong," Bronson spouted before he could think better of it.

"I know," Charli said, sticking her chin in the air. "I weathered the leers and snide comments fine until one day one of the guys cornered me. He was the foreman and tried to pull rank on me as his employee."

Rage hit Bronson so hard he almost stumbled. "What. Did. He. Do?" he demanded.

Charli put up a hand. "Don't worry. It's not quite the story you think it's going to be." Despite her words, she clasped her hands together, wringing her fingers. "He may not have touched me, but he tried. And my fear was almost more than I could handle." She shook her head and looked up again, as if ridding herself of the memories. "Not only did I decide it was time to get in shape so I could protect myself, but I decided I would never be in a position again where someone had power over me."

Bronson took two steps in her direction before pausing again. It didn't quite seem appropriate to try and comfort her by taking her in his arms. He could see why she was so standoffish and didn't work with others. But his fingers twitched with the effort it took to stay back.

"So I became my own boss, and have been building up a business ever since," she stated proudly. "And everything I've gotten, I've earned. The only person who holds power over me is myself." She tilted her head to the side. "And my brother a little, but don't tell him that."

Despite the seriousness of the situation, Bronson's lips twitched. Her relationship with her brother was to be admired, and he couldn't help but feel slightly jealous of their closeness.

With no warning, Charli closed the distance between them and looked up into his face. "I've never wanted a partner before, but you caught me at a time when I didn't have much of a choice."

Bronson waited. It took all his self control, but he waited.

"I can't say I'd necessarily do this again, but..." She gave him a small smile. "I'm glad to be working with you. You're a wonderful guy. You've taken all my bossiness in stride and we've done some good work together." Slowly, she slid her hands up his chest. "And I don't think we should let that go to waste, do you? We can't just stop now."

Bronson knew better than to argue. He let his own hands slide around to her back. With a little tug, he closed the last couple of inches between them. It might not be the smartest thing in the world to keep a relationship going right now with everything riding on his head, but he couldn't argue with the fact that working with Charli was much better than working alone. "Absolutely not," he muttered right before bringing his head down to hers.

He sent a quick prayer heavenward that this new development with the will wasn't going to mean the end of their time together. Hopefully, if they could figure out a plan, this moment was going to be a sweet beginning instead.

CHAPTER 18

"You need to demand a copy of that will," Charli told Bronson as they sat on the porch, eating their lunches.

Bronson nodded, stuffing a chip in his mouth. "I did."

"Yeah, but he still hasn't sent it...has he?"

Bronson's face scrunched up. "Nope."

"Then text him again."

He turned his head to give her a look. "What am I supposed to do? Bug him to death?"

"Yes!" she shouted, nearly upending her soda. "Which is worse? Bugging your brother to the point that he cusses you out, but concedes, or losing your inheritance?"

Still chewing, Bronson picked up his phone from beside him and punched in a few words. Setting it back down, he raised his eyebrows as if to say *Happy Now?*

Charli nodded and took another bite of her sandwich.

"I guess you have experience getting older brothers to do your bidding, huh?" Bronson said with a chuckle.

Charli feigned offense. "I have no idea what you're talking about."

Bronson shook his head, his smile wide and genuine. When his phone chirped, he glanced down. "Well, cuss out number one has happened."

"Ask again."

Sighing, Bronson began a texting argument that lasted close to an hour before Canon finally stopped answering.

By the time the phone stayed silent for more than five minutes, Charli was already working inside again. She paused and poked her head out of the room when she heard Bronson stomp inside. "What happened?"

"Nothing happened," he growled. "My brother just keeps saying I don't need it. He's a lawyer and he's taking care of it."

Hesitantly, Charli stepped farther into the hallway. "You don't think..." She stopped talking, unsure of how to phrase things without sounding petty, or hurting Bronson's feelings.

He paused in his anger and looked at her. "What?"

Charli shook her head. "Never mind. But the point is, legally he can't keep you from seeing that will." She pointed her paintbrush at him. "Tomorrow morning we're going to go see Mr. Filchor. He's the attorney in town. He'll know what to do."

Bronson pushed both hands through his hair, leaving them against the back of his skull with his elbows flared out to the side. His biceps and chest were on full display and Charli held her ogling in check...barely. "My brother is one of the slickest lawyers in L.A. Somehow I doubt your small town lawyer can handle him." He grimaced and dropped his arms. "No offense meant."

Charli shrugged. "None taken, but how will you know unless you try? It's not gonna hurt...right?"

Bronson tilted his head back and forth. "I suppose not." He opened his mouth again, but a loud hissing scream caught their attention and brought the conversation to a halt.

Charli had ducked down automatically, though after thinking about it, it seemed ridiculous. There wasn't anything above her.

"What the...heck was that?" Bronson asked, his jaw tight.

Charli smirked as she straightened, hoping he didn't catch how dumb she must have looked. "I think we just caught ourselves a raccoon."

Bronson's eyes widened. Together, they bolted through the house and out the back door. Sure enough, a spitting and angry raccoon was clawing at the cage that held it prisoner.

"So...uh..." Charli eyed the livid animal. "You need to pick the cage up and put it in the back of my truck." She folded her arms over her chest and cocked a hip, trying to appear confident, even though fear was like a tsunami inside of her right now. That animal was *not* happy and anyone who got too close was going to know it.

"I believe the cage was your idea," Bronson said, taking a step back.

"What?" Charli turned and glared. "You're like this big-muscled guy...so manly in fact, that you told me I couldn't help you on the house, and now you can't handle a tiny, little raccoon?"

Bronson returned her angry stare. "I never claimed to be manly. I just admitted that I was stronger than you. But if you think that raccoon is tiny or little...you need glasses."

"I was trying to help give you confidence." Charli sniffed.

Bronson rolled his eyes. "I think I've got plenty of that on my own, thanks."

"Good." She stepped toward him and patted his chest. "Then you can use it to put the cage in the back of the truck."

Charli quickly stepped away before Bronson could say anything more. She laughed quietly as she walked, glad for once to be the winner of their little arguments. Bronson had a way of kissing her into submission, but she refused to let him use that trick on her again...or at least, at the moment.

She went back into the house, but kept an eye on the window where she could see her vehicle. When she spotted Bronson walking oddly, Charli stepped over to get a better look. "Oh my gosh," she gasped, putting a hand over her mouth to stifle the laughter.

Using a broom, Bronson had put the stick part through the handle of the cage. Holding the cage in front of him, however, threw his weight off balance, so the large man was walking half bent over with his legs stretched wide to try and counteract the dancing cage.

Unable to help herself, Charli headed to wait in the front door.

"Good riddance," Bronson muttered as he dropped the cage in the back of the truck. The raccoon hissed in response and Charli held back more laughter. Bronson made a face at the creature, then turned and headed back to the house. His head jerked when he noticed Charli watching. He buffed his nails on his shirt. "Enjoy the performance?"

"Oh, sure..." Charli drawled. "I've always had a thing for men who walk like they're in their nineties. That hunchback style is dreamy."

Bronson furrowed his brows and started walking very purposefully in her direction.

Charli held her ground, though it was hard. She knew Bronson wouldn't hurt her, but when a predator was on the prowl, it seemed prudent to run. *Especially since it's always fun to be caught.*

Just as he reached her, Charli put her hand to his sternum, stopping him in his tracks. "As much as you probably want to strangle me right now, we need to figure out the situation with the house."

Bronson's predatory demeanor slipped away and he scrubbed his face with his hands. "You're right. We do."

Charli relaxed and started to turn away when without warning, Bronson grabbed her and kissed the living daylights out of her. She felt weak by the time he finished, a sensation Charli had never liked until now.

"Score one for me," Bronson muttered with a wink after he pulled back. Strutting like a newly crowned king, he headed inside, leaving Charli ready to kick him in the backside...or maybe demand a repeat of that kiss.

Right now I'm not sure which would bring more satisfaction.

THE DAY HAD SPED BY, with neither Charli nor Bronson figuring out what they were going to do about the house. On one hand, it seemed stupid to keep trying. The odds of them finishing in time were slim and even if they did pull off a miracle, what would he have to show the judge at the end of the deadline? Bronson had followed Charli home for them to continue their discussion over dinner, and hopefully add Felix's brains to the mix.

"There's got to be something you can do," Charli muttered for the thousandth time. She came over from where she'd been cooking at the stove. "They can't just take your inheritance away from you."

Felix set down the rest of the silverware. "The will trumps all," Felix said. "Unless, of course, you can prove your father wasn't in his right mind when he wrote it." Felix glanced uneasily at Bronson, as if worried the comment was offensive.

Bronson shrugged, his arms folded over his chest as he leaned against the wall. "He was fine and no one will believe otherwise. Dad died in an accident, not from old age or illness. There's absolutely no reason to believe that he wasn't thinking properly before he died."

Felix nodded. "So we can throw that one out." He sighed and scratched his chin, which was covered in at least a week's worth of hair. "Something about this whole situation just doesn't add up. Why only give you the ultimatum? Why not your siblings?"

Bronson made a face, shame heating the back of his neck. He'd already been over this with Charli, so it probably wasn't a big deal to tell Felix, but it never seemed to get easier. "My brother is the golden boy, I guess. He followed Dad's footsteps and is a killer lawyer. My sister is still finishing her degree, but she's already sought after for modeling, so she has a real career lined up as well."

Felix's black eyebrows went up, but he didn't speak.

Bronson couldn't hold his gaze. He loved what he did, but he knew how people saw him. The media spent enough time picking his life apart for Bronson to be very aware of his image. "I've got some great investments set up to capitalize on my trust, but I quit my accounting job a few years ago."

"So you're some kind of lazy playboy?" Felix asked.

"FELIX!" Charli screeched, rushing over to Bronson's side. "He spends his time supporting a charity called Fathers and Sons," she snapped, glaring at her brother.

Bronson put a hand on her lower back, grateful for her defense, but he needed to stand on his own feet with Charli's brother. "It's all right," he whispered to her. Turning back to Felix, he spoke. "She's right. I live off my trust and investing, but I spend my time helping teenage boys who don't have good male figures in their lives. I donate not only money but my time, working as a full-time employee, though I technically take no salary."

Felix's shoulders dropped ever so slightly. "While that's noble and all, I think the main point here is that you're obviously the outcast of the family."

It had been a statement, not a question, but Bronson responded anyway. "It could be viewed that way. I like to say that I'm simply not interested in the fast lane."

Felix grunted and went to the cupboard, grabbing glasses for the table setting. "You're boiling over, Charli."

With a squeak, she rushed back to the stove and pulled the pasta off before it could cause a mess. "Looks like we're ready," she said with a fake grin over her shoulder.

Bronson chuckled and walked up to sit at the table.

After they'd said grace, Felix began talking again. "Did your brother say why the timeline was changed?"

"Said a judge interpreted the will differently than he did," Bronson responded before stuffing spaghetti into his mouth. "This is good," he said to Charli, who flushed and smiled at him.

"So you've got two weeks to finish the house, but the competition doesn't happen for four." Felix's eyes weren't looking at anyone. Rather, he seemed to be talking to himself. "And if you don't have anything to show for your efforts, then you lose the inheritance. An inheritance you need because you want to buy the building the charity is in."

Bronson nodded, his mouth too full to respond verbally.

Felix blew out a breath. "This seems to get more complicated the more I think about it."

Charli grunted and made a face of agreement.

"You seem to have money...why can't you just buy the building now?" Felix asked, leaning his arms against the table edge.

Bronson swallowed. "First of all...have you ever seen what real estate costs in California?" He shook his head. "It makes your little town look like kids' play. So, I probably could buy the building, but it would require taking out a very large loan and I don't think it would be a good thing to have that dragging me down financially for so long. The charity can't afford a lot in rent, so my paying interest on it would be a study in money loss." He shrugged, his fork spinning mindlessly in his noodles. "Then what happens when I want to buy a house? Or start a business of some kind?" Bronson dropped the fork. "I can make the mortgage payments, but it would be much better to have that inheritance. Then I could buy it outright, not having it hang over my head for years, and it wouldn't hurt my living money."

Felix nodded thoughtfully. "Makes sense."

"I could buy something here, no problem. But in L.A?" Bronson huffed. "As much as I want to help those kids, I'm not willing to lose all my income for the next twenty years to do it."

"And you shouldn't," Charli piped up. "No one would ask that of you."

"What if you sold it?"

The table went silent. Bronson tilted his head. "Uh...what?"

"Your brother said it didn't specify what you had to have to show at the end of the eight weeks, right?" Felix continued.

Bronson shook his head. "No. That's been part of the problem. We don't know what the judge will accept."

"Well...what if you finished the house and sold it in the time frame necessary? You'd have a profitable venture to show the judge. Would that be enough?"

Bronson tapped his fingers on the table, the sound loud in the quiet dining room. "I think that just might work," he said slowly, still testing the idea in his head.

"How are we going to get a buyer in just two weeks though?" Charli asked, bringing reality back to the small spark of hope Bronson was starting to feel. "Especially without the house done." She shook her head. "The odds are slim to none."

Felix shrugged. "People buy houses that are in progress all the time. The real issue is finding people to look at it. Our market isn't exactly booming. If it was right on the beach, you could probably find someone looking for a vacation home or rental. But since it's tucked east of town, a local would be a better fit." He scrunched up one side of his face. "And I don't know anyone in the market."

"Me either," Charli said sullenly.

"Well, it was a good thought," Bronson said. Despite the difficulties, he was going to hold onto that hope. It was all he had at the moment. "It at least gives us somewhere to start."

"Right after we see Mr. Filchor tomorrow," Charli added.

Bronson nodded. "Right. Lawyer first, then real estate agent." It wasn't much of a plan, but right now it was all they had.

CHAPTER 19

"Mr. Filchor will see you now," the secretary said curtly.

"Thank you," Bronson said politely as he and Charli rose from the chairs lining the wall.

Charli wanted to stick her tongue out at the rude woman, but she gave the secretary a tight smile instead. Mrs. Munchkin was just a sourpuss and had been that way for years, though nobody knew why. Her husband was very sociable. They were always an odd couple at community gatherings.

"Charli," Mr. Filchor said kindly, holding out his hand in welcome as they walked into his office. "Haven't seen you in ages, young lady."

Charli laughed lightly. "That's probably a good thing, Mr. Filchor. It means your house doesn't need repair and I'm not in legal trouble."

"True enough, true enough," he said with a smile. He turned to Bronson. "George Filchor," he said, offering the same greeting he gave Charli.

"Bronson Ramsay."

Mr. Filchor paused. "Are you related to Canon Ramsay?"

Bronson looked resigned as he nodded.

Charli pinched her lips together. Apparently the lawyer world was smaller than she thought.

Mr. Filchor didn't comment further, solidifying her thoughts that Mr. Filchor's experience with Canon hadn't been a good one. The older man walked around his desk and sat down, waiting until Bronson and Charli were seated as well before he spoke. "How can I help you today?"

Charli turned to Bronson, assuming he would want the chance to speak.

Bronson cleared his throat. "I'm afraid I'm in a bit of a situation with my father's will," he started. For the next twenty minutes, Bronson told the lawyer every last detail.

Charli was exhausted for him when he finished. It wasn't an easy or flattering story to tell and Bronson had spilled it three times in as many days.

Mr. Filchor's bushy white eyebrows had shot up his forehead multiple times over the course of the discourse and now his mustache was twitching, letting Charli know the older man was thinking. "That's quite a story."

Bronson nodded and leaned back, looking as exhausted as Charli felt.

"How close are you to your brother, Mr. Ramsay?"

Bronson frowned. "Uh...not as close as we could be, I suppose."

Mr. Filchor leaned forward. "I need to know if you're prepared to face some difficult possibilities."

"What do you mean?"

Mr. Filchor opened his hands in supplication. "The fact that your brother refuses to let you see the will...a will that your name is in, even though you have purposefully asked multiple times, and one in which he claims has been altered against you...is highly suspicious."

The color drained from Bronson's face and he looked as though he'd seen a ghost. Charli's first instinct was to reach out and grab his hand, but she wasn't quite sure how to go about it. She'd never been the mothering type, but her feelings for Bronson were deeper than she could have ever expected. Deciding her own discomfort didn't matter, she went for it. Relief flooded her when he held onto her fingers like a lifeline. *Must be that touchy-feely part of him,* she mused, though the moment wasn't the least bit humorous. In fact, she was dreading what Mr. Filchor would say next, fearing it would match her own feelings and thoughts.

"What exactly are you saying, Mr. Filchor?" Bronson rasped.

"I'm saying that I think your brother is conspiring against you."

Charli could feel Bronson's muscles tighten and the grip on her hand was painful, but she grit her teeth and waited it out. She could only imagine the emotions running through him right now. It was clear from his history that Bronson wasn't extremely close to his siblings, but it was also clear that he wanted to be. Otherwise there was no reason why he would waste so much time trying to get along with them.

When Bronson didn't speak, Mr. Filchor continued. "As a lawyer, and a sharp one at that, your brother is fully aware of what he's doing." Those large eyebrows pulled together. "He's probably counting on you not having legal counsel outside of himself in order to get away with it."

"But why?" Bronson snapped. "Why would he go to all this trouble?"

Mr. Filchor's gaze narrowed. "How much is your part of the inheritance worth?"

The weight of the question hung heavily in the air. Charli's eyes went back and forth between the two men.

"Five million," Bronson said, his voice hoarse and barely audible, but in the quiet of the office, it hit the space like an electric shock.

If the lawyer was shocked at the amount, he didn't show it, but Charli thought she might pass out from the thought of that much money for one person. Everything she'd ever dreamed of would be hers if she had access to that. The thought was intoxicating and nauseating at the same time.

Mr. Filchor shrugged. "People have done worse for less."

"But Canon has his own money, the trust from our mother and his own part of the inheritance," Bronson argued, though his voice was lacking any real grit. "Why would he want to go after mine?"

Mr. Filchor sighed. "I'm afraid I can't answer that question, Mr. Ramsay. I know your brother mostly from reputation. I've only met him once and frankly, I don't care to do it again. You know him far better than I do, but I can tell you that I wouldn't put it past him." Mr. Filchor leaned back, folding his hands over his rounded middle. "He's a man who likes power. And in his world, money and power are the same thing." Mr. Filchor shook his head slowly. "There comes a point where a man can never get enough."

Bronson shook his head in response and Charli could feel her heart breaking for him. She didn't want him to have to consider this option, but she was grateful to Mr. Filchor for having the courage to say it. It had been on Charli's mind for a while, but she had been too cowardly to hurt her relationship with Bronson.

"No," Bronson stated, sounding stronger than before. "I really don't think he'd do that. I'm his *brother.*"

"And you're standing in his way," Mr. Filchor said softly.

Slowly, Bronson's head turned to Charli, his eyes tortured. "What do you think?" he asked.

Charli closed her eyes, unable to meet his question head-on.

Bronson blew out a long breath, obviously having read her answer without words.

When Charli dared look back up, he was still staring at her, a resigned look in his eye. "Remember what Gary said?"

Bronson frowned. The electrical guy?"

Charli nodded. "He said the wires looked like they had been cut."

"Yeah, but we decided it was the raccoon...didn't we?"

Charli raised an eyebrow and waited. It wasn't fair to spring this many things on Bronson, but as long as the truth was being told, it needed to be told. After Bronson had walked around the house, she'd inspected the wires herself and Gary was correct. It was a clean slice. No animal could have done that. It brought up the legitimacy of the flood in the kitchen as well. But the question was, how far would Canon go to sabotage his brother? And just how far was Canon's reach?

BRONSON FELT AS IF his whole world had been turned upside down. It was almost as bad as the days he'd lost first Janine, then his father. *Will it never stop? How many members of my family do I have to lose before it'll all be over?*

Charli squeezed his hand and he turned toward her. Her sympathy was almost more than he could bear, but he couldn't seem to find the energy to get angry. Instead, he felt drained.

"Remember this is all conjecture at this point," Mr. Filchor stated, as if he hadn't just sent Bronson's life into a spin. "We can't prove anything."

"Maybe not, but it's telling that both you and Charli came to the same conclusions," Bronson said, his voice soft and weak. He didn't like that. He shouldn't be falling apart like a kid going through his first set of finals. He was an adult. Almost thirty years old, for heaven's sake. Crumbling like a termite-infested log was ridiculous.

He leaned forward, dropping Charli's hand and covering his face. His mind was too worked up to think properly. "What do you think we should do?" he asked, his voice muffled.

"First off, we need to get a hold of that will," Mr. Filchor stated firmly. "If you're willing to hire me as your legal counsel, I can formally request it. If you want to go with someone else, I've got a few buddies down the coast that'll take care of you."

Bronson dropped his hands and straightened in his seat. "Is this something you're willing to take on? If my brother feels threatened, I can't guarantee he won't do something to make you regret it." A humorless laugh broke through his lips. "And here I was, just defending him," he muttered, pushing a hand through his hair. He hadn't cut it since he'd arrived in Seaside Bay and it was starting to get in his eyes.

"No one blames you for that," Charli said softly.

Out of his periphery, Bronson saw her reach for him, only to pull back. He finished the movement for her, grabbing her hand once again and resting it on his thigh. Her touch right now was more helpful than she would ever know. "Maybe not, but if I'd just stopped to think about it, it really shouldn't surprise me. Canon is hard and cold. Has been for a long time." Bronson's body deflated, sinking into the cushions of the seat. "He's my mother, but without the depression. Anything he wants, he gets." Bronson blew out a long breath. "Honestly, if it wasn't for the kids, I'd let it go. It's just not worth the fight, and I have all I need."

"No."

Charli's harsh voice caught Bronson by surprise and he turned to look at her.

She was shaking her head adamantly. "He has no right to that money," Charli snapped. "You're a good person, Bron." Her gaze softened just slightly. "You might not need the money, but others do and in the hands of your brother, it'll never help anyone but himself. He doesn't need another house or car, but there are kids who are desperate for what you offer. Adults going hungry. Widows starving for company." She turned more fully in her chair and brought her other hand to the top of the combined ones. "*They* need you to get that money. Because in your hands, it'll make a difference. *You'll* make a difference."

Bronson held her gaze for a long time. Charli had never been particularly loquacious about him and they hadn't had a chance to talk about how she felt with his chosen profession. But seeing the fire in her gaze at the moment was enough to give anybody a jumpstart.

It was at that moment that Bronson realized he'd fallen in love with the kick-butt handywoman. He had come to Seaside looking for redemption and instead he'd found his heart.

In front of a lawyer, who was watching their every move, however, was not the time to confess such things. Instead, Bronson smiled, the one Janine told him could melt even the thickest iceberg, and tried to convey with his eyes how much he wanted to kiss her right now. It must have worked, if her blush was anything to go by.

Turning back to Mr. Filchor, Bronson sat tall. "Okay. We ask for the will. What about in the meantime?"

"In the meantime, we pretend everything is as it should be."

Bronson's eyebrows went up. "So we play along?"

The lawyer nodded. "Yep. Until we can prove otherwise, we have to keep going as we are. Get that house done as quickly as possible and then sell it if you can. That way if we can't find a way to prove the will is illegal, we at least have your actions on our side."

"And if the judge deems them not enough?"

Mr. Filchor sighed. "Then at least we'll know we did our best." He scratched the side of his head. "I can't guarantee that we'll get you out of this trouble, but there are too many odd coincidences to think that this is legitimately legal. Your brother knows the business. He knows exactly what to do to take your inheritance away from you."

"Won't that just make him harder to beat?" Charli asked. Wavy lines marred her forehead and Bronson wanted to smooth them away. He couldn't because of their company, but he would take his time telling her how much he appreciated her later.

"Maybe, but it can also make a man lazy. Canon Ramsay thinks he's got everything under control." Mr. Filchor eyed Bronson. "I doubt he counted on you actually getting help."

"Which just makes me all the more grateful for it," Bronson said. The next few minutes were spent taking down all the information they needed for Mr. Filchor to move ahead as Bronson's legal counsel.

As he and Charli finally left the building, Bronson took a deep breath, feeling like they were breaking out of prison.

"How are you feeling?" Charli asked, her voice cautious.

Bronson looked down and his mouth twisted into a sad smile. "I've been better."

She pinched her lips together and those beautiful brown eyes roamed the street. "Would chocolate help?"

Bronson frowned. "What?"

Charli pointed toward town. "Caro's place isn't very far. Can I treat you to something?"

Bronson stared for a second, then began to chuckle. "Isn't eating chocolate when you're depressed kind of a girl thing?"

Charli laughed with him. "Maybe, but since I'm a girl, I don't really know what else to offer you."

Still laughing, Bronson wrapped his arms around her and pulled her into his chest, kissing the top of her head. "Thank you," he said softly, letting the silky strands of her hair tickle his face.

"What for?" Charli asked. Her cheek was resting against his sternum and her arms wound around his chest.

"For going through that with me."

Charli leaned back enough that he could see her eyes. "Where else would I be?"

Bronson shrugged. "Working? Napping? Reading?"

She laughed. "We're partners, remember? I wanted to be there for you."

Partners... Bronson stiffened at the word, unsure if Charli realized what she'd called him. He wanted her to see him as an equal partner, but despite her apology, he wasn't quite sure where that relationship truly stood.

"Oh!" Charli jumped back. "I totally forgot we were supposed to visit the real estate office. Do you still want to do that?"

Bronson was disappointed to have yet another appointment to keep him from having some time with Charli, but right now, duty called. "Yeah. I think Mr. Filchor's right. We need to move ahead on the assumption that I've got two weeks left." He grimaced. "Is there any chance we can finish in that time?"

Charli took a deep breath, putting her hands on her hips. "Maybe. But it'll require a lot of late nights."

Bronson nodded. "I can pay you more."

Charli shook her head. "No. What you're paying me is already more than enough. I'm just worried about us getting sloppy by being in too big of a hurry, and that won't help your case if this goes before the judge. And I suppose we should get out of the competition. It's too late for that to be of any help to us."

"Let me worry about that," Bronson said, taking her hand and walking to the truck. He stopped when Charli tugged on him.

"The realty office isn't far from Caro's. Why don't we just walk? We can stretch our legs and enjoy the warm weather for a few minutes."

"And get a treat on our way back?" Bronson asked with a smirk.

Charli laughed. "You caught me. I may have a thing for dessert."

Using their joined hands, Bronson pulled her toward him and gave her a quick peck. "That's my treat. When we're done, I'll make sure you get yours."

CHAPTER 20

"Charli!" Nessa, one of the Realtors in their small Seaside Bay office, stood from her desk and came over to greet them as they entered. "What are you doing here?" Nessa leaned closer with a grin. "You finally looking to sell that beautiful house you and Felix live in?"

Charli laughed. "Sorry to disappoint you, but we'll be staying in that place for a long time yet."

Nessa stuck out her bottom lip in a sultry pout. She was a few years older than Charli and had already been through two husbands. From the way her eyes widened when she spotted Bronson, Charli worried the woman was looking for number three.

"Well, well, well, and who are you?" she asked, gliding around Charli with a very noticeable sway in her hips. She held her hand up like a debutante from Regency England.

Bronson's lips twitched as he took her fingers and gave them a slight shake. "Nice to meet you. I'm Bronson."

Nessa sighed and stepped a little closer. "Bronson...such a strong name." Her bright red lips curled into an enticing smile and Charli felt the stirrings of a green-eyed monster begin to build.

Stepping to Bronson's side, she grabbed his hand, raising an eyebrow at Nessa.

"Oooh..." Nessa cooed. "That's how it is, huh?" She winked at Bronson. "We adore Charli around here. Good catch."

Charli went willingly when Bronson pulled her in. "I know," he said smugly.

Charli couldn't help the grin that broke free. She looked up at him and was grateful that his eyes weren't on the flashy real estate agent, but on her. She smiled wider, then turned back to Nessa. "Bronson has a house he wants to put up for sale."

"I didn't even know you were in town, and now you're leaving?" Nessa tsked her tongue. "The town won't be the same without you."

Charli rolled her eyes. "Enough, Nessa."

Nessa laughed and put her hands in the air. "Sorry. I just can't help myself sometimes." She waved them toward her desk. "Come on and let's get this figured out."

"We're almost done fixing up the old Miller house," Charli said as they sat down across from Nessa. "Bronson wants to sell it when we're done."

Nessa nodded and began typing away on her computer. "It's about time someone did something about that dump." She looked to Bronson. "I heard it sold, but I thought it was only a few weeks ago."

"It was," Bronson said.

Nessa looked between the two of them. "So you're flipping it?"

Charli shrugged. "I suppose so." She leaned forward. "But here's the thing, we need to sell it in the next two weeks."

Nessa's jaw dropped. "What?"

The front door opened and Johnathon walked in. "Oh, hey, Charli." He looked beside her and snapped his fingers. "You'll have to excuse me, but I've forgotten your name," Johnathon said, walking up with his hand extended.

Bronson stood and introduced himself.

"That's right. I remember that you're the one who bought the Miller home, but I couldn't quite place the first name." Johnathon put his hands in his pockets. "How's it treating you? Did you manage to get the smell out?"

Charli chuckled as Bronson wrinkled his nose. "We tore out all the carpets," she said. "That made a big difference."

"I'll bet it did," Johnathon said with a smile. "So you've been fixing it up, Charli?"

Charli shook her head. "He hired me. We've been doing it together." She smiled when Bronson's eyes flashed. A short shiver racked her spine at the promise in his eyes. She looked forward to finding out exactly what it meant.

"A team effort, that's great." Johnathon looked to Nessa. "What are you guys doing now?"

"They're looking to sell it," Nessa said sweetly. Her smile was less than sincere. "I guess I get the commission this time, huh?"

Johnathon rolled his eyes. "Leave the office for five minutes and the peasants take over."

Nessa preened. "Finders keepers!"

Charli shook her head. "You two are worse than a brother and sister."

"Whatever," Johnathon quipped. "I've seen you and Felix go at it." He smiled, nodded at the group and headed to his own desk.

"Now..." Nessa straightened her desk. "Let's get back to this timeline you were talking about." She gave Charli a look. "Why two weeks?"

"I can't really tell you all the details, but it's for a good cause."

Nessa's eyes darted back and forth a few times, then she sighed. "I don't know if I can do it in two weeks, but we'll do our darndest." She made a note on a piece of paper. "When can I come look at the house?"

"It's not quite done yet," Charli said warily.

Nessa's head snapped up. "What?"

"We'll be done in the two weeks allotted, but we need a buyer by the time we're done."

"You two know how to keep a gal busy," Nessa said, pursing her lips. Shaking her head, she made some more notes. "Okay. Give me the deets, Char, and I'll search through my clients."

Twenty minutes later, they were outside again.

"That woman is a bulldozer," Bronson said, tugging on his collar. "I thought I left those behind in California."

Charli laughed and pulled on his hand as they began to walk toward Caro's. "There's at least one in every town," she said easily. "Might actually be a few dozen in ours." She grinned over her shoulder. "Catch Bunco night and you'll find them all in one space."

Bronson gave an exaggerated shiver. "Remind me to lock my door at night."

Charli didn't think her smile could get much bigger. Here they were, confronted with a horrible situation, including possible betrayal, and yet just being with Bronson made her feel light and happy. *I'm not sure I'm falling anymore... It's possible I've already fallen.*

The thought didn't scare her as much as she expected it to, but she wasn't even close to being ready to share that out loud. *And now wouldn't be a good time even if I was. There's too much riding on our work at the moment.*

Her eyes automatically drifted to the empty warehouse they were passing. She sought it out every time she walked by and for a split second, Charli considered sharing her dream with Bronson, then decided against it. They had enough going on without her adding her sappy hopes into it.

"What's this?" Bronson tugged her to a stop at the For Sale sign.

"Just an old warehouse that's for sale," Charli said, grateful her voice came out nonchalant.

Bronson stared at it for a moment, then smiled at her. "Our next construction project?"

Charli shook her head. "No way. What we have is enough." Her body relaxed at his joke, grateful that he wasn't really interested, just enjoyed teasing her. "Let's go grab that chocolate and then we gotta get back to work if we're gonna be done in time."

"Yes, ma'am," Bronson said, stepping into place at her side again.

BRONSON SMILED DOWN at Charli, but his mind was back on that building. It looked older and was probably fairly cheap. Ideas began to churn in his head as he considered where his life was and where it was going. He was in love with Charli and when their deal with the house was over, he didn't think he could go back to California.

But he needed a way to keep busy here, a way to contribute to the community...and flipping houses wasn't it. *But what if I brought Fathers and Sons up to Seaside Bay?*

A building like the one for sale would be the perfect place to build a community-type center where they helped those in difficult home situations, or who simply needed a helping hand for a while.

Before he could settle on anything, Charli pulled open the door to Caro's shop and Bronson quickly took the handle from her, late in his gentlemanly duties, but still trying.

"Mmm..." Charli said, her nose in the air. "Smell that chocolate!"

"Sweetie...I got ya covered," Caro said from her place behind the display. She was smiling wide as she waved them in.

Bronson smiled in return. "How goes it, Caro?"

She tilted her head back and forth and put a hand on her hip. "Things are always amazing in here."

Bronson chuckled as Charli rolled her eyes. "Don't feed her ego," Charli said in a loud aside. "Caro can swagger enough to put even Bennett to shame."

Caro gasped and put a hand on her chest. "I do not swagger," she declared in her Southern accent. "I strut, darling. You need to understand the difference."

Bronson shook his head at their antics. It was clear that Charli had a good set of friends and Bronson looked forward to them becoming his as well.

"How goes the reno, handsome?" Caro batted her eyelashes outrageously.

Bronson looked over to see Charli approach the counter. "Pretty good," she said, giving Caro a winning smile. Charli fluffed her hair. "Although I've never had anyone call me handsome before."

This time it was Caro who rolled her eyes. "Give it up, Charli. You knew full well I was talking to your man back there."

Charli leaned onto the counter, meeting Caro nose to nose. "You said it. He's *my* man. And I don't take kindly to flirting."

"Ooohh," Caro said with an exaggerated shiver. "What are you going to do? Build me a fireplace?"

"How about I ruin the one you already have?"

Caro gasped, her hands slapping on the counter. "You wouldn't."

"I would."

"Over a man?"

Charli nodded once, very slowly.

Caro tsked her tongue and looked over Charli's head to Bronson. "Sorry, Bron. You're not worth the loss. I have the most beautiful mantel I just can't live without."

He shrugged. "Don't worry. I've heard that before."

Caro giggled, but Charli moved to get her attention again. "We came in for some cheer-up chocolate."

Caro's humor fled. "What? Why? Did something happen to the house?"

Charli groaned and looked back at Bronson. "Should we tell the story again?"

"You better," Caro said, scowling. "Getting angry like this gives me wrinkles, so spill every bit of it."

Bronson laughed, but tried to cover it with a cough. He wasn't sure whether to pity or admire the guy who would eventually take on Caro. His own spitfire was enough and she wasn't anywhere near as dramatic as Caro.

"I don't know if it's worth your while, but we're kind of in the middle of a battle, so..." Bronson left the sentence hanging, knowing it would put Caro on edge.

"Hold on." Caro grabbed her phone and sent out a text that buzzed in Charli's back pocket. Setting down the phone, she said, "Okay. I've warned the group there's trouble and we need to figure it out."

She leaned with her arms on the counter, her hands folded. "Now..."

They were interrupted when a group of tourists came into the shop and Caro had to stop their conversation to help them.

Watching them pick out their treats gave Bronson just enough time to shoot off a text to the real estate people. He wanted to know more about the building. It would definitely take some time to get his life transferred up to Oregon, but he was feeling more and more sure that it was the right thing to do.

Charli didn't seem to mind that his "job" wasn't a normal one. She'd even implied she thought it was noble and good. There was a lot of red tape involved in building a charity, so the sooner he could get things going, the sooner he could be in Oregon permanently.

Hopefully the situation with the will could be worked out quickly so that Bronson wouldn't have to go back to California to fight everything. But he would if it came down to it. Just because he was leaving California didn't mean he was withdrawing his support of Fathers and Sons. They deserved to keep going and if Bronson could help, that's what he would do. And after settling those affairs, he would come back to Charli. Maybe the two of them could build something else up here.

"Now," Caro snapped after the customers had left. "Spill it," she demanded. "And don't leave out any details."

Charli gave her friend a look, but proceeded to tell almost all of their story. He noted with amusement that she left out anything about their relationship and how it played into the situation.

Caro whistled low and shook her head. "Ya'll are always getting yourselves into scrapes." She grinned and leaned in. "I like it. Keeps life interesting."

"Caro," Charli warned. "This is serious."

Caro slapped her hand on the counter. "You bet it is." She looked up at Bronson. "You'll have to excuse my French, but your brother is a pain in the hiney."

Bronson smiled and frowned at the same time. "You're...excused," he said, not sure whether to laugh or groan. "I might have nightmares about such language, but I'm sure I'll get over it."

Caro waved him off. "Charli can help, I'm sure."

Charli snorted and shook her head. "You're ridiculous."

Bronson watched Caro pace behind the counter, ignoring Charli's derision. "We can't let this guy get away with it. Those sweet little children need that building."

They watched the woman get worked up more and more, her voice growing louder until another group of tourists came in.

After Caro got them settled at the display case, she looked over to Bronson and Charli. "I'll have to think," she said quietly. "Bring Hunky Pants to the flower class next week and we'll get it all figured out."

Bronson laugh-coughed again as he walked with Charli outside. "Hunky Pants?" he asked Charli, who made a face.

"She never could resist a good-looking man," Charli said, her voice sounding distracted. "Do you want to come over for dinner tonight and we'll see if we can't get a new schedule put together?"

Bronson looked at his watch. "That sounds perfect, thanks. I'm gonna run a quick errand before I meet you back at the house, okay?" After leaving a peck on Charli's lips, he took off, back toward the Realtor's office. He wanted to get a few numbers before he went back to the mind-numbing work of renovating. If he was going to try and build something good from the disaster that was his current life, this was hopefully a good starting place.

CHAPTER 21

Charli set the chicken on the table and went back for the salad. She was feeling slightly restless tonight. Edgy even. An unknown urgency about the warehouse was bothering her. She wanted to call and talk to Johnathon and check on the status of the building. She kept having this foreboding feeling that something was going to happen, but she had no idea what it could be.

It's probably due to all the trouble with Bronson's brother and the house. That's enough to make anyone feel weird.

Regardless, she wanted to call the Realtors. She was close to getting paid anyway, so it was probably time to start looking at putting together a proposal and bid. She could just do two birds with one stone this way.

"Smells good," Bronson said, interrupting her thoughts. He rubbed his hands together. "Thanks, Char."

She smiled at him. "You're welcome."

Felix slapped Bronson on the back and Bronson stumbled a little, making Charli wince. She'd been the recipient of Felix's backslaps enough to know that they left a mark. "Have a seat," Felix said with a grin.

Bronson caught Charli's eye and winked at her before following Felix's suggestion.

"You're going to break something," Charli grumbled as she set the last bowl on the table.

Felix scoffed. "If he can't handle a little love tap, he'll never survive with you on his arm."

"I was talking about you," Charli said sweetly, batting her eyelashes at her brother.

Bronson snorted, but otherwise was able to keep his laughter to himself, although Charli didn't try to mask hers, even as Felix scowled at her.

After grace, they began to pass around the food until all their plates were full. "So, Caro sent out a nine-one-one today," Felix began.

Charli paused for a second before going back to eating. "Yep."

"I'm assuming it's about the inheritance situation," Felix said before taking a bite.

Bronson nodded. "Yeah. Caro seems to think we can figure out a plan together."

"What did the lawyer say?"

Bronson made a face and Charli waited for him to speak. She'd taken over at the Realtor's, but this was really his gig and she didn't want to step on his toes. The more she'd worked with him on the house, the more she had come to realize how much she tended to take charge. It wasn't done on purpose or with cruel intent, just a natural part of who she had become over the years. After hurting Bronson so deeply, however, Charli had decided she needed to make a change.

It wasn't that she wanted to let go of her independence or hide what she was capable of, but maybe, just maybe, it was okay to stand back and let others take the lead once in a while. Bronson was also a strong, capable person, and he deserved to show that when the situation called for it.

So she purposefully kept chewing, listening and waiting, letting Bronson run the conversation. As her foot bounced on the floor, however, she realized it was going to be a little more difficult to break her habits than she'd imagined.

"So you're just going to pretend that everything is fine?" Felix asked, his eyes wide in surprise.

Bronson nodded. "That's what Mr. Filchor says." He turned to Charli. "What do you think, Char? We didn't get much of a chance to talk about it earlier."

Charli finished swallowing and put her fork down. "I think he's probably right. We just can't take the chance that no evidence is found to overturn your brother's interpretation of the will. I mean..." She made a face, still feeling bad about speaking of Bronson's family this way. "Even if Canon is doing something illegal, there's no guarantee we can prove it. We might have to take our chances on fulfilling it."

"But if he's working the will, then odds are he won't let you fulfill the terms," Felix pointed out.

Charli's phone buzzed and she glanced down. Johnathon's number from the office was highlighted across her screen and she stiffened. All her feelings of anxiety came flooding back. She grabbed her phone. "I'll be back in a minute," she said, slipping from the table and into a back room. She didn't need anyone hearing her conversation.

"Hello?"

"Hey, Charli!" Johnathon said cheerily.

"Hey, yourself," she said, forcing the trembling in her voice to subside. "What can I do for you?"

"Well, believe it or not, this is a semi-professional call," he said. "I know you said you weren't really interested or anything, but do you remember that warehouse we spoke about a month or so ago?"

Charli nodded, swallowing hard against a blockage in her throat. She'd known. Somehow, she'd known it would be about this.

"Charli?"

"Oh, yeah...sorry." Charli cleared her throat. "I remember."

"Well, the owner was just about to drop the price on it when an offer came in today." Johnathon laughed lightly. "It's a good offer, so I'll be surprised if it doesn't go through, but since you were curious about it, I thought you might like to know."

Charli's eyes filled with tears and she didn't bother to keep them from pouring down her cheeks. "Do...do you know what the buyer wants to do with it?"

"Not really, but that's not information I can share at this time anyways," Johnathon explained. "Nothing is set in stone, mind you. I just thought I'd set your worry to bed since it had all worked out." He laughed again. "Actually, if all goes well, I have a feeling you'll be doing a bit of work there yourself."

"Oh...great," Charli rasped.

"You okay? You sound like you might be coming down with something," Johnathon said, his voice switching quickly to concern instead of triumph.

"Yeah, yeah. I'm fine. Just glad to see it won't be sitting empty, you know?"

"Of course. I knew you'd be interested in hearing. You've always worked hard to keep the appearance of our town up to snuff."

"Thanks, Johnathon," Charli whispered. "I, uh, gotta go though. I'll chat with you later, okay?"

"Sounds good. Tell Felix I said hello."

"Will do." The line went dead, but Charli couldn't move. She stared at the small piece of technology in her hand like it was foreign to her. Her mind spun and her heart physically ached. She knew it had been too good to be true. This shouldn't come as such a shock, after the disaster she'd had trying to secure a loan.

But how could she sit there and let her dreams go up in smoke and do nothing about it? She turned back to the dining room, the men's voices barely carrying to where she stood.

Maybe Bronson can...

Charli shook her head. "No," she told herself. Bronson had enough worries at the moment. He was fighting for those who couldn't fight for themselves. There was no way she was going to burden him with her own problems. Especially since the only person who would get hurt in the situation was herself. She wasn't vain enough to believe that her life trumped anybody else's.

She sniffed as her nose began to run and quickly turned to hightail it to the bathroom. If she didn't want Bronson to know what was going on, she was going to have to fix her blotchy skin and red-rimmed eyes. She cried too little to be able to pass it off as something else.

Turning the water on as cold as it would go, she began to work on cooling off her skin and sent a prayer above that she could make it convincingly through the rest of the dinner.

BRONSON WONDERED WHAT was taking Charli so long, but Felix kept him too busy to go after her. Finally, after what seemed like forever, she came back into the dining room, but something was off.

"Sorry about that," Charli said with a stiff smile. "It was a business call."

Felix grunted and kept going, apparently oblivious to whatever was bothering her.

"Is everything okay?" Bronson asked, watching her face closely.

Charli nodded, but the movement was a little too…eager. "Yep. Fine." She cut into her chicken and went back to eating. "What did I miss?"

"Not much," Felix answered. "We were just going through different ideas, but nothing much has come up." He turned back to Bronson. "I forgot to ask if Johnathon had any clients who might be interested in the house?"

"We spoke to Nessa," Bronson said, his eyes darting back to Charli over and over again. "She said she'd go through her list and let us know."

"Have you asked Canon what he thought of the sale?" Felix pressed.

Bronson shook his head. "No. I haven't brought it up with him. In fact, our conversation yesterday didn't exactly end on good terms."

"It's probably better to keep it to yourself anyway," Charli said. Her eyes didn't meet his, but it was clear she was listening. "If he really is doing something to mess with the will, then telling him your idea will only give him yet another way to sabotage you." She glanced up for a second, her brown eyes dark and sad.

Bronson nodded. "That's probably true." He looked back down at his nearly empty plate. The idea of Canon being so underhanded still bothered him. After all, they were brothers. Yes, Canon was difficult to deal with, but to actually try and steal Bronson's inheritance? It felt like crossing a line and Bronson didn't want to believe it. But he couldn't blame everyone else for accepting it so easily. There was definitely something wrong with the situation. And if Canon was innocent, why was he refusing to let Bronson see the will? Surely there shouldn't be any problem with that?

He took a steadying breath and raised his head only to meet Charli's sympathetic gaze. She gave him a half-smile and Bronson returned it. He wished that they could be alone for a moment. He wanted to hold her and let the world go by for a bit, but it didn't seem like that was going to be his lot in life, at least not for the next little while.

Their playful days of painting each other's faces was over. Now it was time for business, and Bronson feared that would last longer than he wanted it to. Now that he had decided he wanted to stick around in Seaside Bay, he was having a harder time getting himself ready for the work that lay ahead. *It was this lack of motivation that led to this disaster in the first place,* he scolded himself. *Time to step up to the plate. No more taking the easy way out.*

If not for himself, Bronson knew he needed to see this to the finish line for the kids back in California. Too many of them relied on the Fathers and Sons program, something that would have made a huge difference in Bronson's own life when he was younger. The least he could do was make sure others got the chance he didn't. Maybe he could help save them a few years of heartache or bad choices along the way.

"Bronson?" Charli was looking at him expectantly, half out of her chair. Her hand stretched in his direction.

"Oh, sorry," he muttered, handing her his plate. "Thanks."

Charli nodded and took the dishes back to the kitchen.

Bronson got out of his chair and began to help, bringing in the food and helping put it away. "I wash, you dry?" he asked as he closed the fridge.

Charli laughed in that low, husky way of hers. "We have a dishwasher, you know."

Bronson grinned. "I know, but it's kinda fun to work together, don't you think?"

Charli gave him a look, that smile still playing on her face, and nodded. "Sure."

Bronson glanced over his shoulder as he heard noises coming from the other room.

"Felix turned on the game," Charli supplied. She paused. "You sure you don't want to go join him?"

Bronson shook his head. "My mind's too wired up to concentrate on a game. Plus, I'd rather be in here with you."

Charli's cheek turned light pink and she put her focus back on the sink of suds she was creating.

Stepping up behind her, Bronson caged her in. He took in a deep breath, enjoying the sweet smell of her shampoo. "What was your phone call about?" he asked, hoping the question wasn't too personal, but also trying to figure out why she'd been upset when she came back.

When Charli grew stiff against him, he knew she shouldn't have asked. "Just business," she said curtly.

Sighing, Bronson backed off. When she closed up like this, it made him feel like she didn't trust him, and Bronson was grateful he hadn't spilled his feelings to her yet. It would take time for her to be willing to open up, but he could be patient.

Charli turned and gave him a sheepish look. "Sorry. I didn't mean for it to come out quite so sharp."

Bronson nodded. "It's fine. Let's just get this job done."

Charli stepped aside and Bronson started scrubbing, handing her the dishes when he finished. They worked in silence for the first few minutes, until Charli shocked him by sharing a few words. "The call was from Johnathon."

"Oh?" Bronson tried to act nonchalant, but inside he was doing a victory dance. "Does he have a buyer for the house already?"

Charli shook her head, toying with the glass in her hands. "No. He, uh, wanted to let me know that a property I'd been watching had an offer on it."

Bronson froze. *It can't be.* "What property is that? Another house to flip?"

Charli shook her head. "It doesn't matter," she said. "He said it's a good offer and will probably go through."

"What did you want it for?"

Charli pinched her lips together and Bronson was sure she would refuse to share any more. She'd already given him more than he expected, much to his delight and now worry. "I want to open a store."

Dread began to pool in his belly. She hadn't acted interested in the warehouse they'd passed today, but depending on what kind of store, it would be a useful property. "You don't want to do reno work anymore?"

Charli looked up at him with glassy eyes. "I haven't really shared this with anyone except Felix, but my real dream is to restore furniture."

Bronson's eyes widened. "Really?"

"Yeah." Charli put the glass away and came back for the next one. "I love stripping it down and cleaning it up, then restoring it to its former glory." She sighed and leaned her hip against the counter. "I think that's why I was so interested in history. Something about making old furniture beautiful again is like bringing it back to life. A little piece of time sitting right in front of us." She gave him a wistful smile. "Do you know what I mean?"

"Yeah..." Bronson smiled back. "Why don't you go for it? Isn't there another property that would work for you if the one you want is gone?"

Charli shook her head. "I don't have enough money for a down payment yet," she admitted, tucking her hair behind her ear. She glanced sideways at him. "That's why I asked so much from you for the job."

Bronson forced a chuckle, feeling more and more uncomfortable. "At least now I understand why you gave in. Desperation makes us do rough things sometimes, huh?"

Charli nodded and turned, bumping her hip with his. "It's not like it's been all that bad though. I got to know you and that's been a pretty big bonus." She stretched on tiptoe and kissed him.

The kiss was short and sweet, but it didn't mix well with the guilt swirling through his system. Bronson knew without her having to say that the warehouse he'd just offered on was the property she wanted. The woman of his dreams had just lost hers because he'd gotten greedy.

He smiled at her and turned back to the sink. Somehow, he had to fix this...along with the mess from his inheritance. That bright outlook he'd been viewing felt far more ominous than it had before.

CHAPTER 22

Charli took a break from her work to stretch her neck and groan. They'd been working nonstop ever since Canon dropped the new timeline bomb on them. The progress was amazing, but with only one week left, things were going to be cutting it close. *Of course, that doesn't matter if we don't find a buyer.*

Nessa had brought a few people by, but no offers had come from the showings. At this point, Charli was starting to think they needed a miracle.

"Hey!" Bronson poked his head in the room she was working on.

"What's up?" Charli asked, smiling at him.

"Mr. Filchor finally got that copy of the will. He said we should come in this afternoon to see it."

"That's great," Charli said, her feeling of doom lightening ever so slightly. Finally! Something was going their way. "I can't believe how long Canon fought him on it."

Bronson's smile fell. "Yeah...that only confirms to me that you guys were right. Canon has to be up to something to be stalling like this. To have to get a judge's order for him to hand it over is telling."

Charli stood up and walked over, wrapping her arms around him. "I'm sorry," she whispered against his chest. They'd been so busy she hadn't had a chance to really offer her sympathies. Both of them had had their heads in getting the house done. Or at least, partially. Charli had also come up with another idea that she was hesitant to bring up, but had to try.

Bronson's strong arms wrapped around her and he dropped his cheek to her head. "Thanks. I always knew my brother was a jerk. I guess I just didn't expect him to use it against me." He sighed.

Charli tightened her hold. "Uh, Bron?"

"Hm?"

She took in a deep breath. "I...have a question."

Bronson lifted his head and Charli leaned back enough to look him in the eye.

"Do you remember when I told you about that building I wanted?" She frowned a little when something like guilt passed through his face, but it disappeared so quickly, she wasn't sure.

"Yeah."

"Well, I was wondering...would it be possible to get my fee early?" She rushed on before he could say anything else. She was so nervous about asking that she wasn't quite ready to hear his answer, fearing it would all turn out for naught. "I mean...I was thinking that if I had the down payment, I could get that loan from the bank and maybe I won't be too late to outbuy that other guy who put in an offer." She stepped away and wrung her hands. "Maybe I'm too late, but I figured at least I could try. Right?" She stopped babbling when Bronson's face fell. "Oh." She knew the answer without him speaking. "I'm sorry." She waved an embarrassed hand through the air. "I shouldn't have even bothered to ask. It was—"

Bronson grabbed her hand to stop the flailing. "It was a great idea," he said, his voice practically dripping in disappointment. "And at any other time, I'd be more than happy to say yes."

"No...it's okay," Charli assured him, pushing a smile on her face, even as her eyes filled with tears. "I need to just let it go."

Bronson tugged her into his chest and Charli grew stiff before collapsing into his hold.

"Let me explain," he said huskily. "I just recently put most of my savings into a new venture. If I hadn't done that, I would have the money to pay you in advance, but it's gone. I won't have what I owe you until either the house sells or until I get my next trust fund deposit, which is in two weeks."

Charli nodded jerkily and sniffed. "I get it. It's all right. I know our original pay date is in several weeks, so I can wait."

"It's not all right," Bronson said sadly. "You're hurting and I want to make it better." He gave her a little squeeze. "Maybe have a little faith. It might still work out?"

She leaned back. "This isn't your fault, Bron." Wiping at her eyes, she pulled away. "So don't feel bad about it. My timing was all wrong and that's nobody's fault but my own. I should never have set my sights on such a big goal to begin with. I can just start smaller."

Bronson deflated and Charli wondered why he was taking this so hard. He had nothing to do with the situation. She technically wasn't supposed to get the rest of her money for another three weeks. It had been set at the time of the competition, or when they'd originally planned to complete the house, so it was a lot to ask for it this early. She understood that.

"When are we going to meet with Mr. Filchor?" she asked, pushing the conversation away. She had tried to prepare herself for a negative response, but she couldn't help but hope. Now that that hope was crushed, Charli didn't want to think about it anymore. The warehouse was out of her reach and that's all there was to it.

Bronson stared at her, looking like he wanted to speak, then shook his head. "In about an hour." One side of his mouth pulled up into a crooked grin. "I told him we'd be dirty and sweaty, but he said he didn't mind."

"Speak for yourself," Charli quipped, tossing her hair back. She put on her best smile, though nothing about it was genuine. "I don't sweat. I sparkle."

Bronson chuckled as intended, though it sounded tired. He stepped forward to kiss her forehead. "That sounds like something Caro would say."

Charli's smile grew more sincere. "Who do you think taught it to me?"

Bronson laughed again. "I better get back to work. I need to finish scaling that countertop before we go."

Charli nodded. "Yeah. That would be a good idea. It takes a while for that to cure." She looked over at the window. "I've almost got these blinds hung. I only have a couple more upstairs."

Bronson nodded. "Right. See you in a few."

He disappeared out the door and Charli could hear him stomping down the steps. Without an audience, she let herself sink to her haunches and put her face in her hands. Fat tears rolled down her cheeks as she said goodbye to the dream she'd had for so long. She knew it wasn't the end of the world. There were other buildings and she was still going to come out of this project with enough money to start her business, but it hurt. She'd had her eye on the building for a long time and it just felt wrong to have it in someone else's hands.

Its location, size and style were exactly what she'd been looking for, and to have been so close yet still lose made her feel like a failure.

Wiping her face on her shirt, she forced herself to her feet. She was stronger than this. One setback wouldn't break her. It couldn't. Charlize Mendez had climbed her way to the top and she refused to relinquish that power. Losing the building might hurt, but it couldn't stop her ultimate plans.

She sniffed and headed to the bathroom to grab a tissue and clean herself up. Bronson's inheritance was much more important and right now she needed to focus on that. Lots of people would be hurt and lose something precious if they weren't able to win this case. Charli's dream was personal and nobody was out anything if she didn't make it. She had a good job, good friends and a wonderful boyfriend she was in love with.

Once they settled his situation, she could look forward to the future, even if it was a little different than she'd planned.

I HAVE TO TELL HER. Bronson's mind chanted the words over and over again. He still wasn't one-hundred percent positive that the warehouse he'd bought was Charli's, but there were only so many buildings for sale in this small town.

He'd tried calling the Realtor the next morning in order to call off the deal, but Johnathon had informed Bronson that another person had thrown in a second offer. If Bronson didn't buy it, it would still be gone.

He had decided to hold onto the building and wait. He was too busy right now with Canon to do anything anyway, so it wasn't going to hurt anything to let the building sit empty for a while longer. Maybe he would offer it to Charli, if indeed it was the one she wanted, or maybe he'd still go through with his idea of starting a chapter of Fathers and Sons. Really, it didn't matter because nothing was happening right now. It would take weeks for the paperwork to be final and Charli didn't have the money to make a move anyway.

Bronson winced. He felt bad about turning her down. He would have paid her anything he could if his bank account wasn't on the verge of being emptied. Between the house repairs and the down payment for that new property, he simply didn't have what he needed to give her right now. He got paid from his trust in just a couple of weeks, so he could pay her soon, but he still felt like a sleazebag for not being able to offer it now.

He pulled into the parking lot at the lawyer's office and checked his rearview mirror for Charli. She'd been right behind him the whole time. Stepping out of the driver's side, he hurried over to open her door when she stopped.

"Thanks," she said with a smile.

Bronson grit his teeth to keep from spilling everything. It was easy to read the sadness on her face and he hated it. *But you don't even know if it's the right building.* Bronson closed his eyes. *Maybe not, but I haven't asked either.* Taking a deep breath, he opened his mouth to do just that, his resolve to stay silent finally filtering away, but Charli grabbed his hand and tugged him forward.

"Hurry," she said. "I want to know what Mr. Filchor found out." She grinned over her shoulder. "Hopefully it's a point in our favor."

Bronson snapped his lips shut and nodded. *Later. I'll tell her later.* They entered the building and the same rude secretary from before gave them the cold shoulder until Mr. Filchor called for them.

"Mr. Ramsay," the lawyer said, shaking Bronson's hand. "Charli." Mr. Filchor smiled widely. He looked them up and down. "You weren't kidding when you said you'd come straight from work."

Bronson rubbed the back of his neck. "Sorry. With the short timeline and all—"

Mr. Filchor put up his hand. "No need to explain. It really doesn't matter." He waved them toward the chairs. "Have a seat and we'll get going."

Bronson made sure Charli was seated before he followed suit. His legs felt restless, like he wanted to get up and walk, but he forced himself to sit still. A lot was riding on what the will said and Bronson was growing more anxious by the second.

Mr. Filchor grabbed a file folder and opened it across his desk. "Your brother finally gave in to the court order," he said, glancing up at Bronson. "It was harder than it should have been to see this."

Bronson nodded his understanding. "Have you read it?"

Mr. Filchor nodded and leaned back in his seat, taking off his glasses. His thick white mustache twitched. "And I'm unsure what to think."

Bronson frowned and leaned forward. "What do you mean?"

"I mean..." The elderly man straightened in his seat. "That from a surface perspective, everything appears to be in perfect order."

"What?" Charli gasped.

Bronson sat stiff as a board. He couldn't tell if Mr. Filchor was telling him it was over, that the will was legitimate, or if he was hint-ing at something more. He tilted his head, trying to get a better read on the situation. "You think it's real?"

Mr. Filchor shook his head. "No. But at first glance, I have no reason to think otherwise." He tapped the papers with his reading glasses. "The language all makes sense and seems consistent. The signatures are all the correct ones. The only thing that stands out is the fact that he requires more from you than the others."

Bronson shoved a hand through his hair. "Well, what about the timeline? Canon told me one date, but then said a judge told him another. What exactly does it say about that?"

The lawyer put his glasses back on, leaned his head back a little and scanned the pages. "My son Bronson will not be given the same consideration as my other children. As a child who refuses to hold down a steady job, I require more of him in order to gain his inheritance."

Bronson felt his hands begin to shake and he clenched them into fists. It was so different from what his father had said to him while he was alive. *He didn't think that. He just couldn't. He loved Fathers and Sons as much as I do.* Bronson was grateful when Charli reached over and grasped his hand. She was getting more comfortable with touching him first and he enjoyed her initiative.

"He must take a job for a time, working each day and having something to show for his efforts before he will be awarded his third of my estate. With a reasonable amount of growth on his part, judged by a court of law, I bequeath a third of my estate upon him. Remember, Bronson, that volunteering is not a job. The work must be a legitimate career that contributes to society and moves toward a goal."

Mr. Filchor set the papers down, once again taking off his glasses. "He couldn't have been more vague if he tried," he muttered.

Bronson fell back against the chair. "So what exactly does all that mean?" he rasped. An ache in his chest made him want to curl up and shut everything out, but that wouldn't help. He hadn't responded in such a way since he was a young boy and his mother would scold him for every little thing. His father's harsh words were heavier than anything his mother had ever managed. Coming from the man Bronson thought he knew, it felt like a betrayal of trust and ruined the love he thought they'd shared.

"It means that a judge can interpret that any way he wants," Mr. Filchor snapped. He sighed. "Sorry. I'm just frustrated. What this really boils down to is the fact that we have to keep playing the game. Right now you have to follow the guidelines given you by the court. Get the house finished and find a buyer. You have what? A week left?"

Bronson nodded, his mind too chaotic to respond verbally.

"Yes. A week from tomorrow," Charli answered for him.

"All right, get everything you can taken care of and I'll work overtime to try and find the flaw here." Mr. Filchor shook his head. "My eyes are seeing one thing, but my gut is sensing another. It just doesn't seem right that a father would hold out on one child but not the others." His heavily browed eyes pierced Bronson. "As far as I can tell, your brother could stand to learn a few things as well, so why pick on you?" He shook his head again. "It just doesn't make sense, especially since you told me he never brought up the subject while he was alive. Usually with caveats like this, it's the continuance of a fight they were already experiencing, not something completely out of the blue."

"Thank you, Mr. Filchor," Charli said, tugging a numb Bronson to his feet. "Let us know when you have news."

"I will. Thank you for stopping by."

Bronson let her lead him outside, not seeing any of the scenery as she put him in her truck and drove him back to the house.

"Come on, Bron," Charli coaxed. "I know you're hurting, but we can't let Canon win." She thrust a hammer in his hand. "Let's get those floorboards in and show him who's boss, huh?"

Bronson nodded. He wasn't ready to talk, but he could work. Charli was right. The only thing he could do right now was push forward. If Mr. Filchor couldn't find a flaw in time, they had to have the house done. His emotions didn't matter. He didn't need to feel happy to swing a hammer. Canon and their father wouldn't get away with this. One way or the other, Bronson was going to make sure he got what was his.

CHAPTER 23

"Are you sure we need to do this?" Bronson asked, tugging at the collar of his T-shirt.

Charli rolled her eyes. "Don't be such a baby," she teased, pulling him toward the flower shop. "It's just a bunch of women."

"That's exactly why I'm worried," he shot back.

Charli paused and looked back at him. "We've only got a few days left, Bron," she said softly. "These are my friends. They want to help."

"A bunch of ladies arranging flowers are going to help us?" Bronson gave her a skeptical look.

Charli snorted. "The class is already over. We're coming just in time to talk to the gang."

"Gang... I didn't realize this was so serious." Though his words were spoken in jest, the two of them immediately seemed to lose the humor of the situation.

Where they stood was no laughing matter. Mr. Filchor was still working hard, but hadn't found the evidence he needed yet, no buyers had made an offer on the house, and they were down to a little less than a week to even finish, let alone have anything else go their way. Charli had missed the class tonight so she could continue to help Bronson, but she wasn't sure it was going to be enough.

After their visit to the candy shop last week, Caro had texted everyone that they would be meeting tonight when the rest of the class went home, to see what could be done and Charli was glad to take her up on the offer. The truth was, they were in over their heads. Charli had high hopes that her friends would have some ideas that could help her and Bronson.

The more Charli threw herself into the fray with Bronson, the less she found herself pining over the building she lost. She could survive, she could move on and find another way. But for Bronson? There was no other way. Fathers and Sons wouldn't make it without his inheritance and Canon didn't deserve to win. It was the principle of the matter.

Not to mention that as soon as Charli recognized that she had fallen in love with Bronson, she found herself working harder for that reason alone. He meant too much to her to allow him to fail.

"Sorry. That was in poor taste," Bronson muttered, pushing a hand through his hair. "If you think your friends can help us, then I'm grateful for the chance to speak to them."

Charli nodded. "They're amazing. Let's give them a chance." Hand in hand, she and Bronson went inside. The bell ringing above the glass door announced their presence.

"Charli," Rose said, walking over with open arms. "We're so glad you two could take enough time off to come."

"We're glad you guys are all willing to hear us out," Charli said back, hugging her friend. Rose always smelled like flowers and Charli loved it. It fit the feminine, sophisticated woman to a tee.

"Always," Rose promised, stepping back and giving Bronson a smile. "What good are friends if we don't support one another?"

Bronson nodded and smiled back. "I believe that's why Charli calls you all amazing."

Charli grinned and shrugged when Rose looked at her. "Duh."

Rose laughed softly. "Well, come on in. Most of the class has gone by this point, and I'll make an announcement to the few that are left." She turned, then spoke over her shoulder. "I made an extra arrangement for you from tonight's class. There are gladiolas, which mean strength or warrior. Plus peonies for luck. And I threw in a couple of irises for hope." She smiled back at them before turning to face the front once more.

Bronson leaned down to Charli's ear. "She takes this flower thing seriously."

"You have no idea," Charli whispered back. "If any of us are struggling in any way, you'll find a vase of flowers at our house. Rose believes they can work miracles."

Charli led Bronson to the back where the scent of flowers was nearly overwhelming. The room was large with tables placed around and flower stems littering the floor. A petite, redheaded girl was picking up the green pieces, carefully putting them in a sack as she worked her way around the room. "Lilly!" Charli called, excited to see the child she hadn't spoken to in forever.

Rose sighed. "Her sitter couldn't come tonight, which means Lilly will get to bed late." She scrunched her nose. "She'll be a bear in the morning."

Charli laughed. "No way. Being cranky isn't in sweet Lilly's vocab."

"Says the woman who doesn't live with her," Rose countered.

Still smiling, Charli let go of Bronson and walked over to say hi to the beautiful child. Tapping Lilly on the shoulder, Charli signed *Hi!*

Lilly's face lit up. *Hi, Charli!*

What are you doing? Charli pointed to the sack Lilly was holding.

Counting.

"Oh," Charli said, leaving her mouth in an open O, and nodding. *How high can you go?* Charli looked over to Rose, making sure she was doing the right movements.

Rose nodded. "Yep. That was right."

Looking back, Charli's eyes widened when she saw Lilly signing quickly and with childish enthusiasm.

Charli held up her hands. "Whoa, little one, you lost me."

Before Rose could step in to translate, a deep voice penetrated the room. "She says she's learning to go all the way to one hundred."

Charli straightened and nodded to Ken, who had just entered the room. "Thanks, Ken."

He gave her a small chin tilt, but his eyes were fixed on Rose, who was standing stiffly.

Lilly surprised everyone by letting out a weird squeaking noise and dropping her back. She raced by Charli and her mother, heading straight for Ken's open arms.

Ken swung the little girl high, her peculiar giggles making everyone smile. "Heya, sweetie," Ken said softly. He cradled Lilly in one arm and used his other to sign with her.

Lilly was obviously delighted as she and Ken began to converse back and forth. The sight made Charli's heart ache with a sad sort of happiness. *Lilly could use someone like Ken in her life.* Charli's eyes drifted to Rose, who looked resigned, but made no move to join them.

Ken and Rose had been dancing around each other for a long time and no one, other than themselves, knew why. Charli was pretty sure that Ken would pursue a relationship without a moment's pause, but Rose seemed to be holding things back.

No one in the group brought it up, however, assuming the two adults would eventually work out their differences, but it had been going on for so long that Charli wasn't sure they would ever be at peace.

When the rest of the men came through the door, Rose headed over to Ken. "Time for bed," she said softly, signing as she went. She tried to grab Lilly, but the child held tightly to Ken's neck. Rose gave Ken a *help me* look.

Ken's smile held more than a touch of mischief to it. "I don't mind holding her while we all talk. You wouldn't want her up there all by herself, would you?"

Rose's eyes widened and she shrunk back, looking frightened for a split second before she got ahold of herself.

"Rose?" Ken stepped forward, his open hand reaching for her, but she dodged him.

"That's fine," Rose said over her shoulder. "But it wouldn't be a bad thing if she took a little nap during the meeting."

Charli stood watching the whole scene play out and was thoroughly confused. Bronson came up behind her.

"What was that all about?"

Charli shook her head. "I have no idea."

BRONSON SHOOK HIS HEAD and turned away from the display. It was clear something was going on between them, but he wasn't privy to the story and didn't really feel like getting into it right now. His head was too full of his own stuff to worry about someone else's at the moment.

"Come on," Charli whispered, pulling him to a set of chairs. They settled down and soon the whole room followed suit.

"Did we really have to meet like this?" Bennett asked, flipping his hair out of his face. "I mean...I'm not really into flowers..." He ducked when Felix smacked the back of his head. "One of these days I'm gonna start wearing a helmet," Bennett grumbled, rubbing the offended area.

"My sister needs help and you can't handle a little floral arranging?" Felix asked, folding his arms over his chest.

Bennett grinned. "In all fairness, I don't think Charli's that into flowers either. She's more manly than I am!"

Bronson felt some anger flare up inside of him, but when Charli laughed, he relaxed again.

"At least you're willing to admit you're a wimp," Charli called out. "Saves me the trouble from having to challenge you to an arm wrestling competition and humiliate you in front of our friends."

Bronson's lips tugged into a grin. He wrapped an arm around her shoulders and brought her head toward him. "Just for the record, I think you're very feminine," he whispered for her ears only.

Charli glanced up, her brown eyes looking like pools of chocolate. "Eh, I'm not, but I'm glad you think so."

"You are," Bronson insisted. "Being feminine doesn't mean you have to wear dresses and tons of makeup. There are other things that make you a lady, and I'm grateful for it." He let his fingers play with her hair and suddenly noticed with embarrassment that the room had gone silent. He tugged on his too-tight collar. "Uh, hey, everyone. Ready to get started?"

A sniffle caught everyone's attention and the woman from the smoothie shop wiped at her eyes.

"Mel," Bennett groaned, throwing his head back.

"Shut up," she muttered. "You're just jealous that you don't have words that sweet. It's no wonder you're single."

Jensen was chuckling as he tucked Mel into his side and whispered something in her ear, which caused the blonde to turn bright red.

"On that note," Caro drawled, "I think we better get started. Those of us without our own boy toys are starting to feel decidedly uncomfortable."

"Hear, hear!" Brooklyn shouted, raising a fist in the air.

Rose stood and cleared her throat. "Thank you, everyone, for coming." She turned to Caro. "You called this meeting. Perhaps you'd like to start it?"

Caro nodded regally and stood up. "Last week, Bronson and Charli came into the shop and I found out they're in a bit of trouble."

She clapped her hands together. "So I figured we'd pull this do-gooder group together again and see what we can help with."

"Do-gooder group?" Bennett made a face. "Is that a word?"

"Might be above your pay grade," Felix quipped.

Bennett put his finger in the air to counter the joke, but Caro stopped him. "Hush now!" she scolded. She turned to Bronson and Charli. "Why don't you catch us all up?"

Charli looked up at Bronson and he stared down at her. "You want to speak?" she asked.

"Not particularly," Bronson said with a sigh. "But I guess it's mostly my story to tell, huh?"

She nodded. "Go get 'em, tiger."

Bronson snorted and straightened in his seat. "I guess if you want to really understand everything, I have to tell you about my family. My mother is...or was, I guess...Clarisse Rhodes."

"I knew it!" Brooklyn shouted. "I knew you looked familiar."

Charli chuckled. "I figured you'd catch that eventually," she said.

Bronson smiled softly, then waited for Brooklyn to relax before continuing. He told them everything. All about his trust, his time with Janine, the deaths that had riddled his past and what he was facing now. "Felix and Caro are aware of all this, as well as Mr. Filchor, who's trying to find evidence of inheritance fraud." Bronson shrugged. "But unless we find it, we have to just keep going on the assumption that I only have a few days left to finish and sell this house."

"Let me get this straight," Ken said. He was leaning back in his seat, Lilly sound asleep on his shoulder.

Even Bronson noticed how at ease the man looked with the girl in his arms and he wondered yet again what was going on between the police captain and the flower lady.

"You think your brother is trying to cheat you out of your inheritance, but you have no evidence for the claim, so you're just playing the game as he sees fit to give it to you?"

"That's about it, yep," Charli inserted.

"And you need the money to save your charity down in California?" Brooklyn clarified.

Bronson nodded. "Though it's not *my* charity. I didn't start it or anything, I just work for them."

"But you're...like famous and rich," Brooklyn said. "Why can't you help out with the building without your inheritance?" She tilted her head like a curious bird. "I'm not meaning to sound crass about your money, but you apparently aren't hurting for it." She pointed to his pants. "I know that brand and no one else here can afford it." She spun her fingers around the circle.

Bronson felt his neck heat and he rubbed at it uncomfortably. "I'm not gonna lie and say I don't have money, but this place in California is above what I have available. My trust doles out a certain amount each month. I'd have to sell off most of my investments in order to pay for that building. Even paying a down payment would be difficult. The place isn't actually for sale. There's no way the owner is going to let me have it easy." He shrugged. "The only way to quickly get the money I need is to use the inheritance."

Brooklyn nodded. "Fair enough." She pursed her lips and folded her arms over her chest. "I mean, it's your money anyways, or it should be, so I suppose you should get it."

"Any thoughts?" Charli asked, sitting up straight. She seemed eager, but nothing was forthcoming. The room was quiet for several heartbeats. "Really?" Charli asked, deflating in her chair. "No one has any ideas?"

"I don't think we can do much about the fraud side," Rose said warily. "Other than pray for Mr. Filchor." Her cornflower blue eyes landed on Bronson's. "But we might be able to help you meet your deadline."

"What did the will say in regards to you having help?" Jensen asked.

Bronson shrugged. "It didn't. Just that I had to have something to show for my work at the end. And it had to be a *real* job." Those words still irked him. Helping people was a real job. Why couldn't his family understand that?

"Then what if a group of volunteers helped you finish the house? If you're not trying to fulfill the requirements for the Homeowner's competition anymore, surely it's okay to have some help?" Rose pressed, leaning forward in her seat. "I'm not a lawyer, but I know how to use a paint brush."

"Yeah!" Caro shouted, almost jumping from her seat. "It shouldn't be that hard. We can all pitch in our spare time and help you finish up. You know...hedge your bets a little."

Bronson looked down at Charli, who was smiling softly. She glanced up at him, then back at the group.

"But I'm only doing it if Charli promises not to bite my head off," Bennett called out.

Charli laughed along with everyone else. She held up her hands. "Your help would be extremely appreciated and I'll do my best not to be bossy." Her eyes met Bronson's. "I've had a bit of practice the last few weeks."

Bronson smiled back. This might not solve all their problems, but at least it helped ease the load. Now they just needed to hope they could find a buyer to finish it all off.

CHAPTER 24

"No, no, no!" Charli moaned, rushing over to stop Caro before she could drip paint on the brand new wood floor. "You have to wipe the brush first," Charli explained as calmly as she possibly could. "Then touch up the spot."

"If I wipe the paint off the brush, how will I have any left to paint with?" Caro snapped.

Charli sighed and pinched the bridge of her nose. "Never mind," she muttered, forcing herself to walk away. She'd promised Bennett that she would behave, but man...it was killing her.

A snicker caught her attention and Charli looked over to see Felix standing in the doorway. His hair was windswept and his pants damp, indicating he had recently finished his time on the boat today. "Troubles, sis?"

"Nope." Charli put her nose in the air. "Everything is going swimmingly!"

"CHARLI!"

She stuck her tongue out at Felix when he laughed harder and rushed to see what the latest emergency was. It felt like today had been one problem after another. Brooklyn kept wanting to add color to the house and Caro complained that it needed more charm. Bennett seemed to think he had to prove himself, so he kept trying to do two-man jobs all alone.

Charli had no idea how good she'd had it with Bronson. He had followed directions, but also been able to do things himself when the need arose. It was obvious that no matter how much she loved her friends, they had no idea what they were doing.

"What?" Charli asked breathlessly as she rushed through the doorway of one of the upstairs bedrooms. Her eyes widened when she saw the shattered window. "What..." She bit off her question. She wasn't sure she could keep from saying something rude at the moment. A broken window was one of the last things she needed right now.

Cooper and Genni were both staring at the window. Genni shook her head and turned to Charli. "Something hit it," she said, her voice softer than usual.

Charli jerked back. "Hit it? What do you mean? Like a kid playing baseball?" She felt a warm presence at her back and had to stiffen her knees to keep from leaning back into Bronson's strength.

"What?" Bronson asked, his voice incredulous. "Where would a baseball have come from?"

Charli shook her head, but walked carefully over to the broken glass. "This window backs up into the woods..." Her voice trailed off as she spotted a dark object amid the glass. "Bronson," she rasped. Gingerly, Charli lifted a rock from the carpet and held it up.

Bronson groaned. "Not again."

"What do you mean, again?" Cooper demanded. His curls were pulled back into a low ponytail today, but his sleeveless shirt showed off his tattoos and large biceps. Although Charli knew he was a big teddy bear, his appearance could be intimidating when he wanted it to be, and right now Charli was a little frightened.

Bronson pushed a hand through his hair. "We've had a few...accidents around the house," he started. "But when the electric wire was cut, we began to think it wasn't an accident."

Cooper cursed under his breath and Genni stepped forward to try and calm him down. "Do you think your brother is behind this?" Cooper asked, his voice slightly calmer than before.

Bronson shrugged. His face had gone blank and Charli knew he was struggling internally again. Who wouldn't at the thought of their own family trying to sabotage them? "I have no way of knowing at this point."

Cooper scowled, but Genni grabbed his hand.

"Was anyone hurt?" Charli asked, looking around for scratches or the like.

Genni shook her head. "No. We were working over here when the window broke."

Charli nodded. "Right." She sighed. "Let me grab some cardboard and we'll get it taped up, then I need to head into town and see if they have any this size in stock. If not, I'll have to order one."

"How long will that take?" Genni asked, her brows slightly furrowed.

Charli shrugged. "Depends." Her eyes drifted to the window. "This isn't an unusual size, so I'm hoping we'll get lucky. Maybe if we don't have anything, I'll be able to find one in the next town over."

She headed downstairs, her mind whirling with this new development. Someone, whether it was Canon or not, was dead set on making sure they didn't meet this new deadline. She grabbed her phone as she went outside. "Ken?"

"What's up, Char?" Ken was still on duty and had told everyone he'd be by later that night.

"I think we're in trouble."

Ken's chuckle floated across the line. "I thought we already were."

"No. There's something else."

"Tell me." His voice grew more serious.

Charli blew out a breath and pushed her hair out of her face. "Someone's trying to sabotage our work. I wasn't sure before, but now I am."

"Explain." The word was short and clipped. Ken was in full police mode now.

Charli told him everything that had happened, finishing with the latest disaster.

"Why didn't you bring this up before?" he asked.

"Because we weren't sure. The wire was the only thing we had and I wasn't completely positive it had been cut."

"Okay. I'll send out a few men to do rounds out that way. And when I come out in a couple hours, I'll look around and see what I can find."

"Thanks, Ken," Charli said softly. Charli had never hesitated to help when a need arose from her friends, but she'd have never guessed that she would be the one needing help. It was difficult to accept it, but she simply couldn't handle it all herself any more. Her gratitude for her friends had never been so strong.

"No problem. It's what I'm here for," he answered quickly. "Be careful and let me know if you see anything else suspicious."

"Will do." Charli hung up and then grabbed some cardboard and one of her utility knives. Fortifying herself, she headed back inside and upstairs. She wouldn't be able to handle it if someone got hurt because of her. They needed to get this project done and get all the ugliness of the situation behind them.

Then she and Bronson could sit down and really figure out where they were going. She knew she loved him, but he'd never mentioned anything of the kind to her, which made Charli a little bit uneasy. Bronson had been open with his interest and feelings from the beginning, but now he was all business. She missed his "touchy-feely" behavior and hoped he wasn't changing his mind about her.

She just had to hope and pray that his feelings were strong enough for him to be willing to stick around for a while after the whole inheritance issue was taken care of.

THE NUMBNESS WAS BACK. Slowly, Bronson picked up the pieces of glass that were scattered across the carpet. He knew they would vacuum up the smallest pieces, but he wanted to get the largest ones out of the way.

"Hey."

Bronson turned to the quiet voice.

Genni gave him a shy smile. "Are you okay?"

Bronson nodded.

She looked hesitant, then put a hand on his forearm. "I know what it's like to feel like a family member betrayed you," she said, her voice still soft. "Hang in there and we'll get this all figured out, okay?"

Bronson nodded again and he felt his back muscles relax ever so slightly. "Thanks," he said hoarsely.

She nodded and began to help him with the glass.

"Don't cut yourself," Cooper said gruffly as he began to help.

Genni snorted, but grinned and between the three of them, they had things mostly in hand by the time Charli came trudging up the stairs with a large piece of cardboard.

"I called Ken," she stated without preamble.

Bronson nodded. "It's for the best. What does he think he can do?"

"He's going to send men on extra patrols in the area and when he gets here in the next while, he said he'll look around for evidence."

Bronson sighed. "Sounds good." He looked around. "Let me grab something for the glass and bring the vacuum up."

Charli let the cardboard edge fall to her feet. "We might need to dump the canister. It was pretty full last time I checked."

"On it." Genni jumped in and hurried out the door. One of her hands was still full of glass and Bronson again looked around for a garbage can.

"There's a bucket in the hall," Charli supplied, tilting her head toward the entrance to the room.

Bronson grabbed it and they all dumped their glass inside. When Genni came back, she did the same.

"Go ahead and dump the vacuum as well," Bronson said. "I'll take it outside." He walked down the steps with the bucket dangling from his fingers, grateful for the chance to think. Things seemed like they were getting out of hand. He had four days left before the deadline. They still needed to finish staining the hardwood floors, plus he had no buyer. And now whoever was trying to stop him was starting to do things far more dangerous than clipping a wire.

Might as well just give up.

Bronson scowled at the words. They were ones he'd listened to many times in his life. Especially when it came to Canon. It never seemed worth risking Canon's anger just to get his own way. Bronson had set his mind this time that he wouldn't let Canon, or whoever was responsible, win, but how could he risk letting Charli's friends get hurt?

How can you risk those kids having nowhere to go?

He growled and practically threw the bucket at the garbage can, only to curse...loudly.

"What did you do?"

Bronson hung his head and turned to see Charli watching him. The sting against his finger let him know in his hurry to dump everything, he'd let the glass fall against him, leaving a nice, long cut. "Nothing."

"It's not nothing." Charli stepped forward, her hands on her hips. "I can see the blood dripping from your knuckle."

Bronson brought his hand up and looked at it. She was right. It was bleeding quite well. He shrugged. "It'll be fine."

Charli stepped closer. "Don't be a baby. Let me take care of it."

"I'm not a baby!" he shouted, causing Charli to jerk and step backwards. Bronson groaned. "I'm sorry," he said. "I didn't mean to snap." His eyes were on the ground and he couldn't find the energy to lift them. He was embarrassed about his behavior, but he was also just plain worn out. His mental and emotional side had been through the wringer lately and Bronson was starting to crumble under the pressure.

"I've got Band-Aids in the truck." Charli's voice was uncertain and that only cut Bronson even more.

He followed her to the truck, each step feeling heavier than the last. Charli started digging around in the cab. "Why don't you go sit on the tailgate?"

Bronson kept his mouth shut and just followed orders. He hefted himself up, careful to keep from touching anything with his bloody hand.

When Charli came to the back, she didn't speak, just silently started to clean him up. She gave him a quick flash of those beautiful brown eyes when she put the antiseptic over the wound, but otherwise stayed quiet.

"I'm sorry." Bronson swallowed hard, trying to ease the thickness in his throat.

"It's all right," Charli said, though she still didn't look at him.

"No." Bronson sighed. "It's not alright. I shouldn't have snapped at you." He took his hand back now that she was done and studied her handiwork. "You've been nothing but a solid rock during this whole thing and here I'm falling apart like a fragile piece of pottery."

Charli's lips twitched and she lifted her face to him. "Actually, I've been pretty impressed with how well you've handled it all."

His eyebrows shot up. "Really? Because I feel like an idiot and a sucker. How did I not see that Canon was behind all this? And how could I have fallen for it? Not to mention, who has a family that is so intent on getting money that they throw their siblings under the bus?"

Charli stepped forward and cupped his cheek.

The move was so gentle and so unlike Charli that Bronson froze for a split second before leaning into the touch.

"I think the fact that you *aren't* like that is what we should be looking at." She searched his face. "People squabble over money all the time, and the fact that you want to love and trust your family is good, not bad. If Canon is behind all this, then we'll get it figured out. In the meantime, we'll just keep doing what we're doing. Either way, Canon won't win. We're going to beat him at his own game because you're better than him. Because you care about others." She gave him a sad smile. "Because you have people who care about you."

Bronson looked at her intently. "Are you one of those people, Charlize Mendez?" he asked softly.

Her cheeks flushed and she pulled away, but Bronson grabbed her hand.

"Because I'm one of the people who cares about you," he said softly.

Charli's eyes jumped to his.

"I think I'm in love with you, Charli," he said, leaning forward a little. His inner voice began to whoop and holler when she matched his movements.

"Good thing," she said, her voice barely audible. "Because I hate to think of the work it will take to train a new partner when this is all over."

Grinning, Bronson closed the last bit of distance between them. She hadn't said she loved him back, but she obviously wasn't opposed to his declaration. Knowing she was slow to act on her feelings, he would count that as a win. And right now...he desperately needed a win.

CHAPTER 25

"Charli?" Charli turned away from where she was caulking the trim. Everyone was scrambling around doing last minute touch-ups, desperately trying to be finished before the deadline that evening. "Yeah?"

Caro stood in the doorway of the bathroom, looking awkward, which was unlike her. "I think you need to see this."

What now? Holding back a groan and a sigh, Charli climbed to her feet. She swayed slightly, grabbing onto the counter for support. They were cutting it too close for comfort on this job and Charli had barely slept for several days. It was too important to her to help Bronson win his inheritance.

She followed Caro downstairs and found almost everyone standing just outside the front door, examining the house. Frowning, she walked out and turned around. "What?" Charli's knees buckled and she grabbed onto the nearest body.

"I've gotcha," Bennett said solemnly. "Bron?" he called over her head.

Charli felt herself being transferred from one set of arms to the other and she let Bronson's strength hold her up while her eyes travelled around the siding of their beautiful Queen Anne home. Spray paint had been smeared haphazardly over the new paint job. Blobs, streaks, drips and even artistic curlicues could be seen across the entire front of the home.

Stumbling slightly, Charli broke free of Bronson's hold and made her way around the side of the house. The red paint continued for a few more feet before stopping.

"It's not on the back of the house," Bronson said stoically. "I think there were too many of us back there working."

"The tile cutter," Charli whispered. "You were working with the tile cutter."

Bronson grunted his agreement. "I'm not sure how they got around front without being seen, but with so many of us doing projects out the kitchen door, it left it unguarded."

Her vision began to blur and Charli turned to Bronson. "Where's the paint?" she asked.

Bronson looked at Charli with a sad sort of acceptance in his eyes. "Don't, Charli. It's time to let it go. We'll continue to look into the will being a fraud, but we can't keep fighting the timeline."

Charli pushed past him, searching for the buckets that matched the exterior paint.

"Let it go, Charli!" he called after her.

"No," she shouted back, her speed picking up as she grew frantic to find the paint. She tripped over tools in the waning light, her heartbeat growing faster and faster the longer the search went on.

Rough hands grabbed her shoulders and spun her around. "It's time," Bronson growled in a low tone. "We still have other options, but we can't keep this up." He waved a hand toward their friends standing on the porch. "Look at them, Char. They're exhausted." He gave her a little shake. "You're exhausted! I've seen you swaying on your feet. You haven't eaten a decent meal or slept well in days." His face broke. "We have to admit defeat on this one."

"I can't," Charli whispered. She was so angry. So exhausted. So...everything. Her eyes flitted to her volunteers. They'd all come to help. It was supposed to be the magic she and Bronson needed to make sure they made the deadline. But instead, it hadn't been enough. Bronson was right. Everyone was tired and near the end. She couldn't keep asking anything more of them. "Send them home," she choked out. She tried to spin out of his hold, but she didn't have the strength. It felt like the last five miles of an Ironman. The point where her body was done and the only thing to keep anyone going was a mental stamina that few ever achieved. She'd made it to the end more than once; she just couldn't find it within herself to give up. Not until the deadline had come and gone.

"Charli." This time Bronson's voice was soft, cajoling. With a long sigh, he pulled her into his chest. "I love you," he said into her hair. "Every stubborn inch."

The tender touch and words were almost Charli's undoing. She felt her body lean into the embrace, ready to let go of all the tension and worry she'd been holding onto these last few weeks, but her mind wouldn't quite let her. *There's still time*, it whispered. *Don't give up. Show Bronson you love him.*

Charli was all too aware that she hadn't told Bronson of her own feelings even when they'd spoken a few nights ago as she taped up his finger. The words had been there, so close to the edge of her tongue, but they were stuck. She knew she loved him, but for some reason, saying it out loud felt so...permanent. Like she could never change her mind or be the same after spilling those three tiny words.

"I'll help the kids another way," Bronson continued, ignorant of her internal turmoil. "It's not worth this. It's not worth you getting hurt or sick over."

Mustering every bit of strength she had left, Charli pushed herself off his chest. She looked up into those dark blue eyes, seeing the truth of what he was saying. He really believed they'd lost. Slowly, Charli shook her head. "I can't," she said, stepping back even farther. "I won't." *It's the only way to prove myself to you.*

If the words couldn't pass through her lips, then she'd show him with her hands. This wasn't as much about winning or losing as it was about proving to Bronson that she was here for him no matter what was going on.

She spun and searched for that bucket again, ignoring the long sigh behind her.

"Here."

Charli jerked her head up to see Felix pointing to a five-gallon paint bucket.

His eyes were frustrated, even as he gave her a small smile. "This is the one you want."

Charli watched her brother for a moment before nodding. "You don't have to stay," she told him, then turned to the house. "You can all go home," she said. "The deadline's nearly here and I'm so grateful for all your help. You've been invaluable these last few days. Go home, shower, and sleep. You all need it."

A loud scoff came from the back of the crowd and everyone turned to see Caro with her hands on her hips. "Well, thank you, Ms. High and Mighty Charlize Mendez," she said in a snarky tone. Tossing her ponytail over her shoulder, she stuck her nose in the air. "But I have a job to do." With a strut worthy of a Paris catwalk, the petite Southern belle headed back into the house, leading the pack, who all followed in her footsteps. One by one, they disappeared back to what they'd been doing before the hubbub.

Bronson chuckled from behind her and Charli glanced over her shoulder. He shrugged when she eyed him. "You gotta give the lady credit. She handles herself."

Charli huffed a quiet laugh and turned back to the door. Her chest warmed as she realized she didn't give her friends enough credit. She knew they'd have good ideas to help her with the house, but now, at the end of the day, when it all counted the most, she'd expected them to go home. To say they'd done their good deed for the week and leave her holding the bag.

Instead, they stood firm. Sticking around to see the finish line, no matter which side Charli and Bronson ended up on.

Charli's vision once again began to swim. These tears had nothing to do with exhaustion and anger and everything to do with knowing she was loved in a way she'd never realized.

"Char?"

She blinked and looked over to Felix, who was holding out a paint brush. Smiling at him, she walked over and took it. "Thank you," she whispered, meeting his dark eyes, so like her own. She hoped he could hear everything those words meant.

Felix smirked. "Anytime."

Together, they hauled the paint up to the house and began to pry open the top. They still had a long night ahead.

BRONSON WATCHED CHARLI walk away, his heart breaking a little with each step. She was so beautiful in her righteous anger. She had no stake in this house, and he would pay her her due as soon as possible, but otherwise, the only reason she could possibly be doing this was for him.

She hadn't spoken the words of love that he'd shared, but right now...Bronson didn't need them. The fact that she was pushing herself past her capacity just to see that he succeeded was more than enough to keep him going.

His eyes drifted to the house and his shoulders fell. How could Canon do it? Or who did Canon have doing it, was the better question. Bronson didn't believe for a moment that Canon had left California to come and do all the dirty work himself. He had to be using an accomplice...but who?

Bronson scratched the back of his head. Slowly, he began to wander around the house. Maybe he could find something that would tell him something. There had been no sign of the person who'd thrown a rock through their window a few days ago, but one of these days, the culprit was going to make a mistake.

They have to.

He touched the paint, noting that it was mostly dry, but just a bit tacky still. Which meant the spray job couldn't have been that long ago. Looking down at the ground, Bronson walked the line of the house. The sparse grass and uneven ground held no footprints or evidence that someone had been there recently.

Bronson sighed and rubbed at his eyes. They were gritty and tired from the long hours they'd been pulling this week. Laughter from inside caught his ear and a ghost of a smile passed his lips. He knew full well that the people inside were here for Charli, but he would be forever grateful for their support. It was no wonder that Charli was as strong as she was with that kind of group behind her.

He scratched at his beard and wondered what it would have been like to have that kind of foundation growing up. His own family was trying to sabotage him, but Charli's friends, only one being a blood relation, were setting aside their own lives in order to help her. The contrast was startling, and created more than a little bit of jealousy within him.

Shoving the useless emotion away, he put his eyes back on the ground. "There has to be something," he muttered. Walking around the corner he paused. A large glob of paint had fallen to the ground and there was a shoe print in it.

Bronson crouched, his senses coming back to life at the possibility of making headway into this mystery. He touched the edge of the paint, but it was dry.

"Probably not Charli, then," Bronson mused. His eyes devoured the ground nearby and was finally rewarded with what he sought. Pulling out his phone, he turned on the flashlight app to get a closer look, since the sun was on its way down the horizon, making it more difficult to make out.

"Find something?"

Felix's voice had Bronson nearly snapping his neck to look over his shoulder. "Maybe," he hedged. He went back to the spot of red. "I think there's a possibility that the painter left a trail." He dropped to his hands and knees and began to slowly wave the light over the ground. "Gotcha," he whispered when he discovered yet another red splotch. The paint left on the grass was small but visible when he knew what he was looking for.

"Looks like they got paint on the bottom of their shoe," Felix mused, bending down and studying it with Bronson. His dark head came up, looking toward the edge of the property. "They probably headed for the trees."

Bronson nodded and stood up, but stayed hunched over. "I'm going to follow these and see what I find."

Felix was also standing and he nodded. "I'll call Ken."

"Thanks," Bronson murmured. Slowly, praying he didn't miss anything, he followed the tiny marks of red until he reached the edge of the forest backing the property. The red had grown smaller and smaller, the spot on the shoe obviously having dried by the time the intruder ran off.

With the footsteps gone, Bronson began to search in earnest through the bushes and trees. As he pushed past a bundle of twigs, a rattling noise caught his attention. He paused and waited, but the noise didn't repeat itself. Slowly, he stepped a little further and the noise went off again.

Bronson dropped the flashlight to look directly at his feet and he began pressing the ground with his toe, finally realizing the noise came from a pile of pine needles and broken branches. He crouched down and sifted through the debris. "Bingo." A single can of used red paint was lying mixed into the debris.

"BRONSON?"

He stood up and looked back toward the house. "Over here, Ken!" Felix shouted, waving the large man in his direction.

Ken came over at a trot, Charli right behind him. "Find something?"

Bronson nodded. "Look."

Ken stepped up while Bronson kept his flashlight on the find. "Niiiice," the police captain murmured. Pulling off his T-shirt, he picked up one of the cans and examined it in the lightbeam.

"Just couldn't keep your shirt on, huh?" Felix quipped as he joined the group.

Ken grinned. "Every man has to take the opportunity to show off when he can," he joked.

Charli snorted and Bronson was relieved to hear the sound. Bronson knew he was well-built, but Ken was like a tank and it was disconcerting to have him right there with Charli so close. "Boys," she muttered, sounding completely unimpressed.

Felix chuckled and slung his arm around his sister's neck. "You're just jealous that Ken's muscles are bigger than yours."

"He wishes!" she snapped, bringing a smile to Bronson's lips.

"I need to get this to the office," Ken said, ignoring the siblings' teasing. "I'm hoping we'll find a fingerprint or two." His eyes darted to Bronson. "Good find. I'll rush this through myself."

"Thanks," Bronson said with a nod. "I appreciate it."

"Come on," Charli said, walking back toward the house. "Let Ken leave and the rest of us can get back to work."

Felix sighed as all the men watched her leave. "She's a determined little bugger, you gotta give her that," he grumbled.

Bronson snorted and Felix grinned at him.

"You sure you want to date her? She's a handful."

Bronson shrugged. "Her tenacity and strength are more impressive than those muscles you mentioned."

Felix narrowed his eyes and tilted his head consideringly. "That...was a very good answer, California Boy." He reached over and clapped Bronson on the shoulder. "Let's go finish that house. This," he pointed to the can in Ken's hand, "is a good find. But I don't think any of us want to leave it to chance."

Bronson nodded, the familiar weight of the situation settling back on his shoulders. "Thanks, Ken. We'll wait to hear from you."

"Yep." Without another word, Ken jogged across the yard toward his vehicle.

Bronson fell into step beside Felix, both walking back to the front of the house where Charlie was painting over the graffiti job. Bronson rolled his shoulders. "Here we go," he muttered, much to Felix's amusement.

"Oh, this is only the beginning," Charli's brother said with a snicker.

CHAPTER 26

"We did it," Charli whispered, relief slowly starting to trickle into her body. Her knees began to shake and her hands trembled. She turned a too-wide smile to Bronson, who was at her side. "We did it."

"MIDNIGHT!" Caro screamed, rushing down the stairs. "It's midnight!" She began to dance in the front room as everyone slowly began to congregate in the small space. No one else seemed to have Caro's endless supply of energy, but their smiles said enough.

"Did we finish?" Brooklyn asked, wiping a hand across her dirty forehead.

Charli choked on the words and nodded vigorously instead. "You did," she finally pushed out. Strong, warm hands wrapped around her from behind and she collapsed into Bronson's chest.

"You're amazing," he whispered in her ear.

"So that's it? You fulfilled the will?" Bennett asked. "You get your inheritance?"

Charli could feel Bronson's sigh at her back. "I don't know," he answered honestly. "Technically, it said I have to have something to show for it. We were hoping to have it sold so that I could present that to the judge, but maybe this'll be enough."

"About that..." Jensen hedged. He glanced at Mel, who stepped up and took his hand with her brilliant smile beaming full force. They turned to Bronson and Charli. "We were thinking maybe we would put an offer on the house."

Charli's eyes widened. "What?"

Bronson stiffened. "You don't have to do that," he said, his voice hoarse. "You've already done plenty for a man you barely know."

Mel's smile grew. "We know, but we've been thinking we'd like a real home after we get married in a few months anyway." Her eyes traveled around the space. "And this one is beautiful."

"It's a big decision," Charli said. "Are you sure this is something you want? Don't you want to see other houses?"

Mel laughed. "We have. And we haven't found a place we like as well as this one."

"So?" Jensen asked, his face expectant. "Are you willing to negotiate with us?"

Charli looked over her shoulder to see Bronson frowning.

He opened his mouth to answer, but his phone interrupted and he snapped his mouth shut. Grabbing it out of his back pocket, his eyes darted to Charli. "It's Ken," he said.

A hush fell over the room as Bronson answered and turned the phone on speaker.

"Bronson Ramsay."

"Hey, man, it's Ken. I've got news."

"What did you find?" Bronson asked, his body visibly tightening.

"I think it would be better if you came down to the station," Ken said, sounding slightly distracted.

Bronson made a face, and Charli grabbed his hand. "Is there anything you can tell me now? Everyone is waiting for answers."

Ken sighed. "I think we know who's causing you problems," he said warily. "But I don't think you're going to want me to just shout it to the world."

"Was it Canon?" Charli blurted, then winced. She really shouldn't have done that. This was Bronson's scene and she didn't need to add to his troubles. She looked up and mouthed *sorry*, but he just shook his head.

"I really think you should come down to the station," Ken said. "Let the crew get to bed and you two come here so we can get this settled once and for all."

Bronson's eyes closed and his head hung. "Sure. We'll be there in a few." He stuffed the phone in his back pocket and looked around. "I don't know how to thank you all enough." His arm slipped around Charli's shoulder and she went willingly into his chest. "I know you did it to help Charli, but I can never truly repay you for it." He grinned, looking ready to melt into the floor. "When everything settles down, I'll treat you all to dinner."

"We'll hold you to that!" Bennett answered, rubbing his stomach. "All this work has given me an appetite."

"Like you needed this to make you hungry," Brooklyn said with a roll of her eyes. She shook her head and started for the door. "I always enjoy a good steak, Bronson." She winked. "Remember that."

Bronson chuckled and Charli bounced against him. "Okay."

"Remember what we said," Jensen said as he and Melody left.

"I will," Bronson said solemnly. "And if it comes to that, I'll let you know."

Jensen smiled and he and Mel left.

"I'm offended that you think you aren't our friend," Caro snapped.

Charli groaned. "Oh my gosh, Caro. Don't you ever get tired of being dramatic?"

Caro fluffed her hair. "Nope. What's life without a little drama?" She grinned and came over to hug Charli, pulling her away from Bronson's hold. "We love ya, sweet pea," she whispered in Charli's ear, making Charli's eyes fill up with tears.

Oh my gosh. I haven't cried so much in my entire life, she thought wryly. Apparently working too hard for too long made her far more emotional than normal.

"And remember, if you ever get tired of Mr. McHotty—"

Charli pushed her away. "Good night, Caro," Charli said pointedly.

Caro snickered and waved at Bronson. "See ya!"

Bennett came up behind her. "Why is it the newcomers always get more attention than the locals? What is it with women and strangers?" he grumbled, glaring pointedly at Caro.

"Maybe because I don't have as many stories about a stranger," Caro shot back, her voice growing softer as they got farther away. "I can still remember you picking your nose at—"

"I DID NOT!" Bennett shouted. Their arguing faded as they disappeared into the night.

Charli shook her head.

"And on that weird note, I think the rest of us will go." Rose smiled softly and led all the rest of the crew out of the house. "I left some daisies in the kitchen," she called out just before leaving. "They're for a new beginning."

"Good luck," Genni said as she and Cooper left.

Charli smiled back. "Thanks."

"Ready?" Bronson asked when the last car had pulled out of the driveway.

"As I'll ever be," she murmured. All Charli wanted was her bed and twelve hours of uninterrupted sleep, but it appeared it wasn't coming quite yet. She grabbed her purse and her keys and walked into the dark with Bronson at her side.

Pausing at her truck door, she looked across the hood at Bronson. "I guess the better question would be...are *you* ready?"

Bronson took in a deep breath. "Nope. But I don't think I have a choice."

Charli nodded. "I know." She climbed into her seat. "But truthfully, we have nowhere to go but up from here."

"I hate how true that statement is," Bronson said through a yawn. He leaned his elbow on the window and put his head in his hands. "Wake me when we get there."

Charli laughed quietly. It felt good to do so. The house was finished, but there was no guarantee the offering would be accepted, and now Ken had something more. It felt like every time she and Bronson thought all was well, something else came up. But it didn't matter. When she gave her heart to Bronson, she did so without caveats. And surely after all was said and done, things would only get better.

She made a face. *Well...eventually. After we take care of Bronson's problems, then I need to tackle my own. Mainly, where can I look for another space for a storefront? After that...then we can move forward.*

BRONSON KEPT HIS EYES closed, but never actually fell asleep on the trip to the police station. A feeling of dread sat heavily in his stomach, taking away the victory of finishing the house by the demanded deadline. Jensen's offer to buy the house only added to the queasiness. It just felt wrong to sell it to one of Charli's friends. Bronson felt like Jensen and Melody were sincere in their offer, but he didn't like the taste it left in his mouth. He would always worry that they were only trying to help out instead of having honestly chosen the home because they liked it.

"We're here," Charli said, patting his knee.

Bronson grunted and opened his door, following Charli inside. Surprisingly, there were several officers there sitting around or working on projects.

"Charli! Bronson!" Ken stepped out of his office and waved them down the hall.

Once they were settled inside, Bronson couldn't stand it anymore. "I have to know, Ken. Was it Canon or not?"

Ken gave Bronson a sad smile. "No. I didn't find any evidence that it was Canon."

Charli gasped while Bronson sighed in relief. He let his shoulders relax and his head hung down as his muscles went lax, releasing weeks' worth of tension.

"Then who was it?" Charli asked, bringing Bronson's attention back to Ken.

Ken turned his laptop around. "Do you recognize this guy, Bronson?"

Bronson studied the man on the screen. He had an ultra-white smile, with a manicured goatee and carefully styled hair. His eyes were a murky shade of green and brown and his skin looked tan, as if he spent time in the sun. Bronson shrugged. "No. He looks like half the men in California."

Ken nodded. "Well, that's exactly where he's from."

"He followed me from California? For what purpose?" Bronson could feel his anger growing. He didn't know this guy from Adam. Why in the world would he be trying to sabotage him?

Ken turned his computer around and clicked a few things before facing it to Bronson again. "How about now?"

Bronson's jaw fell slack. "That's my sister," he rasped. The man from the earlier picture was standing with his arm around Aria, kissing her temple as they both held up champagne glasses for the camera.

Ken nodded, his face solemn. "This is Davis Sorenson. It was his fingerprints on the spray can."

Bronson could feel his heartbeat picking up speed. He didn't like where this was headed.

"I've been in contact with Canon and Mr. Filchor," Ken said, his words slower than before as if he were testing Bronson's reaction. "And I've got an APB out for your sister and this Davis guy."

"No..." Bronson breathed.

"Oh, Bron," Charli whispered in a thick voice.

When she reached out, he clutched her hand like a drowning man with a buoy. Canon had always been difficult to get along with, which made believing him to be the bad guy a little easier to take. But Aria? She was his baby sister. They might not have had the same ideas of life, but he'd always gotten along with her. "So you're saying that Aria is behind all the problems at the house?" Bronson choked out.

Ken shrugged. "We don't know for sure. And won't know until we bring her in. Right now, all I have are some fingerprints and a connection. Only time will tell the rest."

"But why would she do something like this?" Bronson asked, leaning forward. "She's just about to graduate. She has her whole life ahead of her with a modeling career. Why in the world would she be trying to keep me from my inheritance? It makes no sense."

"I agree," Ken said. "But like I said, she's all we've got."

"Sir?"

They all three looked toward the door.

The officer nodded at Bronson and Charli, then turned to his captain. "We found Sorenson."

Bronson jumped to his feet. "I want to see him."

"Whoa, there," Ken said, standing up and coming around to put a hand on Bronson's shoulder. "That's not a good idea."

"Why not? I'm the one he's been trying to hurt. I have every right to confront him."

"Because right now all I have is circumstantial evidence," Ken said firmly. He held up his hand to stop Bronson's interruption. "Those fingerprints could have come from any time, and any lawyer worth his salt will know that." He sighed and scratched the back of his head. "I'll talk to him personally, okay?" He raised his eyebrows and met Bronson's glare with patience.

Bronson was the first to look away, knowing he wouldn't win this battle. "Fine," he ground out. "But I want to know what this guy is doing with my sister and why he's after me. I don't believe that Aria would be mixed up in something so underhanded."

Ken nodded. "I get it. Go home and get some rest and we'll take care of things."

"Come on," Charli said softly. She tugged Bronson toward the door. "Let Ken do his job and when he has news, we'll be the first he tells. Right?" She looked to Ken for confirmation and the police officer nodded.

Bronson let Charli pull him away. He didn't have the strength or willpower to resist right now. "Fine," he muttered again. Turning fully toward the door, he let Charli lead him outside.

"You can sleep at my house tonight," Charli said as she started the engine.

"I can't sleep at your house," Bronson grumbled, folding his arms over his chest. "Just drop me off at the motel."

"Nope. I don't trust that you won't come hounding the officers when they have work to do."

Bronson glared across the cab. "You're being bossy again."

"Someone has to be when you're in such a mood," she stated without batting an eye.

Bronson huffed, but settled back into his seat. "It's still not right."

"Felix will be there. You can have the guest bed and you can count him as a chaperone."

"Whatever." Bronson jerked his head over when Charli started to chuckle. He always loved the low huskiness of her voice, but right now his mind and emotions were in too much turmoil to find comfort in the sound. "What's so funny?"

"I think we've spent most of our relationship with you being the reasonable one, trying to calm down me." She grinned as she looked at him. "It's sort of nice to know that you have a breaking point." Her smile fell. "I'm sorry about your sister though. That had to be hard to hear."

"We haven't heard anything," Bronson argued. "For all I know, that guy is using her to get what he wants."

"True," Charli responded, though he could tell through her tone that she didn't believe it.

"Aria has no reason to do something like this," he said, his voice soft. "Someone had to put her up to it."

Charli reached over and patted his knee. "It'll all work out," she assured him. "We've come this far. If we can finish renovating a house in six weeks, we can conquer anything."

Bronson thought back on the support that Charli had brought with her to the project, and for a second, he believed the words. *But this has nothing to do with them. This is all on you.* The tiny voice in the back of his head dispelled the hopefulness she was trying to share. They might have made it through the deadline, but now the situation was out of their hands. If Aria really was involved, then no one, not even Charli or her friends, could fix it. This was all Bronson and his messed up family.

CHAPTER 27

Charli's phone buzzed on her nightstand the next morning, but she ignored it. When it went off again, she groaned and turned, but was too slow. "Whatever," she grumbled, pulling the covers back up to her chin. She was past the point of exhaustion. They'd finished their project late and then spent time at the police station, and all the lost hours of sleep were catching up to her. Now that she was comfortable and flat on a mattress, she didn't want to move for a week.

"Char?" Felix's voice came through her door as he pounded on it.

What now? "I'm sleeping!" she hollered, snuggling down even further.

"Charli, you need to get up."

"No."

"Ken just called." Felix's voice dropped. "They found Bronson's sister last night."

Charli stiffened. *Oh no.* She jumped to her feet and opened the door. "What?" she asked breathlessly.

Felix grinned. "If only Bronson could see you now," he teased, his eyes going to her head.

Charli grimaced as she put a hand up and realized she had a terrible case of bedhead. "Shut up," she snarled, punching her brother in the arm. "What did you say about Bronson's sister?"

Felix's humor fled. "They caught her last night, and some guy. Ken just called because he couldn't get a hold of you."

Charli slapped a palm to her forehead. "Crud," she muttered, knowing that those were the calls that had just come through. "I need to shower and take Bronson over."

"He's already gone."

She jerked to a stop. "What?"

Felix picked at his nails, not quite meeting her eyes. "He was up early, too agitated to sleep, I think. Headed out to the station before my first sailing this morning."

"Your first..." Charli glanced to her nightstand and realized it was past ten in the morning. "Oh my gosh," she whispered. *How did it get to be so late?* She turned back to Felix. "How did he seem?" she asked, already dreading the answer.

Felix let out a loud breath before his eyes met hers. "Not good."

Nodding firmly, Charli backed into her room. "I need to shower really quick."

Felix backed up. "I have a bad feeling that he's gonna need you today."

Charli's brows furrowed. "Me too," she said quietly.

Taking the world's fastest shower, Charli didn't even bother to dry her hair, though she knew it would dry into a half-curly mess by the end of the day. Right now, she just didn't care. The idea of Bronson handling this all alone broke her heart and she wanted to get to him as quickly as possible.

Grabbing an apple, she darted out the door and forced herself not to speed down Main, though it was tempting. She parked and put her head high while walking inside, as if she belonged.

"Heya, Charli," the front desk secretary, Mabel, said.

"Hi." Charli smiled back. "I understand that Bronson Ramsay is here. He's probably with Captain Wamsley. Can I see them?"

The secretary eyed her a moment, then nodded. "Let me ask the captain."

Charli shifted her weight from foot to foot as Mabel spoke into the phone before finally waving her back. The station was bustling this morning, in contrast to the quiet feel last night, which only agitated Charli's nerves. *If Bronson has been here that long, then something's happened. I wonder how he's taking it.*

She knocked lightly on Ken's door before opening it, relieved to find Bronson inside. "Hey," she said softly, hesitating slightly at the threshold. It just now occurred to her that Bronson hadn't asked her to come, nor invited her. Maybe he wanted to handle this alone, and she, bossy woman extraordinaire, had come barging in like it was her right.

Bronson's smile of relief quickly helped ease her sudden worries and he waved her over. "Morning, sleepyhead," he said with a tired smile.

She slowly came over to the chair beside him. "I think you need to be a sleepyhead a little more," she quipped, still keeping her voice soft. She lightly touched the bags under his eyes. "Why didn't you wake me?"

He gave her a crooked grin. "Because you're too beautiful to be marred by this kind of makeup." He pointed to his dark circles.

Ken cleared his throat and Charli jumped, feeling guilty, though she wasn't sure what for. She turned to her friend. "What have you discovered? Felix said you brought some people in?" She watched Bronson out of her periphery, feeling bad when he winced at her question.

Ken stared at Bronson for a moment as if asking permission before answering Charli. "We caught Aria Ramsay and Davis Sorenson at a hotel a few miles down the road," he said in a business-like tone. "They're in separate rooms at the moment and we were just about to head over to interrogate them."

Charli turned to Bronson. "Do you want me to come? Or would you rather be alone?"

His large, warm hand gripped hers. "It probably won't be pretty, but if you're up for it, I'd love the company."

Charli nodded. She could be strong for him. Her own problems weren't going anywhere, so they could wait. "Then let's get this over with."

A very somber group walked down the hall to the areas where the suspects were being detained. Bronson and Charli were ushered into a room adjoining the one Ken would be in, where a window allowed them to see the proceedings.

"You sure you want to be here?" Bronson asked as he wiped his hands on his jeans.

Charli took the clammy hand and held it between her own. "I want to be wherever you are," she said.

Bronson's shoulders sagged a little and he gave her a short smile. "You might regret those words when you discover just how terrible my family is."

The door opened and a man in a tailored suit briskly walked in.

Bronson shot to his feet. "Canon?"

Charli's eyes widened. Bronson and Canon looked little alike. They shared the same stunning eyes, but otherwise, they seemed to come from two different worlds. Canon was crisp and orderly in every aspect of his appearance, where Bronson's ruffled hair and week-old beard made him appear almost homely next to his brother.

"Bronson," Canon said curtly. His eyes dropped to Charli and narrowed. "Who are you?"

Bronson tugged Charli to her feet. "This is Charli, my girlfriend."

One eyebrow rose. "Your girlfriend?" He snorted. "Figures you'd be busy with things other than your job."

"Don't start," Bronson growled. "She's been an integral part in making sure the house was done in time." Bronson slumped back into his seat, taking Charli with him. "Not that that matters anymore."

"Probably not," Canon admitted to Charli's surprise. "But maybe we need to see what dear old sister has to say before we pass judgment."

Charli's eyes were darting back and forth between the two men, but she didn't speak a word. Part of her was concerned that if she did, Canon would snap her head off. He wasn't as large as his brother, but his presence was far more intimidating. *No wonder he's been called a nightmare in the courtroom.*

"You think she's guilty?" Bronson asked, his voice shaking.

Since Canon had taken a seat behind them, Charli couldn't see his face, though she dearly wanted to turn around to look. It took a few seconds before the lawyer answered.

"Yes."

CANON'S RESPONSE MADE Bronson's heart beat so hard, it felt as if it were trying to break free of his chest. He had wanted to be wrong. He wanted to go back to thinking of his baby sister as a baby sister. A beautiful, growing woman who had the world at her feet. But after spending several hours this morning with Ken, digging through her college, or lack of college, career...Bronson's opinion had soured.

Apparently, Aria had been kicked out almost six months ago, citing a drug problem they were unable to resolve. How Bronson had never heard of the situation was beyond him.

I wonder if Canon knew...

Bronson almost turned around to ask his brother, but he kept himself facing the window. What good would it do to argue about such things now? They were where they were, and the only thing to do was to figure out what happened next.

"Aria Mariah Ramsay," Ken said in a formal tone as he entered the small empty room. He put a folder down on the table and took a chair. "I've met some of your family recently."

Aria snorted. "Really? Would that be my perfect oldest brother? Or perhaps the family screw-up middle child?"

Bronson was taken aback by the vitriol in her voice. He'd never heard her speak that way before. She was the darling of the media. Just as stunning as their mother, but less volatile. Though Bronson had seen her throw a few tantrums in her time, this wasn't like her at all.

Truth be told, he barely recognized her at all. Aria had always been thin, especially as a woman who wanted to do modeling, but right now she was so skinny, he could see veins and bones protruding from her body. Her face, which had enchanted millions, was now haggard and sharp. Dark bags hung under her eyes and her clothes practically fell off her body. Even if he had no idea what had happened at college, Bronson would have recognized the signs of drug abuse. His sister had gone from bright and beautiful to a washed-up addict.

"Both, actually," Ken said casually. He shuffled some papers, then looked her in the eye. "What brings you to Seaside Bay? From what I understand, you've been going to school in California."

Aria scoffed. "Don't pretend you don't know. There's only one reason you would have picked me up, since I was just sitting in my hotel room watching a movie when you arrived." She leaned forward. "I want a lawyer."

Ken studied her.

"I think she got that from you," Bronson grunted, sending his comment over his shoulder.

"I'd say good girl," Canon responded, his voice less sharp than before. "But in this case..." His voice trailed off and Bronson turned to see a break in Canon's normally perfect facade.

In a word, Canon looked...weary.

The man who commanded court rooms, brought fear into his opponents and ran his family like a military compound was breaking.

Canon let his eyes meet Bronson's and for a split second every doubt, fear and regret the slick lawyer had was visible. The speed of a blink, however, had it disappearing and Canon stood. "I believe that's my cue."

Bronson watched, his jaw slack, as his brother made a grand entrance into the room. "Good morning, Captain Wamsley."

Ken nodded. "Canon."

Aria had been sitting back in her chair with a smirk on her face and it faltered at their greeting, before she plastered it back into place. "Hello, *brother*. Ready to spring me out of here?"

Canon grabbed an empty chair and sat down. "No, actually. I don't think that would be in your best interest this time."

This time?

Bronson felt as if he'd been sucker punched. "What is going on?" he asked no one in particular.

Charli squeezed his hand. "I think Canon's been keeping secrets," she whispered.

Bronson groaned and let go of Charli to put his face in his hands. "How much worse can this get?"

The words were like a prophecy as Aria jumped to her feet, screaming at her brother.

"You're taking his side!" she shouted. "How can you do that? I'm your sister. Your ONLY sister, and you would choose Bronson and his stupid charity over me?" She pushed her hands into her hair, looking like she wanted to yank it out from the roots.

"I'm not taking anyone's side," Canon said calmly, looking like he didn't have a care in the world. "As your legal counsel, I believe it's in your best interest to cooperate." His voice dropped and Bronson had to strain to hear what happened next. "You can only get caught so many times before you pay the consequences."

Aria hissed, looking wild in her anger. "You want to know why I'm here?" she said in a deadly tone. Her face jumped between the two men. "Because Bronson is an idiot."

Bronson flinched and Charli scooted closer to him.

"She's not in her right mind," she whispered, clinging to his arm. "She's probably in withdrawals at the moment."

So she noticed, he mused distractedly. It would be a miracle if Charli wanted anything to do with him after this.

"Mr. Goody-Two-Shoes is about to inherit five million dollars, and what does he want to do with it?" Aria threw her hands in the air. "He wants to buy a crappy building so a crappy charity doesn't get kicked out." Her laugh was dark and humorless. "Can you imagine? What makes those people so special?" She spun quickly and slapped her hand down on the table, making it shudder.

Bronson had to give credit to the men in the room. Neither one gave her any emotional response to the outburst.

"Those people don't deserve that money. They didn't earn it. All they earned was a ticket to the poor house."

"Are you saying that you deserve it?" Ken asked, still looking detached from the situation.

"Of course, I do!" Aria screeched. "It was my father's. It should be mine."

"You already got your part of the inheritance," Ken said smoothly. "And Bronson is your brother. Why begrudge him his part?"

A terrifying smirk crept across her face and she slunk to the chair, sitting down. "And let him waste it?" Aria clucked her tongue and slowly shook her head. "Him helping those people would be like throwing it away. Which would just be a rotten shame. That kind of dough could get me back in business."

Charli gasped and Bronson felt as if his heart had stopped. "She was *selling?*"

"So you...what? Wrote a fake will?" Ken tilted his head, watching her curiously.

"No," Aria scoffed. She folded her spindly arms over her bony chest. "I had Davis do it. He's a law student, you know."

Ken nodded and gave a grunt that could have meant anything. "Why bother sabotaging the house, then? If the will was going to get you the money, why did you feel the need to go after him physically?"

"The dolt was going to win!" Aria's voice was shrill again. "The first thing he did when he got to this podunk town was find someone to help him, and it was working!" She snarled. "I couldn't let that happen." In the blink of an eye, Aria was smiling again. "So I took matters into my own hands." Her face tightened and she slammed a fist on the table. "Until last night when Davis got lazy. I *told* him he should have looked harder for that can he dropped." She spit some curse word that would have made a sailor blush.

Charli's grip tightened on Bronson's arm. "I think we should go," she said. "You've heard enough."

Bronson shook his head. "No. No more running. I want to know it all." Charli didn't respond, but she didn't leave, for which Bronson was secretly grateful. The next hour was spent listening to Aria spew hatred for him, their father and eventually Canon as well, as she talked about needing to maintain a certain lifestyle in order to be happy. Nothing more was truly revealed other than for Bronson to recognize that his sister was gone. In her place was a shrew who was so deep into the dark underbelly of society that she didn't know right from wrong anymore.

He waited after she was removed from the room, knowing Canon would stop by before he left, and Bronson didn't have to wait long.

"I'm flying out this evening," Canon said by way of greeting when he opened the door. "I'll work on a defense that will end with Aria in rehab."

Bronson didn't know whether to admire his brother's way of keeping aloof or be saddened by it. "Why didn't you tell me?" he asked, referring to the fact that this wasn't Aria's first offense. Apparently, Canon had been running interference for years behind Bronson's back, and that might have hurt more than anything else at this point. It made Bronson feel weak, as if Canon thought he couldn't handle the weight of the problem.

Canon sighed and pinched the bridge of his nose. "Now's not the time—"

"WHY?" Bronson shouted, rising to his feet. His hands were clenched and the sterile space suddenly felt too small. "And what about the will? Why did you refuse to let me see it? Why push the part that you suspected was wrong?"

Canon's face was like a statue, solid and unflinching. "I was trying to uncover things on my own without involving the police, and that meant you were caught in the crossfire. In order to be able to dig behind the scenes, I had to act as if nothing was wrong, which meant treating the will in public the exact same as I would anyone else's inheritance. I apologize that you were hurt during that time."

The betrayal pulsing through Bronson's chest was enough to strangle him. The room felt too small and there wasn't enough oxygen, but he still needed to know. "But why not say something? Why not let me know what was going on and let me help?"

Canon looked him in the eye for a moment. "One of us deserved to be free." After another heartbeat, he was gone and Bronson's trembling knees gave out, bringing him back down to his chair.

He barely felt Charli's hand on his back or her words of comfort. With those few words, Bronson realized he'd misjudged both his siblings. And now he couldn't help but wonder if maybe it was too late to fix.

CHAPTER 28

Bronson barely spoke for the next week and Charli was going out of her mind with worry. Things had been wrapped up at the police station. Aria and Davis had been formally charged, Canon was handling the details and the original will had been revealed.

There was nothing left to do, but Charli still felt ill at ease and she knew she wouldn't feel better until she was able to help Bronson out of his funk.

Not that she would blame him for having a hard time. No one wanted to have all their family secrets spilled and discover that what they thought they knew wasn't even close to the truth.

"Hey," Charli said softly as she came inside her home to find Bronson sitting in the front room.

He smiled at her, looking more awake than he had in several days. "Hello, beautiful."

Charli carefully sat down on the couch, aware that her clothes were dusty from her recent job. "Did you eat lunch yet?"

Bronson shook his head. "Nope." He shut down the laptop on his legs. "And I heard a rumor that you've got a thing for Melody's smoothie bowls, so would you like to go get one?"

A flutter of hope lit in her chest at his invitation. Maybe he was finally coming out of his depression. "I'd love to, but I'm filthy." She looked down at her work overalls.

Bronson chuckled. "Who cares?"

"I do!" she argued, but her smile gave away the fact that she wasn't upset.

"You met with Mr. Filchor looking worse than that," Bronson pointed out. He set aside the computer and stood, offering his hand. "Come on. Nobody'll notice."

"Says the guy who's clean," Charli grumbled, letting him pull her out the door.

The ride to the smoothie shop was quiet but comfortable. Bronson held her hand the whole time, which was more affection than she'd received in the last several days combined. There was a part of Charli that was worried that she was losing Bronson.

The house was done, the mystery was solved and their relationship was going nowhere.

He's been hurting, she reminded herself. *Give him time to grieve and come to terms with everything that's happened.*

The words were on repeat in her brain. She'd been telling herself that since everything happened at the police station, but the more days that passed, the harder it was to believe.

He still held her hand, but there'd been no words of reassurance, no celebration of their accomplishment, no talk of the future, no kissing or hugging. And considering how much Bronson seemed to thrive on touch, Charli knew that wasn't a good sign.

She blinked rapidly, trying to clear her vision. The last thing she needed at the moment was to let Bronson know she was hurting. It would probably only drive him away even faster than he was already drifting, and she knew it was selfish, but she wasn't ready to let him go.

She loved him. Truly and deeply. They'd already been through the depths of purgatory together and it had only made her even more determined to see them work out as a couple. She knew his secrets, but she was losing the man.

Her actions at the house and support during the family situation apparently hadn't been enough.

Bronson parked and they got out, heading inside. The line was long and Bronson whistled low under his breath. "Looks like Mel is popular today."

"It's warm," Charli explained, trying to inject some enthusiasm in her tone. "It's always packed when the sun comes out."

"Makes sense." He huffed a laugh. "She should move down to California. She'd be packed all the time."

Charli nodded. Her thoughts had taken a bad direction in the car and now she was struggling to keep her head above water. Usually she just stayed busy and it helped her forget her own heartache. Now that she was still, it was coming back in full force.

It took a half-hour and a chat with Mel to get them out the door and on the sidewalk.

"Let's walk," Bronson said, taking her hand and starting down the side of the street.

Charli sipped her favorite fruity concoction, but it sat heavily in her stomach.

"I owe you an apology."

She snapped her head in his direction. "What?" Bronson gave Charli a sad smile and her heart faltered.

This is it. He's going to break up with me.

"I'm sorry."

When he didn't say anything more, Charli nodded and pulled her hand away. "It's okay. I get it," she said softly. She was going to be sick, and as soon as she was by herself, she planned to cry until she couldn't cry anymore. She turned to go, but his hand stopped her.

"Where are you going?" he asked, looking confused.

Charli frowned. "You just..." Her eyebrows twitched and she scrunched her face. "I was leaving because you just broke up with me."

Bronson's eyes widened and his face blanched. "What?"

She opened and closed her mouth a few times. "Uh...I'm lost."

He dropped her hand and pushed his own through his hair. "I'm such an idiot," he muttered. Spinning back to her, Bronson grabbed the back of Charli's neck and met her lips in a hard, sensual kiss. When he pulled back after a moment, they were both breathing heavily. "I wasn't apologizing because I was leaving. I was apologizing that I've been shut down for the last few days."

"Oh," was all Charli managed. Her emotions had done a complete reversal and she wasn't quite sure which way was up anymore.

He chuckled and kissed her forehead before stepping back. "Come with me," he said, grabbing her hand once more and leading her more purposefully down the sidewalk. "I know I haven't been myself," he began as they dodged other people. "But I promise my feelings for you haven't changed." He looked over and winked, the old Bronson starting to shine through. "If anything, they've only gotten stronger."

Charli felt her cheeks flush. Now she felt like the idiot. Somehow, she'd put two and two together and gotten seven.

He squeezed her hand. "I'm sorry that my behavior led you to believe otherwise," he said softly.

Charli shook her head. "No. I shouldn't have jumped to conclusions."

Bronson jerked to a stop. "Nope. No blaming yourself here. I've been absent. I should've seen how this was affecting you and I didn't." He turned her so they were looking straight at each other. "I'm sorry, Charli. I've been working through so much this last week, and despite the fact that you've been through the whole ordeal with me, I shut you out." He sighed and looked away. "But I think I needed to. I needed time inside my own head to force everything into its place."

"I get it," Charli said, interrupting him. "I need space sometimes too."

He grinned. "I know, which is partly why it didn't occur to me that you'd think I was getting ready to get rid of you." His eyes turned slyly to the side and Charli followed, only now noticing that they were standing in front of the old warehouse. "In fact," he continued, "if you'll have me, I plan on giving you very little space for a long time."

BRONSON WATCHED HER eyes widen as she looked around. "I don't...I don't understand."

He took her smoothie and his own, setting them down and out of the way before turning her to face the building. Then he stepped behind her and wrapped his arms around her waist. "You once told me that you had your eye on a building, but it had been sold before you could get it."

She nodded jerkily.

"Is this the building?"

She nodded again and Bronson gave an internal sigh of relief. He had been *almost* positive this was the place, but with all the chaos, had never actually asked.

"I happen to know the new owner," he whispered in her ear. She stiffened in his arms and Bronson ploughed ahead. "He wants to hire you as a partner to help him fix it up."

Charli spun, nearly knocking him in the nose. "You bought it?" she gasped.

Bronson nodded, stuffing his hands in his pockets.

"How?" She shook her head, a few tears trickling down her smooth cheeks. The look of betrayal in her eyes hit him square in the gut.

"I didn't know," Bronson rasped. "You didn't tell me until afterwards that you had any plans for it."

Her face fell and her chin nearly touched her chest. "I know," she relented. "I...was afraid to share my dreams, because I was still struggling to open every part of myself to you."

Bronson dared to reach out and put his hands on her upper arms. "Do you think you can let me in enough to work with me again?"

Charli raised her face, her eyes going back to the building as she wiped away her tears. "What are you wanting to do with it?"

Bronson swallowed hard. "I've got a couple of options, and I was hoping you would help me decide."

She looked back at him. "Okay."

"My first thought had been to build a Fathers and Sons chapter up here in Seaside Bay."

Her eyes widened. "Would you be around to run it?"

Bronson nodded and slowly began to pull her in closer. "But I also had another thought." The moment between them grew thick as molasses, and Bronson had a hard time keeping his eyes off her lips. He'd been deprived of them too long, but he needed to settle this with her first. "A beautiful woman planted the idea in my head that this would make a great showplace for restored furniture."

Charli put a fist over her mouth as a broken sob slipped through her lips.

"Which do you think would be a better fit?" he asked, slowly wrapping his arms around her back. When she was settled into his chest, he brought his lips to her hair. "Keep in mind that if we put in a furniture place, I'd have to rent it out to this bossy woman who likes to think she's in charge."

He laughed when she leaned back and punched him in the shoulder.

Her smile died a moment later when she met his eyes. "It feels wrong to take this opportunity away from those kids," she admitted. "What kind of person would I be if I said to go for the restoration store?"

Bronson shook his head. "A normal one," he assured her. "I can always find another place for a chapter here. Now that my inheritance is on its way, I'll have enough left over from the sale down in California to put a down payment on something here."

"Are you sure?"

Bronson nodded. "Charli...would you be willing to help me renovate this old building and then rent it from me?" He brought his nose down to hers. "If you're nice, I might even let you work out a rent-to-own option."

"Nice?" Her lips curled into a sly smile and her hands slipped behind his neck. "How nice would I have to be?"

"Very nice," Bronson teased back. "You'd have to let me be all touchy-feely with you and go on dates with me and spend time working with me."

"Would I have to call you boss?" she asked, pursing her lips in thought.

Bronson flared his eyes. "I hadn't thought of that, but it's a good one—oof!"

She punched him again.

"Enough already," he said, laughing. "This is not the way to start things off with your new boss."

Charli grew serious. "No," she responded. "But this is." Raising up on her tiptoes, she brought their mouths together and the world held still.

Bronson wrapped his arms tighter around her and let Charli's touch soothe the inner corners of his mind that were still raw. It would take some time for him to recover completely from the betrayal of his siblings, but with Charli near, Bronson knew it would happen.

He'd already informed his brother that he was staying in Oregon during the conversations they'd held while Charli was at work. Despite the fact that Bronson had shut down emotionally for a few days, he'd actually accomplished quite a few things. He wasn't quite done surprising Charli yet.

As if she could read his mind, she pulled back. "Where are you going to stay?" she asked breathlessly. "I mean, I know we have room at the house, but..."

Bronson shook his head. "It wouldn't be right for me to stay with you and Felix." He gave her a crooked grin. "I was actually thinking that Brooklyn could use some of her good fashion sense to help me furnish my new place."

Charli's eyebrows shot up. "You have a place in mind?"

"I have a place," Bronson said, waiting for her to catch on.

She stared hard, then opened her mouth in an 'O'. "You're going to stay at the Miller place?"

"Why not?" Bronson asked. "I already own it."

"Geez," Charli lamented. "I think you own more land in Seaside Bay than I do and you just got here!"

He laughed and tugged her back in. "It wasn't quite intentional," Bronson said softly. "The first one was under duress and the second was an opportunity I couldn't pass up."

"I guess it doesn't matter," Charli said against his T-shirt. "I'm just glad you have a reason to stay."

"The properties have nothing to do with why I'm staying," Bronson corrected her. He pulled back just enough to see her face. "I told you that I love you, Charli. That hasn't changed. And even though I know you're not to that point yet—"

"But I am!" she shouted, looking surprised at her own outburst.

He froze. "You...are?"

Charli nodded slowly, her lips pinched together. "I know I have a hard time speaking my feelings, but I do. I love you, Bronson. I've loved you for a long time now. I've just been too scared and distracted to say the actual words." She grimaced. "I did kind of hope that my actions would speak louder than words, but I still should have said something."

With a whoop, Bronson hugged her close and lifted Charli's feet off the ground. She stumbled when he put her down. "I've changed my mind," he said, cupping her cheeks and kissing all over her face.

"Hmm?" Charli hummed, her eyes closed as she enjoyed his attention.

"I don't think I can be your boss anymore." He left his lips against her forehead. "I think we should just be partners."

"Oh, good," Charli breathed, grabbing his neck to hold him still. "I've always enjoyed a good partner." She tugged and Bronson met her halfway.

Partners...colleagues...boyfriends and girlfriend...Bronson knew it really didn't matter what they called each other. All that mattered was that Charli was his for now and eventually he'd make her his forever.

EPILOGUE

"It's beautiful," Caro breathed as she admired the dresser Charli had brought out from the workshop yesterday. "I don't know how you do it."

Charli grinned and put her hands on her hips. "It's because I'm not afraid to get dirty," she teased.

Caro looked at her with a raised eyebrow. "I know how to get dirty. I just don't go out in public that way."

Charli laughed. "Touche."

Caro sniffed. "As gorgeous as this is, I think I need something smaller. You know, more like a jewelry box. Grandmother always did have a thing for the fancy stuff."

Charli nodded. She'd had her shop open for two months now and her inventory was moving quicker than she could have ever expected. At the rate she was going, she was going to have to hire someone to run the front so she could stay buried in the workshop, cleaning up pieces.

She still ran the odd job around town when occasion warranted it, but most of the inhabitants of Seaside Bay had been thrilled to see her move forward into something new.

"I don't have anything restored," Charli said slowly, her eyes looking around. "But I do have something I made."

Caro perked up. "What? You made something?"

Charli shrugged as she walked to the display where the box sat. "I've been testing out different woodworking techniques and built this as a test pilot." She grabbed it off the shelf. "I'll give it to you for a box of chocolates, if you're game."

"I can't do that," Caro said defensively. "It's got to be worth way more than that."

Charli pursed her lips and shook her head. "Nah. It was just for fun." She handed the box to Caro. "See what you think."

"Ooh, Charli, it's beautiful!" Caro cooed. "You're amazing!" She shook the box slightly and frowned. "Why does it feel like there's something in there?"

Charli jerked back a little. "What?" She reached for the box. "Maybe I left some wood chips inside. I'm sorry. Let me clean it out."

"Hey, beautiful." Bronson suddenly appeared at her side and Charli jumped a little.

"Oh, hey!" she said, tucking a stray hair behind her ear. She was probably a mess at the moment. "Where did you come from?" She tilted up for his kiss as his arm went around her waist.

"Meeting got done early," he explained, shifting her so her back was to his chest. The Seaside Bay chapter of Fathers and Sons had officially opened about a month ago and Bronson was the head of it. Being in charge meant he spent less time with the kids, but it kept him busy, which he enjoyed. "Whatcha doing?" he asked, his chin resting on her head.

"Caro was looking for a gift for her grandmother, so we ended up at my jewelry box," Charli explained. She reached for it again. "But we think I left some junk inside, so I'm gonna clean it out."

She took the box and lifted the lid, then almost dropped it. There wasn't a speck of dust or wood inside, but there was a rolled piece of paper. And the bow holding it together seemed to sparkle in the overhead lights.

"Let me take that," Bronson whispered, reaching out to hold the box.

With shaking fingers, Charli picked up the scroll and abruptly began to cry. A diamond solitaire was the source of the sparkle and she couldn't quite bring herself to untie it.

Bronson, having set down the box, took the paper from her hands and undid the knot. "I've been thinking," he said softly in her ear. "We've been business partners for a few months now and as much as I love it, I think I'd like a change."

He took her left hand and stretched out her fingers while Charli watched, mesmerized, at his actions.

"I don't really need another business partner. What I need is a life partner." He unrolled the paper and held it so she could read the fine print. "Would you, Charli Mendez, be that partner? As an added incentive, I'm offering you the papers for your store. I don't want you to think that I have any power over you, but that we stand as equal partners in everything. Just you and me...forever."

Charli frantically wiped at her face, the weight of the ring feeling new and odd on her hand. "You know...I never cried until after I met you." Ignoring Caro's snort, Charli turned in his arms and looped her hands around his neck. "But I don't need the building," she said. "I just need you. I love you."

"Perfect," Bronson said with a wide smile. "Because when we're married, it'll be both of ours anyway." He winked. "I just wanted to sweeten the pot, so to speak."

Charli laughed a little, then rose up on tiptoe and paused at his lips. "You might want to turn away, Caro," Charli called out. "We're about to get touchy-feely in here."

"My work here is done!" Caro said, walking to the front door. "But I still want that box!" she hollered right before the front door closed.

"So is that a yes?" Bronson asked as soon as they were alone.

Charli started when she realized she hadn't really answered the question. "That's a yes," she clarified. "But if you don't kiss me right now, I might have to rethink it all."

"Bossy, bossy," Bronson teased before giving her a slow, soft kiss. He spoke against her mouth. "I like it."

Charli began to laugh, but he cut her off as they celebrated their new venture. Never in a million years would Charli have expected to take on a partner, nor for that partner to become a permanent part of her life. She'd been doing it all herself for so long that she'd forgotten what it was like to have another set of shoulders to rely on.

She sighed as he deepened the kiss, reveling in every moment of his attention. It was attention she was going to keep for herself for a long...long...long...time.

Thank you for reading
Charli and Bronson's story!
I hope you enjoyed reading it
as much as I enjoyed writing it.
Not quite ready to be done yet?
Want to read the stories for the other
members of the Bulbs, Blossoms and Bouquets group?
Don't miss a romance!
[Her Unexpected Roommate][1]
[Her Unexpected Second Chance][2]
[Her Unexpected Partner][3]
[Her Unexpected Rival][4]
Her Unexpected Catch
Her Unexpected Star
Her Unexpected Delivery
Her Unexpected Protector

---

1. https://www.amazon.com/Her-Unexpected-Roommate-Blossoms-Bouquets-ebook/dp/B08PPXK15R
2. https://www.amazon.com/gp/product/B08T63NT34
3. https://www.amazon.com/gp/product/B08WJJ3FQH
4. https://www.amazon.com/gp/product/B08YX11KNY

Other Books by Laura Ann
lauraannbooks.com[1]

BULBS, BLOSSOMS, AND BOUQUETS
Her Unexpected Roommate[2]
Her Unexpected Second Chance[3]
Her Unexpected Partner[4]
Her Unexpected Rival[5]
Her Unexpected Catch
Her Unexpected Star
Her Unexpected Delivery
Her Unexpected Protector
THE GINGERBREAD INN[6]
Three cousins come to help their grandmother run an inn during the Christmas season when mysterious happenings nearly ruin everything.
Book 1-3[7]

---

1. https://lauraannbooks.com/

2. https://www.amazon.com/Her-Unexpected-Roommate-Blossoms-Bouquets-ebook/dp/B08PPXK15R

3. https://www.amazon.com/gp/product/B08T63NT34

4. https://www.amazon.com/gp/product/B08WJJ3FQH

5. https://docs.google.com/document/u/0/d/1nMuKsy0G7OO4aQ-ZiFUjBMS4aN-JRGzwhT5Iq5fMKKwA/edit

6. https://www.amazon.com/gp/product/B08N4JD51P?ref_=dbs_p_mng_rwt_ser_shvlr&storeType=ebooks

7. https://www.amazon.com/gp/product/B08N4JD51P?ref_=dbs_p_mng_rwt_ser_shvlr&storeType=ebooks

SAGEBRUSH RANCH[8]

When city girls meet cowboys,
true love is on the horizon.

Books 1-6[9]

LOCKWOOD INDUSTRIES[10]

The Lockwood triplets started a personal security company.
Little did they know it would double as a matchmaking business!

Books 1-6[11]

OVERNIGHT BILLIONAIRE BACHELORS[12]

Three brothers become overnight billionaires.
Will they discover that love is the real treasure?

Books 1-5[13]

IT'S ALL ABOUT THE MISTLETOE[14]

---

8. https://www.amazon.com/gp/product/B089YPCF6X?ref_=dbs_r_series&storeType=ebooks

9. https://www.amazon.com/gp/product/B089YPCF6X?ref_=dbs_r_series&storeType=ebooks

10. https://www.amazon.com/gp/product/B083Z49VL3?ref_=dbs_r_series&storeType=ebooks

11. https://www.amazon.com/gp/product/B083Z49VL3?ref_=dbs_r_series&storeType=ebooks

12. https://www.amazon.com/gp/product/B07RJZL29J?ref_=dbs_r_series&storeType=ebooks

13. https://www.amazon.com/gp/product/B07RJZL29J?ref_=dbs_r_series&storeType=ebooks

When 6 friends brings fake dates to their high school reunion, mayhem and mistletoe win the day!
[Books 1-6][15]
[MIDDLETON PREP][16]
If you enjoy fairy tale romance,
these sweet, contemporary retellings are for you!
[Books 1-9][17]

---

14. https://www.amazon.com/gp/product/B082F8FTHY?ref_=dbs_r_series&storeType=ebooks

15. https://www.amazon.com/gp/product/B082F8FTHY?ref_=dbs_r_series&storeType=ebooks

16. https://www.amazon.com/gp/product/B07DYCWRQL?ref_=dbs_r_series&storeType=ebooks

17. https://www.amazon.com/gp/product/B07DYCWRQL?ref_=dbs_r_series&storeType=ebooks